Praise for Katharine's Books

AGAIN, MY LORD

"This series is groundbreaking in the Historical Romance genre."
The Reading Wench

"Deeply romantic and wonderfully enchanting. This book made me feel all the feelings. A truly magical romance."
Maya Rodale, *USA Today* bestselling author

MY LADY, MY LORD

2014 RITA® Award Finalist
Romance Writers of America

"Breathlessly romantic and original… charming, clever, intelligent, and entertaining"
Romantic Historical Reviews (Best of 2014)

THE EARL

"This is historical romance at its best."
All About Romance (Desert Isle Keeper)

"Tender and gripping."
Bookpage (TOP PICK!)

"A rollicking page-turner… entertaining and emotionally satisfying."
Publishers Weekly (*Starred Review*)

THE ROGUE

"A strong and independent female protagonist."
Library Journal (*Starred Review*)

"The chemistry between them is electric ... Saint is easily one of the finest romantic heroes I've read in quite some time."
All About Romance (Desert Isle Keeper)

"The desperate yearning—and dangerous secrets—between the star-crossed lovers had my stomach in knots until the very end of this hypnotic book."
Amazon's Omnivorous (Best Romances of the Month)

"Powerful, suspenseful and sensual."
RT Book Reviews (TOP PICK!)

HOW A LADY WEDS A ROGUE

Recommended Read!
Woman's World Magazine

"Emotionally touching and sexually taut."
Kirkus Reviews

HOW TO BE A PROPER LADY

Ten Best Romances of 2012
Amazon Editors' Choice

"Everything fans of historical romance could want in a book."
Joyfully Reviewed

Captive
Bride

A Regency Ghost Novel

Katharine Ashe

CAPTIVE BRIDE: Copyright © 2012 Katharine Brophy Dubois

Cover design © Carrie Divine/Seductive Designs

Image: inarik/Depositphotos

Image: FairytaleDesign/Depositphotos

ISBN 9780991641260

Published by Billet-Doux Books

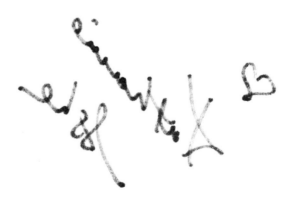

To my author friends.
I love you dearly.

Chapter One

October 1822
Hart House
Yorkshire, England

"No, Lord Cheriot, I will not marry you."

The nobleman's emerald gaze, fixed on Beatrice Sinclaire clipping roses with steady hands, was not wide with surprise. Neither was it awash in pain, shadowed with hopelessness, or taut with longing. Nor were the eyes that followed her movements skeptically sharp, calculatingly narrowed, or enigmatically hooded. Instead, the gentleman seemed perfectly at ease.

Anticipating this odiously measured response, of course, had shaped Bea's reply in the first place.

The ribbons on her hat fluttered in the late autumn breeze. She tilted up her face toward him.

"But I thank you for the offer," she added.

His smile stretched wide across a handsome face made all the more appealing by the smile.

"You say that every time. Exactly the same words. Heaven knows I have invented at least a half dozen— no, I'll merit, a dozen different ways to beg your hand. But you haven't bothered a bit to spice up your response with variety." The baron's merry gaze shifted to a bob of rusted blooms at his elbow. "You've missed a few here, Bea."

"If you please, my lord, I prefer you to address me as propriety demands."

"If you insist, peagoose." His eyes sparkled. "Miss Sinclaire, that is."

"Thank you, Lord Cheriot." The clippers opened and closed in even efficiency between Bea's fingers. Brown-edged and limp-petaled, spent roses dropped to the carpet of green at her feet.

"Thank you, Lord Cheriot," the tall, impossibly broad-shouldered gentleman echoed as he wandered to a wrought-iron bench settled amidst shrubs thinned of their gold, pink, and white treasures. Lifting the tails of Weston's best bottle green superfine coat with unself-conscious grace, he reclined upon the incommodious seat as though it were covered in down-filled cushions. His long legs stretched out in an attitude of insouciant serenity. "If I were a man to be driven mad, Miss Beatrice Sinclaire, you surely would have accomplished the thing by now."

"Then I am glad you are not so predisposed. I do enjoy your company, and I don't believe inmates of Bedlam are permitted visitors."

"I should think a man's wife ought to be allowed to visit him once in a while," came the quick rejoinder. "You know, I won't let up asking. And when you have finally accepted me, I will insist that you call me Tip. Or perhaps I would like my given name better from you. A fellow ought to have a say in that sort of thing." He paused. "And I will call you Bea whether you like it or not."

"You're sounding boorish, you know."

Tip snorted a laugh. A wavy, dark brown lock tumbled forward over his eyes.

"No wonder you won't marry me. Never mind the Lord Cheriot-ing you are so fond of. Why, to hear the way you speak to me, a stranger would think I was your brother."

Firming her smile, Bea allowed her fingers to slow and her gaze to slip sideways beneath her hat brim. His attention was settled upon her, his brows high, quizzing.

She swallowed a sigh.

If only he *were* her brother. If he were Thomas, he would

not insist on asking for her hand in marriage, a habit Tip had formed early in their friendship just after Bea's sister, Georgianna, broke his heart by marrying her childhood beau. And if Tip were her brother, instead of teasing her ceaselessly as he did every time he came to Yorkshire, he would busy himself haring off on some wild escapade, spending his allowance inappropriately, and making trouble for the family. Most especially, if he were her brother she would not have harbored for seven interminable years the consuming wish that he would once look at her and see *her*, rather than a poor reflection of her lovely, brilliant sister.

Alas, Lord Peter Cheriot was not related to Bea in any manner, despite his repeated proposals of marriage. But she had lived a lifetime of loving too well those who did not love her well in return. She simply could not bear for Tip to settle for her while ever after longing for a woman he could not have.

Nearby, the shrubbery rustled and the butler stepped through a gap in the hedge.

"Miss Beatrice," he said in a harried tone. "I have been searching for you all about the place."

"Really, Perkins?" Familiar tension ticked Bea's stomach. Her mother must be especially tetchy for Perkins to fret so greatly that he would come all the way to the garden.

Tip slouched back into the bench as the butler approached.

"This just arrived, miss. It is from Master Thomas. In *Wales.*"

"Wales?" Bea reached for the letter. "Thank you."

Perkins disappeared, this time through the rose trellis, a man relieved of a heavy burden.

"Thought your twin was on a repairing lease in Scotland, not Wales," Tip commented as Bea pried open the wax seal. "What scrape has he gotten himself into now?"

"I hardly know," she murmured, chancing another look at her companion. Lord Cheriot seemed to be absently studying the roses hanging over his shoulder. Then the words scribbled across the page seized her attention.

A handful of silent moments later, moments marked with
Bea's churning emotions, she again met Tip's gaze.

He swallowed, a visibly hard movement of his throat
above his elegantly knotted cravat.

"You've got the damnedest eyes, Bea," he said in a strange
voice. "Very pretty, I mean—Have always admired . . . Miss
Sinclaire?" He rose with a jerk from the bench and moved
forward. "Bea? What is it? You have that look your sister used
to get when—"

Bea's whole body wavered toward the bush. She darted a
hand out for support and her palm caught on a thorn. She
gasped and grabbed it to her waist.

Tip grasped her shoulders.

"Here now, my girl." His light grip steadied her.

Bea gulped in a breath. The shallow scratch on her skin
would surely stain her favorite lemon muslin. But she had
accomplished what she wished by wearing the fetching gown.
He had offered for her again. However much she knew he did
not mean it sincerely, she liked to hear the words. His voice
was so lovely and deep, his smile breathtaking.

He hovered close, his hands wrapped around her arms.
Bea's heart beat in quick little flutters like the wings of
hummingbirds that darted about her garden. She drew out of
his hold and straightened her back, hiding the letter in the folds
of her skirt.

"Dear me," she said. "I daresay I have been standing too
long in the sunshine. I will catch my breath and then go in for
a cup of tea. Will you join me, my lord?" She made to turn
away.

A firm hand impeded her.

"Oh, no you don't, missy. I saw your face. And I never
even imagined you were capable of swooning."

"I did not swoon. I became momentarily dizzy due to the
sun."

Tip frowned. It did not in the least mar his easy good
looks. It would be a great deal easier to withstand her feelings
for him if he weren't so dreadfully handsome. And kind. And

solicitous. And . . . *him.*

"What is it this time?" he said. "Is he in the suds again and calling for your pin money to square him with the sharps? Lord, the fellow will never learn."

"No, Tip, it isn't like that. Thomas is not in debt again. Well, he is, of course, or he would be in London now instead of Wales. But that is not why he has written."

His mouth turned up in the slightest grin and his hand slid from her shoulder to the letter tucked in the fabric of her skirt. Bea gripped the paper tight. His gaze met hers. A mere breath separated them. Tip's eyes looked oddly intense.

With a little breath of panic, she released the letter.

He settled back upon his heels and read the missive through.

"It's nonsense," he said.

Bea snatched away the foolscap.

"It is not nonsense. Thomas is in trouble, and I must help him. And if you tell Mama what he wrote, I will never speak to you again, Peter Cheriot." She tugged her hem out of the rosebush, arranging the gown around her legs. Tip stepped back, watching without comment. But he looked far too sure of himself. Bea's eyes narrowed. "Don't doubt me."

"Oh, I don't. I won't tell Lady Harriet. But you aren't going alone. If you imagine I would let you, you are not the sensible girl I have known you to be these past seven years."

"My father is in town. I will write to him today and beg his assistance."

"Ah, I see. Then, let us go forthwith to the parlor and I shall dip the pen into the ink for you, ma'am," he said with a lifted brow. Bea held her tongue and he offered a knowing grin. "I didn't think so."

Of course he knew perfectly well she would not enlist the aid of her father. Mr. Alfred Sinclaire disliked only one thing more than his wife's constant complaints and criticisms: his son's wastrel ways.

"This is not your business," she insisted. "And I will thank you to stay out of it." She grabbed the basket of gardening tools and took a step forward.

His hand enclosed hers wrapped around the handle. Heart in her throat, Bea did not chance looking up. He spoke close beneath her hat brim, his breath stirring the tendrils of hair that escaped her braid.

"Yes, thank you, Lord Cheriot," he said. "I would be delighted for you to accompany me to Wales to help rescue my scapegrace brother from the castle in which the idiot believes he is being held captive."

She opened her mouth to object but he continued.

"I am in fact so enormously grateful, my lord"—his voice was low—"that when the job is done I will be more than happy to consent to becoming your bride." His hand shifted, and he pulled the basket from her grasp.

He moved toward the house. For a moment, Bea watched him go, his shoulders disappearing beneath the trellis thick with foliage.

Pulse tripping, she started after him.

She caught up with him just shy of the house. "You cannot do this. Gwynedd is several days' ride away, and you despise riding in carriages."

"I will ride alongside." He did not look back at her.

Bea absolutely did *not* wish to stare at his wide back and muse upon how a man could look so wonderfully virile whilst carrying a basketful of flowers. But she could not seem to prevent herself.

"You will be missed here," she said in as steady a voice as she could manage. "Lord and Lady Marke have been looking forward to your visit. Little Avery has not ceased singing your praises since the last time you came to York. And Mama expects you to play whist with her before you leave the county. She says I play too poorly to bother."

"Marke and his family will go along perfectly well without me. They know I only hole up with them because they are closer to Hart House than the posting inn." He swung the servant's entrance open, dropped the basket on the ground, and gestured her toward the door.

Bea faced him, clasping her unsteady hands at her waist.

"What about Mama?" More importantly, what about the days it would require to travel to Thomas, days of agonizing intimacy on the road, at inns and in private parlors? What about the lack of any other company to save her from being alone with him, so easy to achieve in town before Mama had moved to Yorkshire permanently, even possible here, but certainly not on such a journey? What about her poor heart, so wretchedly determined to withstand his nonchalant attentions? It would not stand a chance in such close quarters. "She will be enormously unhappy if you leave so soon after arriving."

He stepped toward her and reached for her chin, tilting it up. His fingertips were warm, sending tiny jolts of forbidden pleasure into her belly. Steeling herself for the tingling thrill that went through her every time she met his gaze, she turned hers upward. As always, his eyes were alight.

"As your mother's happiness is not my primary concern," he said quietly, "that argument, my girl, is not particularly effective."

"She depends on you when you are here."

He seemed intent upon studying her face one feature at a time.

"She depends on you," he said. "Too heavily. I only endeavor to amuse her to take some of the burden off your shoulders."

"You are very good to her." Bea spoke across the lump in her throat. "You always have been, since Papa sent her into rustication. She despises it here."

Tip did not respond, but his brow compressed. His fingers slid away and he gestured for her to precede him into the house.

"Ready to brave the dragon?"

"You simply cannot come." Bea wrung her hands, which he watched with interest. "Thomas will be livid to discover I have involved you."

"I don't care a jot for your twin's sensibilities. And I can and indeed will escort you to Wales. Would you like me to inform Lady Harriet, or would you prefer to do that task yourself?"

"I will, of course." Bea's palms were clammy.

"It is not as though you haven't saved his hide plenty of times already." He followed her through the entryway toward the parlor.

"I have never before *gone* anywhere to help him," she murmured.

"You have only spent every penny of your pin money and played peace broker between him and your parents at every other turn. But this time I will be there to lend you moral support." He smiled.

Bea nearly groaned aloud.

The gold parlor, decorated with Egyptian silks and claw-footed furniture, glowed with sunshine. Lady Harriet, opulent in sea-blue organza, reclined on a yellow satin divan. With limpid cerulean eyes so unlike Bea's dull brown eyes, she stared out the French windows onto the terrace as though longing to go into the bright day.

Bea stifled her irritation. Mama never went outside unless moving from the front door to the carriage. She was merely putting on a show for her husband's aunts.

Bea went to the two elderly ladies sitting opposite Lady Harriet, a contrast of cool and cozy nobility. Icy-eyed, silver-haired Lady Marstowe shared little in common with her pleasantly rounded, cockeyed, smiling sister-in-law, Miss Julia Dews. But they were excellent traveling companions and came from their brother's house in London to Hart House each October without fail. Bea welcomed the relief. When the great-aunts were in residence, Mama insulted her much less often.

"Dear me, Beatrice, must you drag in all that dirt? What a horrid mess you are," Lady Harriet said languidly. "Good morning, my lord. How do my neighbors, Lord and Lady Marke, go along?"

"Very well, to my knowledge, ma'am. My ladies." He greeted the great-aunts with a bow, offering Aunt Julia an especially lovely smile.

Bea kissed her mother on one pale cheek. Her face powder made Bea's nose itch.

She gathered her courage.

"Mama, Thomas has written to me. He is in Wales and requests my assistance with a matter of some delicacy."

"Wales!" Lady Harriet's wan hand fluttered over her breast. "Whatever did he go there for? The Welsh are all so tiny, and wretchedly dark."

Tip chuckled softly. Lady Harriet did not seem to notice.

"I would like to go," Bea said, tucking her hands into her skirt.

"Go? Why, of course you may not go. What would I do without you? I daresay I would be obliged to speak to that wretched Perkins. He does not care for me above half. And that dreadful Mrs. Hobbs never listens when I tell her how I want lilies, not chrysanthemums, in my dressing chamber."

"Mama, lilies are not in season and you told the gardener you wished to grow only gardenias in the hothouse this year, so he has done that. Perhaps you might have those cut for your dressing chamber?"

"Gardenias," her mother said upon a groan. "How wretchedly common. You should not have allowed him to do that. Next year you must be more forthright with him, Beatrice."

"Yes, Mama."

"No, you cannot go. You will be obliged to take along my maid, and the two of you are the only ones who know how I like my hair arranged." She draped a hand over her brow.

"I cannot ask Papa for assistance with this matter, Mama." Bea forged ahead. "And Kievan is in Ireland with Georgie and the new baby, of course. Lord Cheriot has graciously offered to escort me to Wales." *Please let her mother forbid it.*

"What a dear, *dear* man you are," Lady Harriet extended her hand for Tip. He bowed over it, and she smiled. "The responsible, caring brother my Beatrice never had to support her, I daresay."

Bea bit the inside of her cheek. Mama didn't care a fig whether anyone supported her in anything. But, *brother*? Must she be so cruel?

But Mama had no idea. No one did, just as they did not know that Tip had ever proposed marriage to her. He had never asked her parents for permission to court her. A man did not do so, after all, when he intended only to tease.

"Harriet," the dowager Lady Marstowe intoned, looking down her nose through a lorgnette, "it is entirely improper for Lord Cheriot to escort your daughter on such a lengthy journey without a suitable chaperone, maid or no maid present."

Bea clasped her hands tightly together.

Lady Harriet set her disinterested gaze upon Bea. She sighed theatrically but with all delicacy.

"I daresay Aunt Grace is correct, Beatrice. You must not go off to rescue Thomas," she said, proving her indifference to both of her youngest children in one listless utterance.

"Perhaps, Lady Marstowe," Tip said with a charming smile, "you would act as chaperone to Miss Sinclaire on this occasion. Miss Dews, might you be convinced to come along as well? I understand that Wales in this season is exceptionally salubrious."

Lady Marstowe's lips pinched together, but Aunt Julia's hazel eyes danced, setting them even further askew.

"That sounds lovely, Peter," Julia said. "Dear Gracie, do let us go along. I have never visited Wales and I suspect this will be my last opportunity."

"Never say it, ma'am," Tip said. "You appear as youthful as a spring stream."

"Well, I am not," Lady Marstowe said sharply. She frowned at the baron. "But I will go. It will certainly be more interesting than sitting in this parlor listening to your complaints, Harriet."

Bea glanced at Tip, but his attention was fixed on her mother, particularly intent.

"Well, you all may as well desert me! Everyone has since Alfred left." Moisture glimmered in Lady Harriet's pale eyes.

"Yes, go, all of you, and take your maid too. Leave me to my lonesome misery." She turned her face away and sighed again. "But before you leave, Beatrice, do instruct Mrs. Hobbs to tell the cook that I simply abhor sole with lemon sauce."

"Yes, Mama." She did not bother pointing out that she had not left her mother's side for more than a day in the four years since her father announced he would no longer see his wife. "Thank you for allowing it. I will return as soon as I am able. Aunt Grace and Aunt Julia, I am very grateful."

"It's bound to be the loveliest lark." Aunt Julia chortled, endeavoring to untangle cream tart from her knitting wool.

Bea turned to Tip. "My aunts and I will do very well traveling on our own, my lord. You needn't bother yourself, and I am certain Cheriot Manor calls you."

"It can wait," he said with a quick smile and turned to her mother. "I will take my leave of you now, my lady. Please allow me to make arrangements with your coachman as I depart."

The lady of the house waved an indolent hand. Bea went with him to the front door.

"Thank you," she said. "You are kind to lend us your assistance."

"Ah, a change in attitude seems to have come over the lady. How refreshing." He grinned. "But don't bother with that, Bea. I have business in that area I should see to anyway. I'm glad to have the excuse to go along."

Of course. Business. Why else would he have offered?

He donned his hat and sketched a light bow as Perkins opened the door.

"Until tomorrow, then, my girl." He went out. On the third step he turned and looked back at her. "Don't think of leaving without me."

"I—"

"You will not."

He tipped his hat at a devil-may-care angle that choked Bea's breath in her throat, and continued down the stair and across the drive. She stared after him, as always. She had done it so many times she had memorized the precise shape of his back and the length of his confident strides. Then Perkins closed the door, and she returned to the parlor for her afternoon dose of humiliation.

~o0o~

Hillsfarne Lodge
Yorkshire, England

Tip had the most pressing urge to hit someone. Glancing about the parlor of Hillsfarne Lodge, however, he saw no one even remotely resembling Thomas Sinclaire's blue-eyed, golden-haired good looks, so unlike his twin sister's deep brown eyes and luxurious, coffee-colored tresses. Thomas took after his mother.

Tip's host sat opposite him in a comfortable chair before the fire, nursing a glass of port. Naturally, Tip could not hit Marke, even in the absence of the true target of his wrath. The thrashing he ached to deal out must wait until he reached Wales.

"Upon your advice," Marke said, "I bought the matched grays from Chance."

Tip swung his attention to his friend. Fifteen years his senior, Averill Marke was a fine fellow. He was also astoundingly decent for never minding that Tip used his home as an inn when he came to visit Bea at Hart House three miles distant.

Marke and his wife never remarked on it. Until a few years earlier, Lady Marke had been companion to Tip's sister, Elizabeth. And when Tip visited, he entertained their young son and offered his host advice on horses. It seemed payment enough for using them so shabbily.

"Like them, do you?" he asked without much enthusiasm.

"They're not in the current fashion, grays, of course." Marke sipped at his brandy. "But very fine. You have an enviable eye for horseflesh, Cheriot, and an impressive knack for knowing a winner."

"You mean those races at Newmarket, I suppose." Tip's fingers wrapped around his crystal goblet. "Had to recoup my father's losses somehow, didn't I? That slate merchant you put me in contact with has turned me a tidy profit, too, by the by. I am indebted to you."

"Glad to be of assistance. A man can't have enough good advice when it comes to trade." Marke looked away uncomfortably. He engaged in trade of necessity.

Tip didn't mind it much, and his investment in the Welsh slate quarry was now proving convenient. While she was clearly resistant to his escort on this journey, Bea couldn't very well deny him the right to look into his business affairs, even if she could deny him herself—again and again.

"I'm heading to Wales tomorrow, actually," he said by way of announcing his early departure. "Don't think Lady Marke will mind me decamping so abruptly, do you?"

"Nancy always enjoys your visits, but she will understand, certainly. Are you concerned about the quarry?"

"No. No worries there. Only, I would like to see it once, meet the quarry master, shake hands and all that."

Marke assessed him.

"You have a dangerously honest air about you, Cheriot, but a clever eye nevertheless. No wonder you do well with tradesmen and horses."

"I will accept that as a compliment, old man." Tip stood to leave.

The parlor door opened and Lady Marke entered. Her compact form glided toward them as silently as she had always moved when living in Tip's family home. That, of course, had been before his father died four years ago and his mother a year later, both in the typically dramatic, brutal fashion with which they had done everything.

Nancy rested her hand upon her husband's shoulder. He reached up and grasped it.

"Are you off to bed now, my dear?" Marke said. "So

early?"

"I chased Avery around all day playing soldiers and am absolutely ragged."

"My lady," Tip said, "although I always enjoy your hospitality, I must depart early tomorrow."

"Tomorrow? Have you been thrown out of Hart House after only one day? I will not believe it. You have not visited in months."

It felt like an eternity.

"No. All are in fine fettle there. Miss Sinclaire is traveling into Wales on an errand and requires an escort."

"Beatrice is going to Wales? Whatever could she have to do there?" Lady Marke's eyes narrowed. "It is Thomas again, isn't it? He is in trouble."

"I will leave that information to the lady to impart to you if she so wishes." Tip bowed his farewell and moved toward the door. "For my part, I have found that business calls me to Wales conveniently at the same instant she wishes to go." A twinge of guilt prickled him for forcing his company on Bea for this journey. But he would not allow her to hare off into the wilderness without a man's protection, and he wasn't about to let any other man have the job.

"Rather too convenient, I would venture to say," the baroness remarked. She folded her arms in an attitude of mild intolerance.

Marke gazed at his wife with measured affection and a hint of pride.

Chest tightening, Tip turned away. Regrettably, he had not been made from the same stuff as Marke, the sort that admired without adoring, the sort that could settle into a comfortable love match without wishing to tear out his heart and hand it to the lady upon a plate, then tear hers out as well. No, he came from the sort of poor sod who met his end in a ditch on a road, and drove his lady-love to a similar fate not long after.

Even before his parents' deaths, though, Tip had recognized Beatrice Sinclaire's rational spirit. That she was pretty as could stare, with silken hair that would ever escape its confines, thick-lashed doe's eyes, and a sweetly curved figure did not escape his notice, of course. A young man on the town—still at university when he had made her acquaintance—was far from immune to those sorts of enticements.

But after that first season his susceptibility to her charms had only grown. Now each time he saw her it grew more difficult to pretend he didn't want her, more than life itself, it sometimes seemed. Like his foolish father, he felt far too deeply. And every time she refused him—for God knew what reason, although Tip had plenty of theories—his fuse shortened.

But Bea was not his mother, as reckless and passionate-natured as her husband. If Tip could keep a cool head in control of his heated heart, he felt certain Bea would see to the rest.

"Tip?" his hostess said. "You have stayed with us in order to visit Hart House at least seven times in the past two years."

"Keeping a running account, are you, Nancy?" He tilted a teasing brow. "Wouldn't have thought it of you, but I will pay my board if you like."

"Don't be ridiculous. You will not tell me even if I ask directly, will you?"

"If you mean to inquire about my devotion to Lady Harriet, you are correct. With all due respect, it is none of your business." He smiled, a jaunty twist of his lips that rarely failed to please.

Nancy's eyes softened, but her arms did not unfold.

"Tease all you wish," she said. "But I suspect you are not as single-minded in your visits to Hart House as you believe. Lady Harriet's situation is not unlike your own mother's at one time. I know Lady Cheriot depended upon your company enormously in those months after your father's death. You were a great comfort to her."

If the words had come from any other than the person who had shared his family's home and affection for years, he would have laughed aloud and changed the subject.

"You have always been very clever, haven't you, Nancy?" he said. "Too clever on occasion."

"Is that an insult, Cheriot?" Marke said.

"Certainly not." Tip bowed. "A compliment to your esteemed wife."

"Ah, good then."

"One doesn't need to be clever," Nancy continued, "to be astonished over the fact that you have not yet come to the point. Or if you have, that she has not accepted you."

"May I remind you that Lady Harriet is already married, however unconvincingly these past several years?" He kept his tone insubstantial. "It would not be the thing for me to pay her formal addresses, you know."

Nancy's arms unwrapped and she slapped her hands against the skirt of her frock. "You are hopeless. You will not tell me, so I cannot help you. And Beatrice won't, either. You both deserve to go on like this for another two years, or twenty."

"Trust me," he said as evenly as he could, "it has already gone on far too long for my tastes." Not a mere two years. *Four.* Four interminable cycles of seasons since that fateful evening when across a ballroom Bea had lifted her shining gaze to his, and he was lost.

He bowed again, met Marke's impassive study with a nod, and left the parlor.

~oOo~

October 20, 1822

Today he proposed in the rose garden. I wore my yellow sprigged muslin, the one he has admired before.

Diary, I am a ninny. I should not wear gowns he likes or meet him without Mama or a maid nearby. But it is very difficult after so many years to remain on formal standing with him.

He stood before me and said, 'Will you do me the honor of becoming my bride, Bea?' He calls me Bea despite my objections. It makes my toes curl up deliciously in my slippers.

Before he left he cast me a Very Dark Look, warning me not to depart for Wales without him. I have enlisted the chaperonage of the great-aunts. Aunt Grace certainly will not allow me and Tip any privacy. A blessing and a curse, at once.

I know very well, Diary, that I ought to have turned him off once and for all this time. I wonder if he still pines for Georgie. He mentions her infrequently now. Someday, no doubt, he will meet a lady who finally breaks the spell my sister cast on him, and love her as well or perhaps even better. In the meantime, his visits here seem to be a habit for him. I am a habit for him, from a time when visiting me allowed him to be close to Georgie, whom he could not have.

I am very wicked to feel so excited. A dark castle, a villainous lord, and Peter Cheriot—all at once! If I were a less sensible person, I might swoon. (I will consider it a miracle if I return home with a functioning heart.)

~oOo~

Chapter Two

Gwynedd, Wales

From a corner of the carriage, Lady Marstowe glowered. Bea did not mind it. As soon as they had left Hart House it seemed as though a cool, encouraging hand pressed her along, a voice whispering in her ear that, for the first time in years, she was free.

Free.

At least for a bit.

"If you want the facing seat, Aunt Grace, I will be glad to switch with you. Or Peg could," she added, smiling at Lady Marstowe's maid. The maid she shared with her mother had remained at Hart House. Easier not to fight it, as usual.

"I cannot abide the facing seat." The dowager's narrow cheeks drew tight with displeasure. "Why isn't Lord Cheriot riding in the carriage with us? Have you offended him?"

"I told you, Aunt Grace, he prefers to ride." He was one of the best horsemen around. Everyone agreed, and Lord Marke and Bea's brother-in-law, Kievan, spoke of it regularly enough. Tip always ignored that sort of praise, of course. He was the least vain man she had ever known.

"It is better this way," the dowager countess grumbled. "It is unsuitable for a young gentleman and lady to be in each other's pockets the way your mother tells me you and he are. Isn't his estate in Derbyshire? How often does he come to Yorkshire?"

Not often enough.

"Every few months or so," she replied, "when Lord Marke needs advice. He is setting up an impressive stable," Bea murmured, hoping her great-aunt could not see the warm flush rising in her cheeks.

"I understand Lord Cheriot has hopeful mamas all over London setting tea just for him," the dowager clipped. "He is a baron, young, wealthy, and handsome as well. Still he comes to Hart House in the middle of the fall session. Impossible."

"Peter is a lovely boy," Aunt Julia chirped. She dug into her knitting bag, her cap hanging upon springy gray curls over one twinkling eye.

The dowager fixed Bea with a hard stare.

"Why are you not yet wed, Beatrice?"

Because when they had lived in town before Papa left, any time a gentleman seemed to show any interest in her he invariably disappeared without a trace after a few encounters. Because her mother had swiftly wearied of chaperoning Bea to entertainments at which her friends were not present. Because at the ripe old age of fifteen Bea had lost her heart to the man who still owned it.

"I have not received an acceptable offer, Aunt Grace."

"Well I don't wonder at it, with Harriet dragging you to Yorkshire the moment Alfred turned her off," the dowager said crisply. "But it does not deter that young man from making the trip. What have you done to him, gel?"

From practice, Bea's hands in her lap remained impressively still.

"Done to whom, Aunt Grace?"

Lady Marstowe's ice-blue eyes narrowed.

"You have offended him, haven't you? Or you are playing fast-and-loose with him. It must be one or the other."

"I am sure I don't know what you mean, Aunt." Her heart raced like one of Tip's prized thoroughbreds. "Lord Cheriot is very kind and he dotes on Mama exceedingly."

"He treats Harriet with much more consideration than she deserves," the dowager muttered. "But he is not a brother to you like that fool woman believes."

"Do you remember, Grace," Aunt Julia said, "that visit to Hart House two years ago when Harriet insisted we sit out on the lawn all afternoon so that she could oversee the planting of the cherry trees and enjoy conversation at the same time? You developed the most disagreeable heat disturbance."

"Harriet is a selfish fool." Aunt Grace frowned. "She never thinks of anything but her own comfort."

"Dear Peter came that afternoon to see Beatrice," Aunt Julia continued, "but when he observed your illness he went right out and found the doctor. At night. Himself! I don't think he even considered sending a groom."

"Hm." The dowager's lips thinned, pulling wrinkles around her mouth.

"He was mourning his beautiful mother then." Julia sighed. "Still he came to visit our Beatrice, didn't he?" Her entire cherubic face creased into a smile.

With moths fluttering about her belly, Bea drew aside the window curtain. Whatever Aunt Grace said, Tip did in fact treat her as Thomas did. He liked visiting because he could be at his leisure with Lord Marke and Nancy, as well as with her and Mama. In York he never had anything to worry about—grain prices, sheep shearing, Parliament bills, or conniving mothers. Certainly not the latter. And, of course, in York he could hear news of Georgie from her and Mama.

Outside the carriage, mists blanketed the landscape, wrapped about gnarled, lichen-covered trees and hovering above grass the exact color of Tip's eyes. Stone fences crept along hillsides, white sheep rising out of the gray like droplets of spring snow yet to melt. Wales was full of mountains in this northern part, but Bea could not see more than a hundred yards in any direction.

Tip rode along the other side of the carriage as he had for days already. He had been a lovely escort throughout the journey, arranging lodging along the road, conveying Aunt Grace, Aunt Julia, and Bea to their chambers after dinner and greeting them with a smile each morning. He regaled them each evening with stories, and explained about the caravans of wagons piled high with slate for which they were obliged to make way several times on the narrow highways.

If this trip accomplished nothing else, it convinced Bea once and for all that he truly had no idea of her feelings for him. He smiled, teased, and laughed, and he served Bea and her great-aunts with unhesitating gallantry. But he might have been a hired courier for all the intimacy he showed her.

It was, of course, much better this way.

Bea stared out the window, the clip-clopping of hooves, creaking of carriage works, and clattering of jumbled stones on the road echoing dully through the fog.

Then, quite abruptly, the curtain of fog lifted and Bea's breath caught.

Ahead, atop a rocky spur amidst a forest of dark evergreens and twisted oaks and elegant ash trees, a stone castle rose in dark, solitary splendor. Built on a massive scale, yet compact in its position tucked against the mountain face, the fortress loomed above the valley. Tip had told them that most of the castles in northern Wales were built in the Middle Ages, to help the English king gain control over the rebellious Welsh peoples and their copper, slate, gold, and silver-rich lands. This castle certainly looked darkly medieval, mysterious and sinister.

"Gwynedd Castle, my lord," the coachman called down. The team pulled the carriage to the right, climbing a narrow, exceedingly bumpy track toward the castle.

"Beatrice, bring your head inside," Aunt Grace commanded. "You will catch your death from the chill."

Bea obeyed. But she did not draw the curtain. Her pulse beat so swiftly she could hear it.

It was more than she had hoped. More than she had imagined and dreamed. Closeted with her demanding mother in the countryside for four years, she'd not had one adventure, not even a spark of excitement. The only true pleasure she had—other than Tip's infrequent visits—came from the novels she borrowed from the lending library in York.

Now she had her chance. She only prayed that what Thomas had written in his letter about the castle's master was true. It could not be. Still, her spine shivered in eerie delight.

The mist seemed to close in on them again as they ascended, as though beckoning them into its haunted embrace. They continued to climb along the hillside, at once doubling back, then again, until they reached a slight plateau. Bea stretched across the seat and opened the other curtain.

The castle was huge, much bigger than it appeared from below. Rising in a double set of rounded towers flanking a central portal, a wall easily a hundred feet high stretched along the ridge of the hill to meet yet another thick tower. Crenellated battlements were pierced by long, narrow slit aperture windows, and here and there a judiciously placed stone hawk completed the portrait of power and strength. Fog encompassed the remainder, rolling down the thick gray stone to unfurl on the grass below. It was all positively ghastly.

And *wonderful*.

The carriage ground to a halt and Tip opened the door.

"My ladies," he said, offering his hand. Lady Marstowe took it and descended; then Tip handed Aunt Julia down. He turned to grasp Bea's fingers.

"You look as though you have seen a ghost," he whispered, effectively doubling the number of words he had spoken to her privately since they had left Yorkshire.

She smiled, afraid her voice would not function properly. The combined proximity of a formidable castle and the man she adored tied her tongue.

"Why, Bea, I believe you are hoping to do exactly that." He chuckled.

"This stone heap is certain to be cold and damp." Lady Marstowe scowled. She beckoned to her maid. "Peg, bring my shawl, and prepare the warming pan as soon as we are within. Why hasn't a footman come out to greet us yet?"

Bea's knees quivered deliciously as they moved forward, possibly because of the monumental building they approached or Tip's hand covering hers upon his arm.

"Thomas wrote that Lady Bronwyn keeps the house now," she said, "with her grandmother, who is apparently frail."

As though on cue, the portcullis lifted into the heavy portal and behind it a thick, iron-bracketed door swung open. Through it sailed an angelic creature.

"Oh, you have come!" she exclaimed, her voice a tinkling of the sweetest bells imaginable. In a porcelain-perfect face warmed by rosy cheeks, her eyes sparkled like gentians touched with dew. Ringlets of black hair tumbled about her neck and tapered shoulders, a cluster of white silk flowers tucked behind one ear with a white ribbon. Gowned in a frothy confection of snowy lace and muslin, she floated to them upon tiny feet clad in peach satin slippers.

Bea was dumbstruck, although perhaps only because the lady of the house did not quite suit her surroundings. She certainly suited Thomas's brief description in his letter: young, maidenly, and excessively beautiful.

Tip did not seem quite as flabbergasted by the girl's exceptional loveliness. He bowed over her hand.

"My lady, am I to guess that you are our hostess? We thank you for the gracious invitation to your home," he said, then drew Bea forward.

Bea dropped into a curtsy. "Good afternoon, Lady Bronwyn. My aunts, Lady Marstowe and Miss Dews, and I are happy to have come. And may I present to you Lord Cheriot?"

The angel's delicate hand grasped hers and drew her up with surprising strength.

"Oh! You must be Miss Sinclaire, for I see your brother's intelligent gaze in your eyes." She giggled infectiously and pressed Bea's hand between both of hers. "I will not have you calling me anything but Bronwyn. I am so happy to make your acquaintance, and thrilled that you have come to visit me on such short notice." Her sparkling gaze shifted to the elderly ladies. "Oh, dear, I am remiss," she exclaimed. "My lady and Miss Dews, you must be cold and weary from the journey. Allow me to show you and your maid to comfortable quarters."

"Your housekeeper will do." The dowager coolly assessed the girl.

Lady Bronwyn's face fell.

"Oh, I fear Grandmama and I haven't a housekeeper any longer. The castle used to be filled with servants, you see, until Lord Iversly returned. Now none will stay. He has frightened them all away except Cook, thank goodness, and her husband, Mr. Dibin. He is the butler, though he was the groom before. They are both very sensible and say Lord Iversly cannot scare them off. Most of the servants I brought with me from London were English, you see, but Cook and Mr. Dibin are Welsh, of course."

"What sort of man frightens his servants?" Lady Marstowe glared. "Is he cruel, or does he chase the maids' petticoats?"

Bea could not resist glancing at Tip. He lifted a brow. Clearly, he did not approve that she had not shared with Aunt Grace the entire contents of Thomas's letter.

"Oh, no," Lady Bronwyn exclaimed. "He isn't that sort of man. At least, it does not seem so." Her brow wrinkled, but it cleared just as quickly. "But do come inside. I will bid Cook brew some tea."

Thomas appeared beneath the castle portal.

"Bea!" His brow furrowed. "And Cheriot? Aunt Grace, and Aunt Julia? Why have you brought them, Bea?" he demanded, striding forward.

"That is hardly the way to greet your devoted sister after she has traveled such a distance at your request, Sinclaire," Tip said.

Bea grasped her brother's hands.

"It is good to see you, Tom. Mama and I have missed you."

Thomas at once looked sheepish, his light curls surrounding his face in a boyish manner.

"Yes, well, a fellow gets busy, of course." He shifted his attention to Tip. "How do you do, Cheriot? What brings you to Wales?"

"Lord Cheriot has business interests in Porthmadog," Bea supplied. "He graciously offered to escort us here. I am sure he will wish to be off first thing tomorrow to see to his affairs."

"I am in no particular hurry," Tip said laconically, casting her a sideways glance. "And I have a notion to meet this Iversly who frightens off all but the most steadfast of servants."

Thomas's brow lowered.

"Aunt Grace." He bowed with stiff formality.

"Scapegrace," she muttered, and turned toward the castle.

"Thomas, you young scamp." Aunt Julia accepted a kiss from him upon her cheek.

"Oh, let us all go inside and get comfortable," Lady Bronwyn said, fluttering her lashes at Thomas as he took Aunt Julia's arm. Bea was not in the least surprised. Despite his often-shabby manners, her handsome brother always attracted the prettiest girls.

Thomas smiled gently at his hostess and followed her through the massive portal with Aunt Julia.

"So, now we may comprehend your brother's great interest in Wales," Tip murmured at Bea's shoulder as they moved through a heavy passageway lit by torches. They ascended a cramped, winding stone staircase into another narrow corridor and then through a truncated entryway, all of stone, offering no adornments but severe pointed arches.

True to Lady Bronwyn's word, no footman stood ready to open the door she approached. Thomas did instead, gesturing them all inside. The chamber was broad and hexagonal, obviously one of the enormous towers Bea had seen from the outside. Given its size, it was surprisingly cozy within. Thick, colorful tapestries draped the walls, rugs lined the tiled floor, furniture of recent date filled the space, all illuminated by the glow of a brace of beeswax candles and a merrily crackling fire.

Bea sat beside Aunt Julia upon a brocade sofa, but Aunt Grace remained at the door, perusing the chamber with lifted lorgnette. Lady Bronwyn pulled a bell rope and smiled charmingly at everyone.

"I hope your journey passed smoothly." She dimpled.

"Very well, thank you." Bea cast a glance at Thomas, who was staring at Lady Bronwyn like a boy at a new puppy, as any gentleman might when confronted with such loveliness.

Bea's gaze shifted to Tip. He was looking at her, not at the young beauty.

"Oh, Beatrice," Lady Bronwyn said, sitting beside her and grasping her hands again in delicate fingers. "I have so *longed* for a friend." Her eyes dimmed. "I have not gone out in quite a few weeks, of course."

"Aunt Grace and Aunt Julia," Bea said swiftly, "wouldn't you like to go to your chambers and rest a bit before dinner?"

"I said as much before, didn't I?" The dowager glared at their hostess, but she seemed peaked.

Lady Bronwyn leaped up. "Oh, yes, of course!"

Tip offered his arm to Aunt Grace.

"May I see you to your chamber, my lady?"

"No." She batted his arm away. "I am perfectly capable of seeing myself there, if this girl doesn't get us lost on the way."

"Oh, my lady, you are so diverting." Lady Bronwyn's giggles faded into the corridor as she led the great-aunts away.

Tip turned from the door and gave Bea a long, steady look before shifting his attention to her brother.

"What's going on here, Sinclaire?"

"Not sounding so friendly now, are you, Cheriot? I wondered why you'd come."

"Gentlemen." Bea stood and moved toward her brother. "Let us not adopt threatening postures yet, shall we? We have only just arrived. Thomas, Lord Cheriot has come along to assist you, as I have. Your note, however, left us with some questions."

"I should say so," Tip put in.

Bea cast him a speaking look. She placed her hand upon her brother's arm.

"Tell us what is happening, beginning with how you came to be here. Mama and I believed you to be in Scotland. That is what Papa wrote to us in his last letter, although admittedly that was some months ago."

"I'd intended to go to Scotland. But Charlie begged me to come here instead."

"Charlie?"

"Charlie Whitney. You know, Bea. I brought him home on holiday three years back or so. Stirred up a lark with the carolers, if you remember."

"Yes." She nodded, vaguely recalling a young gentleman in his cups the entire visit.

"Well, Charlie's pater told him he had to come up here to meet his betrothed. Never set eyes on the girl, but said she was an impressive heiress and he'd fixed him up good, only the contract left to finalize, but p'raps he wanted to eyeball the chit before the thing was all signed and sealed."

"And Mr. Whitney asked you to accompany him?"

"Charlie's never been much for filial responsibility." He cracked a grin. "Thought we could take in the sights on the way, have a go at the local ales and a few black-haired—"

Tip cleared his throat. Thomas's gaze shot to him, then moved guiltily back to Bea.

"Go on," she said. "So you set out to meet his fiancée. Then?"

"Then we arrived, Charlie saw how it was, and he hightailed it out of here before a fellow could blink twice."

Bea shook her head.

"I fear I am lacking perfect understanding, Tom. You arrived here?"

"Yes." His gaze shifted back and forth between Bea and Tip, his brow questioning.

"Do you mean to say that Lady Bronwyn is Charlie's betrothed?" Bea asked.

"Not any longer." Thomas scowled. "He stayed here for all of three hours before he told her he wouldn't have her and that her grandmother could give her dowry to the dogs for all he cared about it."

"Good heavens," Bea murmured. "But she is very beautiful and seems charming."

Thomas's blue eyes shone with sudden fervor.

"Aphrodite embodied. An angel on earth."

"I daresay." A grin tugged at Bea's lips. Warmth gathered

at the nape of her neck. She glanced at Tip and again found him watching her. She turned her gaze to the lavishly appointed chamber. "And wealthy, you say?"

"According to Charlie's father."

"What did he find to be so repellent about her that he left in such short order? Or is he merely a cad?"

Thomas shrugged.

"He's a good enough sort of fellow. At least I thought he was until this. Now I'm convinced he's a sorry coward."

"Coward?"

Thomas peered at Bea's face for a moment.

"Didn't you read my letter? I explained it all in plain English, Bea."

"I read it, of course. You did not mention how Lady Bronwyn's servants had all abandoned her, however. Why did they leave?"

"Iversly came back, just as she said, and frightened them all off."

"Yes. This Lord Iversly . . ." Bea's spine prickled. "When did he return, Thomas, and from where, exactly? Your letter did not mention him."

"Of course it did." His brow screwed up and he looked back and forth between her and Tip again as though they were slow tops. "He's the ghost."

~o0o~

August 6, 1822

'*Won't you marry me, Bea, and have over with these ridiculous refusals? It begins to grate on a fellow.*'

This constituted Lord Cheriot's highly intimate and wondrously gallant proposal of marriage to me this afternoon.

Can I be blamed for declining? I do not understand why he will not leave me in peace and go bother some other wretched spinster-in-the-making. Or he might even try proposing to a lady who deserves his oh-so-charming nonchalance. I have it on excellent authority (cousin Amelia spent the season in London) that he is considered a prize on the Marriage Mart. Of course he is. He admitted to me today, however, that he is weary of town. Little there interests him, he said.

Sometimes he looks at me very oddly. Then he speaks of light matters, a glimmer in his teasing eye, and my heartbeats slow again to nearly regular speed. Never entirely though. My heart beats for him.

It will always beat for him, no matter how shabbily he treats me. I am horrified to admit this.

I should accept him once, merely so that he will suffer a touch of the misery he thrusts upon me each time he asks. What a surprise that would be for him! And a terrible awakening. Ah ha! Perhaps next time, Diary, if I am courageous (and if there is a next time), I shall. But then I would be obliged to cry off afterward. Or to marry him.

I suppose it would not do to accept him, after all.

~o0o~

Chapter Three

"Thomas, we are already here." Bea frowned. "This is not necessary."

Her brother fixed an irritated look on her.

"I can't expect you to see the right of it. Only a girl of real understanding, like Lady Bronwyn, would—"

"That is enough, Sinclaire."

Thomas's gaze darted to Tip, momentarily repentant. Bea's remained averted, but pink colored her cheeks.

"I'm sorry, Bea, I didn't mean to be unkind," Thomas said, too begrudgingly for Tip's taste. But it seemed to mollify his sister. She set her slender hand on her twin's arm again.

"Thomas, what on earth leads you to believe that a ghost haunts this castle?"

"He doesn't precisely haunt the entire castle. Only Lady Bronwyn." His face grew stormy. "He intends to marry her."

"To whom?"

"To himself!"

"Oh, I see." Bea's hand dropped.

"It don't seem as though you do." The petulance had returned to Thomas's voice. "I tell you, Bea, the villain says he'll haunt her until she promises to wed him."

"A *ghost*, Thomas?" Her brow creased again. "How can a ghost marry anyone?"

"I'm certain I don't know," he admitted. "But he intends to do it."

"How do you know that?"

"He told her, of course."

"He did? That is interesting. And why doesn't Lady Bronwyn simply leave?"

"At first she chose not to leave because her grandmother is too frail and can't relocate. But when she finally attempted escape, he wouldn't allow it."

"How singular."

Thomas crossed his arms in an attitude of exasperation and looked across to Tip.

"What do you think of this, Cheriot?"

"I admit . . ." He paused. "It strains credulity."

Bea's lips quivered, but her cheeks remained bright. Feverishly so. Her soft eyes too. She looked peculiarly agitated and astoundingly pretty.

Tip's mouth went dry.

"Well, I believe Lady Bronwyn," Thomas said staunchly. "What's more, I've heard him speak."

"You have? You've really heard him?" Bea's fingers twisted together, her quickening breaths now apparent through the slight movement of her lovely breasts. "What did he say?" Her voice was a wisp of its typical serenity.

Unthinkable. Beatrice Sinclaire's voice did not waver. Ever. Except, perhaps, once. On the third of November, 1821. Tip would never forget it.

And now again.

He stared at her, thoroughly transfixed.

"He wasn't speaking to me at the time," Thomas said. "He was telling Lady Bronwyn that she wouldn't require a bridal trousseau." He glowered. "He enjoys taunting her."

"Gracious me. He sounds beastly," Bea said, her tone nearly level again. Tip released a slow breath.

"He's an awful beast," Thomas said forcefully.

"Why did he choose Lady Bronwyn, Tom? Why is he haunting this castle, and her in particular?"

"He was once lord here, hundreds of years ago."

"Hundreds?"

Thomas nodded. "Seems so, though only briefly. Then he was cursed."

"Ah. He is not merely an ordinary run-of-the-mill ghost," Tip said, leaning back against the doorpost. "He must be cursed as well. Intriguing."

"Yes," Thomas said peevishly. "The curse requires him to remain at Gwynedd Castle until he finds a bride who will marry him. A living woman."

"Dear me," Bea put in. "What did he do to deserve that fate?"

"Isn't clear. He hasn't been straight with Lady Bronwyn, and he won't speak to me at all."

"Did he speak to Whitney?" Tip inquired mildly.

"Yes. He told Charlie to sod off, so the bottomless looby did."

Tip could not prevent himself from grinning. Thomas was only four years his junior, but he wore his emotions on his sleeve like a lad of ten.

"Thomas," Bea said quietly. "Must you speak in such a manner?"

"Apologies, Bea," he scowled.

"Your sincerity no doubt touches your sister," Tip murmured.

Bea's feathered brows were drawn.

"Thomas," she said, "if Lord Iversly has been trapped here for so many centuries, why hasn't he yet had any luck in finding a bride?"

"Would *you* marry a ghost?" Thomas asked incredulously.

Bea's cheeks glowed even brighter, and quite abruptly pretty became *stunning*.

Tip's breath shortened. He had never seen her features suffused with so much feeling. With him she laughed, quipped, and demurred. Now passion was all over her face. Good Lord, merely watching her blush tightened his breeches uncomfortably. Now who was the boy?

"No, of course I would not marry a ghost," she replied a bit unsteadily. "But you and Lady Bronwyn said he only just returned to the castle. Where has he been?"

"Sleeping, apparently."

"What do you mean, sleeping? Ghosts sleep?"

A simple, rational question. Tip hoped this lasted. Her

cool, measured sense he could manage well enough.

"I don't know if his sleep is like ours," Thomas said, as though indeed discussing a rational subject. "But he went away for a time, not leaving the castle mind you, but not often bothering the inhabitants for a few decades, apparently. Nearly a century, in fact."

"Really?" She seemed intrigued again, her dark eyes sparking with keen interest.

Tip took in a slow pull of air.

"Why did he wake up, as it were?" she said.

"Well," Thomas flicked an uncertain glance at Tip. "You see, the curse has a stipulation."

"What is it?" Bea asked.

"It seems that Iversly must marry a maiden," he spit out the words.

Silence followed this revelation.

Finally Bea spoke.

"A maiden?"

"You know, Bea." Thomas rubbed his brow. "A virgin."

"Yes, Tom, I know what a maiden is," she said in a low voice. "Intimately." Her gaze slid to Tip. Now even her lips looked pinker than usual. Nearly red. Shapely and full. Beautiful to the point that the fall of his breeches was not now in the least bit suitable for public.

Tip nearly had to turn away, but the door opened behind him and Lady Bronwyn entered, calling Bea and Thomas's attention. Bea seemed to study their hostess with renewed interest.

"Oh," Lady Bronwyn said, "now Lady Marstowe and Miss Dews are settled, with a nice hot pan and a pot of tea and biscuits. Cook bakes the tastiest ginger biscuits. You must have some, Miss Sinclaire. Oh, may I call you Beatrice?"

"Of course."

"Oh, Beatrice, we shall have so much fun now that you are here! I cannot go beyond the estate boundaries, but still there are the stables, and picnics to be had if the weather clears, and the gardener clipped walking paths before he left in July.

Perhaps they will still be usable."

"Have you and your grandmother been here only a few months, Bronwyn?"

"Oh, Grandmama has been here for eons. I was with my mother's sister in Bath for several years, though not yet out in society. But I grew up in this castle. He was not here at that time, of course. There were no eligible maidens in residence then, you see. Only little girls, old matrons, and men." She sighed, a theatrical trill of sound that filled Thomas's eyes with longing and left Tip cold. "I wish I had believed in the curse then," she continued. "I certainly would not have returned to be with Grandmama this summer if I had known it to be real."

"I daresay," Bea said.

"Oh, but where is the tea? I will fetch it myself. Cook must be very busy preparing dinner all alone in that enormous kitchen. Beatrice, would you like me to show you to your chamber so that you may freshen up?"

"Yes, thank you." She moved toward the door, meeting Tip's gaze as she passed. Her thick lashes fluttered ever so slightly, then she smiled.

Tip's cravat grabbed at his throat, abruptly too snug. Remaining aloof from her during the journey had accomplished nothing except to make him more desperate for the sight of her, for her voice, words, scent, touch.

It was the opposite of what he had intended. But that seemed to be his perpetual trouble. Always the less he saw of her, the more he wanted her. Then when he finally had her near, he wanted her even nearer. He was the greatest idiot alive to imagine she would relent to his suit now simply because he escorted her here. Her comment about his business in Porthmadog made it clear she wished him gone already.

Thomas cleared his throat.

"I'm sorry, Tip, if I don't seem myself today." He thrust out a hand. "I'm glad to see you here."

"Thank you, Tom. I regret to find you embroiled in this situation."

"I don't regret it." Thomas shook his head. "I couldn't

wish myself elsewhere. Not for a thousand guineas."

"Lady Bronwyn?" Tip could understand how a man might admire a girl as beautiful and vivacious as the castle's chatelaine. He wouldn't, of course, but his tastes ran to women with rather more in their heads than hair and feathers. One woman, in particular.

"She is perfection itself," Thomas said upon a heavy exhalation.

Tip's stomach soured. *Perfection itself.* His father's favorite phrase to describe his wife, the woman he practiced infidelity upon for over twenty years despite his vows of devotion.

"Is she?"

"I mean to save her from her fate," Thomas said firmly. "I would take her away from this dratted castle straight off, but the curse traps a maiden here as soon as she arrives. Lady Bronwyn can't leave. You can see now, I've got to find a way to release the curse and rescue her. That's why I wrote to Bea. She's so clever and levelheaded. I don't know how we got to be twins. She always knows precisely how to— Tip?" His brow wrinkled. "Cheriot?"

Tip's jaw had locked. With extraordinary effort, he loosened it enough to speak.

"I do not know how you came to be twins, either, Sinclaire." His voice sounded dangerously low, even to him. "But then, you do have something in common: She thinks only of your well-being, and so do you."

"I beg your pardon! I have only Lady Bronwyn's safety on my conscience."

Tip gripped his hands into fists to prevent himself from employing them.

"And what of your sister's safety? Did you pause one moment in pursuit of your conscience to consider hers?"

"Bea is perfectly safe. Why, she's the most sensible girl . . ." Thomas's words stumbled. Slowly his eyes went wide. "Oh, good God," he uttered. "I didn't even think!"

It didn't matter that this whole cock-and-pony story wasn't real. Thomas believed it to be, and so his unthinking behavior was no less noxious. But he rarely ever thought of his sister before himself. He used her when he needed her, in the same manner that her entire family did. Except perhaps Georgianna. Tip knew that Georgie cared deeply about Bea. Unfortunately, that caring did Bea little good all the way across the Irish Sea.

"It is a lucky thing for you that this is all a hoax, Thomas," he said, "or I would level you right now."

Thomas's brow lowered.

"This is no hoax, Cheriot. It's perfectly real. Mark my words, you'll see—or hear, rather, because he isn't visible to anyone but maidens." He moved toward the door. "I must go speak with Bronwyn now. That is, Lady Bronwyn. She said something else about the curse, a detail, I can't quite recall, but I think perhaps—I don't know. I will see you at dinner," he said and disappeared through the doorway.

Thomas Sinclaire was an inconsiderate pup. And his ghost story was a Banbury tale. But Bea believed him. Recalling her bright eyes and quickened breaths sent hot pressure into Tip's groin again. He hoped to Hades he had managed to keep the desire from his gaze. But the moment had surprised him. She surprised him.

If he were honest, she usually did. Each time he made the journey to Yorkshire to feast his senses on her for a few days, she revealed something of herself he had never seen before. Another tantalizing hint.

It had happened like that in Aldborough four years earlier.

He had gone to York on a whim, wanting to see her but not realizing quite how desperately. He arrived late at the assembly rooms to find her dancing, graceful ease in each step. But he already knew she danced well. He had been to plenty of parties she attended in London, paying her his careless attentions for two years when he was on holiday from university.

On this night she sparkled in the crowded, overheated hall. As the patterns of the set took her about the room, she watched her partner and the other dancers. Eyes luminous, she sought their gazes, and when they met she smiled, her doe's eyes lingering with pleasure and gentle longing, her lips curved in a reflection of enchantment.

Watching her, something had tightened in Tip's chest, something vital and alive. Already at twenty-three he had tried to dampen that sort of feeling. He had seen the damage it could do to a man. But staring at Bea that night, he let it have rein.

Then she laughed—at her partner's witticism, perhaps—throwing her head back with full-throated delight, her lovely neck a column of warm cream, and Tip could not breathe. When the set ended, in a haze of bemusement he stepped forward. Her gaze met his, illuminated with dazzling joy, and Tip lost his heart.

He realized only later that night, when she refused his hand, that in point of fact he had lost his heart to her the moment he had met her years earlier.

"You gaze at her with lust."

Tip started out of his memories. He'd had the very thought mere moments ago. But the voice that spoke was not inside his head. Instead, it echoed through the chamber from no clear direction, low and gravelly, and peculiarly accented. Not altogether English.

Or, rather, not recently English.

He pivoted slowly on his heels, studying the tapestries draped over the heavy walls. Nothing stirred in the chamber, no feet beneath the wall coverings, no figure crouched behind a table or chair.

Tip folded his arms.

"I beg your pardon?" he ventured. He may as well discover now if wanting Bea and not having her for so long had driven him to madness already.

"You do so when she is not watching," the voice rumbled. "When none are watching."

A shiver passed across Tip's shoulders, but now he knew it was not his conscience speaking. The voice was too different from his, rougher and flat-toned.

"Except you, I presume?" he replied.

"You wish to bed her."

Tip couldn't blame the fellow for being observant, whoever he was.

"Perhaps," he admitted.

"Why have you not? Are you not man enough?"

Tip's neck bristled.

"Who are you? Show yourself."

"I am Iversly. This is my home in which you sojourn."

Tip released a breath. No game-playing, after all. Just clear, simple bamboozling.

"I understood that this house belongs to Lady Bronwyn's father, Lord Prescot. Why don't you come into the open where I can see you?"

"I stand before the tapestry that depicts a scene of hunting, by the north wall, near the window."

Tip's gaze shifted to the spot. There was nothing there, of course.

"You cannot see me," the voice continued, "because you are not a maiden."

Tip couldn't help chuckling.

"Not remotely."

"Why do you seek to conceal your desire for her?" The disembodied voice said. "Why have you not taken her to wed?"

"Who?"

"Ach! You are a fool." The voice rang with contempt.

"And you are a villain, or so I am told."

"Insult me in my home again, lad, and I will show you my displeasure."

"I daresay. But how, I wonder." Tip moved toward the tapestry. Chill air cut across the chamber despite the thick fire in the hearth. "Do you throw objects, or are your methods more subtle? A loose board in the floor of a high battlement? A rusted nail in my wardrobe? I understand that some ghosts get up to those sorts of tricks. Are you among those?"

The voice grumbled wordlessly. Tip lifted a brow, straining to catch the direction from which the sound came.

"Ah, so you have no true corporeal powers, then," he said.

"I understand that is the way of most specters. Even ill-tempered ones." He made a slow perusal of the chamber again, then looked to the tapestry, leisurely studying the hunting scene picked out in vibrant blues, reds, greens, and gold. A pack of dogs were bringing a young stag to the ground, leaping onto its long back, biting its flesh, drawing blood. The hunters, mounted on decorated steeds with bows at the ready and arrows nocked, closed in. "You know," he said, "I am not at all certain you have the right to call me lad. Your voice sounds too young. How old are you?"

"Five and thirty years I lived as a human. Since then centuries have passed, and now I am nearly as old as these mountains." He sounded weary. Given the circumstances, Tip didn't much sympathize.

"I doubt that. In which century were you born?" The more questions he asked, the more likely the fellow would be to make a mistake.

"I fought for King Harry when the blood of French princes and mercenary scum mingled upon the soaked fields of Agincourt."

"Ah, that long ago," Tip murmured. He would unmask this humbug soon enough.

"The girl is beautiful." The voice dipped deep.

Tip paused before responding.

"You speak of your intended, I suspect."

"No."

Tip's spine stiffened. This went too far.

"My lord," he said firmly, "afford me the pleasure, if you will, of refraining from commentary on Miss Sinclaire. She is not your business."

"She is a maiden."

"Which should not merit your interest. Haven't you already chosen your bride, or am I mistaken?"

Silence greeted him.

"The curse stipulates a Welsh bride," the voice finally said, hollower than before.

Tip shrugged. "Well there you have it. Lady Bronwyn it

must be, or none."

"The Sinclaire maid's veins run with Welsh blood. A drop only is needed to fulfill the curse."

"How would you know of her ancestry?" Perhaps he had associates outside the castle gathering information. Thomas had been here more than enough time for clever thieves to investigate his family. The bamboozler would be a fool to make an assertion that would be easily denied by the lady herself, after all.

"I do not know it," the ghost said. "I sense it."

"Ah." The ruffian would suffer for this. Whoever he was, and his confederates, Tip would make them pay.

"But the black-haired girl came here first, so she it must be," the voice continued with peculiar heaviness. "Soon she will be my bride, whether she wishes it or not."

"You know," Tip strolled toward the center of the chamber, "in this century we do not force women to the altar."

"Neither did we in my era. But this time there will be no altar, nor priest. Only a marriage bed, then death. Blessed, peaceful death."

Tip's blood ran cold. Lady Bronwyn seemed a flighty, careless girl, but she did not deserve this cruel fraud.

"Excellent, my lord," Bea said, entering the room. "I am glad you are still here. I had hoped to speak with you before—" Her voice slid to a halt.

Tip turned to her, masking his emotions with her as always.

The back of his neck prickled. Her lovely gaze was fixed on the lower portion of the hunt tapestry. She curtsied toward the tapestry and turned to Tip.

"Lord Cheriot, will you be so kind as to introduce me?"

Chapter Four

"As you see, Bea, I am alone, except for your lovely self, of course."

"Given the circumstances, my lord, this is not really the best time to tease." Bea moved forward, glancing again at the gentleman by the wall. In the flickering firelight and candles he seemed all dark angles. He was tall, nearly of a height with Tip although thicker-bodied, and dramatically dark, from the slash of black hair crossing his brow and shadow of a beard upon his jaw to his ebony eyes. All about him hung an air of cold gloom. And there was something strange about him, something oddly insubstantial.

In comparison, Tip's masculine vibrancy and warmth was like a breath of life.

"Please," she said to him. "Introduce me."

Tip's eyes took on a guarded look.

"I assure you," he said. "I would do so if there were another person present in the chamber with us."

"He cannot see me. Only maidens can see me." The gentleman's voice sounded across the broad chamber, both deep and thin at once, like a hard winter wind, present one instant with powerful force, vanished the next.

A shiver slithered up Bea's spine. Her gaze slid to Tip's. His emerald eyes seemed bright.

"Of course he can see you," she said to the gentleman. "You are standing less than four yards away. Who are you, sir?"

"Iversly." He bowed. "Enchanted, my lady."

Bea blinked in surprise. She had imagined Lord Iversly an invention of Lady Bronwyn's imagination, created to bring Thomas to heel. It was frankly something of a relief to see that he was a real man, although not at all the sort of fellow with whom she wanted her brother to compete. He had a harsh, muscular look about him, and was at least a decade older than Thomas.

"I am pleased to make your acquaintance, my lord. I am only Miss Sinclaire, however."

"But you are of royal stock," he replied. "One of your English forebears bedded a Welsh princess and begat a child upon her."

"Why, that is perfectly true." She nodded. "It happened a very long time ago, and of course it was not quite that unseemly. They were married. But how do you come to know about that?"

Tip had gone entirely immobile beside her, his lips a white line.

Lord Iversly replied, "I can smell it on you." The fire in the grate seemed to recede, the mists outside invading the chamber as though attracted by his words.

Tip's brow lowered.

"Beg the lady's pardon for that."

"Why must I beg her pardon for speaking the truth? My senses are uncommonly acute—those I have remaining, of course."

"Those you have remaining?" Bea asked Lord Iversly, but she could not take her eyes off Tip. He seemed to be avoiding looking directly at their host. That was not at all like him.

"Smell, sight, hearing," Lord Iversly replied. "Alas, taste and touch were stolen from me when I perished, or this immortality would be considerably more interesting, no doubt." He pushed away from the wall and moved to a candelabrum. Lifting his hand, he passed it slowly through a flame, holding his palm in the fire for a long interval then presenting it for her inspection. "You see?"

His skin was unmarked.

Bea's breath petered out. She turned to Tip. His face was taut, his cheeks pale as he stared unfocused across the chamber.

"Can you see him, Bea?" he said.

"Yes, of course," she said, somewhat shaken by his intensity and Lord Iversly's trick.

Tip took a quick, hard breath and turned to her.

"I cannot."

"Because you are not a maiden." Iversly's voice mocked, the sound hollow and seeming to come from everywhere now.

Bea stepped back.

"Oh, no." Lady Bronwyn's voice wavered in the doorway. "He is here."

"Drawn by beauty, as always, my lady," Lord Iversly replied, a wicked glint in his black eyes.

"How charming," Aunt Julia said. "A ghost who knows the value of flattery."

Bea's great-aunts entered, but Lady Bronwyn hesitated, Thomas hovering behind.

"Aunt Julia," Bea said, pushing back her shoulders. "Lord Iversly is not a ghost, after all, as you can see."

"I cannot see anything of the kind," Lady Marstowe said sharply. "Lord Iversly, show yourself this instant and cease this foolish charade."

Iversly's face grew, if possible, more shadowed.

"I shall take my leave of you at this time," he intoned. "But I shall return." He crossed to the door. Lady Bronwyn leaped out of the way, Thomas flattened his back to the wall, and Lord Iversly passed them by and was gone.

"There, you see," Bea said bracingly. "Ghosts do not use doors."

"He does occasionally," Bronwyn said, trembling noticeably. "At least to leave. Usually he arrives any which way and at the most unexpected moments." She clutched her shawl and Thomas hurried to assist her.

"Do you see now?" he said. "He is real. The curse is real and we must find a way to save Lady Bronwyn."

"This is preposterous." Lady Marstowe sniffed.

"Or wonderfully sentimental." Aunt Julia nodded. Her cap was tied atop her unruly gray locks at a slant and bobbed to one side like a blancmange on a tilted plate.

"I beg your pardon to disagree, Aunt Julia," Thomas said. "There is nothing whatsoever sentimental about Iversly. He is a monster intent on ruining this poor lady's life."

"Thomas, you are a besotted fool," the dowager said sharply. "A man who does not exist cannot ruin anyone's life."

Lady Bronwyn's cheeks went from white to red.

"You heard him, Aunt Grace," Thomas said. "He stood right in this chamber and spoke to us."

"A magician's trick."

"A very good one, I should say." Aunt Julia nodded again.

"Julia, do not encourage this foolishness."

"But he was here, I tell you," Thomas insisted.

"He was, Lady Marstowe." Lady Bronwyn's voice was thin. "Oh, why won't you believe me? I saw him!"

"So did I." Bea's words brought all eyes to her.

While the others spoke, a tingling energy had crept into her, drying her damp palms and stilling her shaking. Excitement sizzled through her.

She had seen a ghost. She had *spoken* with him. It was by far the most thrilling thing that had ever happened to her. Except for meeting Peter Cheriot.

"I saw him too," she said to Lady Bronwyn. "Could you describe to me his appearance?"

"I believe you," Thomas mumbled to the girl, but Bronwyn was already crossing the room to grasp Bea's hands.

"He is odious," she said, squeezing Bea's fingers.

"But exactly how?"

"He has black hair and horrible black eyes and he smirks at me, just as he did there." Her gentian eyes clouded. "He wears a black tunic, shirt, and stockings."

"Hose, I believe they were called," Bea offered.

"And awful, tall boots that do not make any sound when he walks."

Bea's blood hummed. A tingle of fear still wriggled through her, but it only added to her exhilaration.

"Why does he use the door to leave, do you imagine?"

"To be odious," the girl repeated with an eloquent shudder.

Clearly Lady Bronwyn was too close to the matter to be of critical use.

"Beatrice, you cannot believe this child," Lady Marstowe said.

"I do, Aunt Grace. I saw him, and I spoke with him before you all arrived. He passed his hand through a candle flame without flinching. He also told me that I have a Welsh ancestor, which is true. Thomas, had you mentioned that to anyone here?"

"I didn't even know it!"

"You see, Aunt Grace, Lord Iversly is a ghost."

"Well of course he is!" Thomas exclaimed. "The question is not whether he is a ghost, but how we will prevent him from forcing Lady Bronwyn into marriage."

"It seems so, Tom." Tip's voice was especially deep, but even. Bea met his gaze. It seemed shadowed, and there was a crease in his brow.

She had dragged him into this. Well, not precisely. He had insisted on coming along. But he had not expected this, certainly.

"You needn't remain," she said quickly. "Neither of us believed Thomas's letter, of course. You did not bargain for this when you offered your escort, and you have business elsewhere. We will not take it amiss if you leave."

"Of course we will, Cheriot," Thomas stated. "I can't defeat this fellow with a bunch of women."

"Thomas, your gallantry does you no justice," Tip replied, then turned to Bea again. "My business can wait."

She had rarely seen him so somber or speak with such lack of animation. She could only recall one occasion on which he had looked so emotionless, the time he visited Yorkshire while he was still in mourning from his mother's death. He had been so grave then, so unlike himself.

"I would not wish you to—"

"I am remaining." His tone was unflinching, his jaw hard.

A thrill of pleasure skittered through her. Before, he had thought the whole thing nonsense, and he had not actually seen Lord Iversly. But now he believed her and intended to help.

"The last sane mind in this party has fled, I see," Lady Marstowe said, then barked at Lady Bronwyn, "When do you serve dinner here, girl?"

"Oh, I beg your pardon, my lady." Lady Bronwyn's eyes glittered. "I am only enormously relieved you are all here. You cannot imagine what a terror this has been for me. Then Mr. Sinclaire arrived and promised help." She laid eyes full of gratitude upon Thomas, then turned. "Thank you, Lord Cheriot and dear Beatrice. You are infinitely kind."

Tip did not smile. Bea bit the inside of her cheek.

"Dinner?" Aunt Julia chirped.

~o0o~

Strain hinted about Tip's mouth throughout the meal. He did not once look at Bea, and he continued unusually sober. Everyone else was wrapped up in the ghost. Bronwyn and Bea were obliged to repeat the details of his appearance several times, and Thomas recounted each occasion on which he had heard Lord Iversly speak. Tip remained largely silent, not offering his own testimonial although Bea was certain he had been speaking with the ghost when she entered the parlor.

The party returned to the parlor after dinner to take tea, but the great-aunts did not remain long before rising to retire.

"Lady Bronwyn," the dowager said, "does Iversly wander the corridors at night, dragging chains and that sort of nonsense?"

"Oh, no. He stays in the master suite, I believe. At least," her voice quivered, "that is what he told me."

"The villain." Thomas took her arm. "I will escort you to see your grandmother before you retire, if you wish," he said gently and led her from the chamber.

"The poor dear," Aunt Julia said, although Bea could not

say whether she meant Lady Bronwyn or the sickly grandmother they had yet to meet. Bronwyn's grandmother was of a delicate nature and apparently frightened of Lord Iversly. Thomas insisted this was the reason he had stayed on after his friend fled, although Bea wished he had thought to engage a more effective chaperone for the maiden.

She glanced at Tip across the parlor. His gaze rested on her, peculiarly enigmatic.

"Beatrice, come along," Lady Marstowe ordered. "Julia."

Bea obeyed, but Aunt Julia paused.

"Peter dear, aren't you going to bed too? It has been an awfully fagging day."

"Of course, ma'am." He offered his arm to Julia.

Their bedchambers were all clustered about a central keep, with Bea's around a corner along the dark, stone corridor, and Bronwyn's, Thomas's, and Tip's just beyond.

"Don't allow Lord Iversly's jingling chains to keep you awake all night," Aunt Julia said with a seraphic smile and closed the great-aunt's bedchamber door.

The intimacy of the narrow corridor, lit only by the stump of a torch, with Tip just behind her, closed in on Bea swiftly. She went the few yards to her bedchamber door and paused. He was near enough to touch, tall and dark in the shadowed passageway. She crossed her arms, hugging them to her for warmth.

"You really should leave here," she said.

"I will not. I have already told you so."

"This trouble has nothing to do with you."

"You are involved. It does now."

Bea tried to discern his expression in the dimness.

"But you do not like this," she said. "I can see that."

"Why don't you allow me to decide what I do or do not like, hm?" He leaned one broad shoulder against her bedchamber door, as though perfectly at ease. "It's a bit like one of those novels you enjoy so much, isn't it? The stories featuring horrid villains and helpless maidens."

Bea's eyes snapped wide.

"I do not enjoy those sorts of novels."

"Of course you do."

Her cheeks got positively scalding.

"How would you know that?"

Tip's gaze shifted, as though studying her blush.

"I have accompanied you to the lending library in York at least half a dozen times, my girl. I am not blind."

Bea begged to differ. For years he had not been able to see how much she loved him.

"Of course you have. I just never thought you would—" She halted and bit her lower lip.

The light in Tip's eyes seemed to flicker in the torch-glow.

"You never thought I would what, practical, sensible Miss Sinclaire? Notice your shameful secret?"

She swallowed hard. Then frowned. Why must he always tease her? He never teased Georgie; he always treated her with complete respect.

"I never thought you would care enough to notice," she said shortly.

He pushed away from the door, coming within inches of her.

"I care. Always have." A slight tilt of his mouth cut a crease in his cheek. Warmth trickled into Bea's veins. She did not care for his teasing, but his smile made her want to laugh and cry at once, filling her with sweet longing and fear that it would all disappear, that he would finally find another lady he could love, cease visiting York, and she would never see that smile again.

Her pulse raced, but she smiled back. She could never resist his good humor, especially now, seeing it for the first time since Thomas told them about Iversly.

Tip's eyes took on a peculiar glint, the same she had spied earlier in the parlor and again at dinner.

"You like this," he said.

Bea's heart turned over. She liked standing in the corridor with him alone in the middle of the night? Most assuredly. Like a pathetic, dream-starved girl.

"This?" she managed to breathe.

"The ghost story."

Oh.

"It is not a story. It is real."

"I still cannot believe it, yet I feel deuced foolish not to have realized it sooner." He ran his hand through his dark locks around to the back of his neck. The gesture was so unconscious, so boyish and manly at once, it sent a delicious ripple through her. The corridor seemed very narrow.

"It isn't your fault," she said. "Who would have believed this sort of thing could truly happen?"

"You did." His tone did not accuse. It sounded oddly bewildered, and his eyes looked bright.

"Well, Thomas wrote of it."

"You wanted to believe it, didn't you? You wanted the ghost to be real, and you are happy that he is. Aren't you?" He looked at her so fixedly, as though he hoped she would deny it.

She could not deny it, not even for him. She'd had so few adventures in her life. *None*, in truth. She simply could not regret this one, however horrifying it might seem to a rational person. She may as well admit it to him. She was fairly certain he would not tell anyone, especially not Mama; he already knew her nasty little predilection for darkly dramatic prose.

Cheeks hotter than ever, she tightened her arms and met his regard directly.

"I did hope he would be real, and I wanted to be able to help. I cannot imagine a more exciting activity to be engaged in just now."

"I can." Tip's voice sounded rough.

"What?"

He looked even odder than before, his eyes intense, like emeralds glinting from within a shadow. He put his palm on the stone behind her head and leaned in.

Her heart slammed against her ribs. They had never stood this close, not even while dancing, and that was years ago. He seemed so large from only a few inches away, so masculine and broad, his chest a wall of heady possibility right before her. If she unwound her arms she could touch him, place her palm on his coat and feel his body that looked so firm and powerful, as she had wanted to do for years. *Longed* to do.

Her breaths shortened. She fumbled behind her for the door handle.

"I-I think I will turn in now."

"Not." His breath feathered across her brow. "Just." He bent his head. "Yet."

His lips brushed hers.

Chapter Five

His lips barely lingered, a soft caress of wonderful heat that stole into her. Like satin thread it twined between her lips and across her breasts to explode in unruly sizzles all through her middle and, wickedly, between her legs where she always grew hot when she fantasized about him kissing her.

But this was not a fantasy. It was spectacularly, miraculously real: his lips pressing to hers, his body so close, his scent and heat all around her. A sigh escaped her.

He stepped back abruptly, blinking several times.

"I should"—he spoke haltingly—"should go."

She nodded. Her lips tingled. Her *everything* tingled. She tilted forward into the corridor, attracted like a magnet to his pole. They could write it on her gravestone like that: *Beatrice Sinclaire, spinster, unappreciated companion to her wretched mother, human magnet, b.1799–d.1822.*

"I will—" He took a sharp breath. "Good night, Bea." He turned and disappeared down the corridor.

Clutching the door handle, she gulped in breaths of air acrid with torch smoke. It smelled like summer flowers.

Peter Cheriot had kissed her. She floated ten feet off the ground. One hundred feet. *Miles.* The sensation might not last. But for now, heaven seemed entirely hers.

She did not know why he had, but she would not even think about that. Not now. Not yet. She would simply allow herself to feel, remembering the sensation of his lips touching hers so intimately. Reliving the swirling delight in her body. Reveling in it all.

He had kissed her. Finally.

It had taken only seven years.

~oOo~

What in the devil had he been thinking?
Nothing. Not a damn blast thing. One moment he was
watching the pink flush steal into Bea's lovely cheeks, her eyes
glimmering with excitement, and the next he was kissing her.
In an instant he realized the mistake. At the gentle touch
of her full lips, his cock went hard as rock. If he hadn't halted
the kiss immediately—frankly, before it truly got started—he
might not have been able to stop it at all. Four years of
frustrated lust for a woman was no small thing to control.
Tip fell back against his closed door and put his hands to
his face, sucking in an enormous breath.
Dear God, she felt good. And it hadn't even been more
than a tantalizing hint, the most fleeting touch.
He wanted more. He wanted to touch every inch of her,
to caress the tender place behind her knees, the palms of her
hands, her breasts—*her beautiful breasts*—her tapered waist, and
her sweet, taut sex until she begged him for release. He wanted
to strip her naked and take her in every way that would ensure
her greatest pleasure and his own, in every way *imaginable*. He
wanted to be deep inside her when she called out his name in
ecstasy, her rich eyes fevered with need that only he could
satisfy.
He had never in his twenty-seven years halted a kiss so
swiftly. Not even close.
How had he let his discipline slip like that? So many times
before he'd had the same opportunity with her, and he always
stopped himself. He was a gentleman, for God's sake, a man
of cool, rational sense. If she wanted him, she would accept his
offer of marriage. Until then, he didn't have any business
kissing her.
She had not shied away.
She had *sighed.*
Tip shuddered, heat sliding through his body. He could

not bear it much longer. But nothing would quench his hunger except her soft, supple curves, her hands on him, her lips and tongue. It was far too long since he'd had a woman. He wanted only this one.

Dear God, was he mad? What was he doing here in this remote castle trying to stave off his desire for the one woman he had ached for—*for years*. He was imbecilic to have come, idiotic to remain, and even more foolish to not march right back to her bedchamber and show her in no uncertain terms how marriage to him could be remarkably enjoyable indeed.

He groaned and shifted to relieve the pressure in his groin.

He must be insane. He certainly was not in his right mind tonight—not since earlier in the parlor when she had glowed with eagerness over that damn ghost.

"Damn ghost," he muttered. An angle of moonlight slanted through a window, illuminating the bedchamber in a silver glow. No fire burned in the grate, a consequence of Lady Bronwyn's cowardly servants.

"Blasted ghost. You don't frighten me," he mumbled, arranging wood in the hearth and searching about for a taper.

"Yet she terrifies you," a deep voice said over his shoulder.

Tip stood. His gaze rounded the vacant chamber.

"Do you derive a perverse pleasure from intruding on a man's privacy in this manner?" He folded his arms.

"I take no pleasure in the misfortune of others." A pause. "Any longer."

"Then tell me how to save Lady Bronwyn from your villainy." The words tasted peculiar. Speaking them felt peculiar. The ghost was real, and Tip had to admit he was conversing with it—with a man who had once lived but no longer did.

"I am not the villain," Iversly replied. "The curse binds me."

"A quibbling difference."

"Not to me."

"How can the curse be broken?" Tip persisted, not in the least enjoying conversing with someone he could not see.

From what Bea and Lady Bronwyn said, the fellow was a dark character, but someone he could take easily enough. He wished he could fight the lout. It might serve to dissipate some of the frustrated lust in his blood now.

"For me," Iversly said, "there is nothing you can do to undo the curse. For the lady, you need but relieve her of her maidenhead."

The face that flooded Tip's imagination was not Lady Bronwyn's. He bent again to the hearth and lit the taper.

"Leave, Iversly."

For a moment the ghost did not speak. Then, "Have you no other questions for me?"

Flame flickered before Tip's eyes.

"Do you know of other dead?" he said. "Can you speak with them or see them?"

A long silence followed. Tip remained motionless, waiting.

"Have you someone with whom you wish to communicate in the world of shadows?" the ghost finally replied.

"You might answer my question before I consider yours."

"No." Iversly's tone seemed thinner than usual, unsubstantial. "I am alone in this exile from humanity."

Tip nodded.

"As are you," Iversly added.

"I am not in exile," Tip countered.

Silence met him. It stretched through the chamber for long enough that finally he concluded Iversly had left. He sat back on his heels and ran his hand through his hair.

He ought to do exactly what Bea wished. Leave. He should see to his business in Porthmadog and return to Cheriot Manor where he had plenty of work to keep him busy. She did not want him here, and he didn't need a blasted ghost putting foolish thoughts into his head.

But now that he had tasted her lips, however fleetingly, he could not leave her. Not until she promised him much more.

In all practical matters, he was an excellent bargain. Her

sense of duty to her mother was strong, of course, but Tip feared the reason for her refusals had less to do with Lady Harriet than with the late Lord and Lady Cheriot and their infamous marriage.

Bea had never said a word to suggest it, but no woman of sense would want anything to do with that sort of alliance. Tip was not entirely blameless, either. In his younger days he hadn't been overly discreet. He had made a dash on the town, eagerly indulging in one loose-screw pursuit after another, including courting Bea's sister, Georgie. Of course, that had been largely for show.

But that had all changed the moment his father died. In the four years since then, Tip had adopted a downright staid existence. He was a model gentleman, the sort any lady would consider an unexceptionable husband.

But Beatrice Sinclaire was not any lady. She was the only one who with a glance turned his mouth dry and with a touch made him randy as a goat. That she harbored a passion for adventure only stoked his desire, to his chagrin.

He wasn't surprised. The foolishness was in his blood.

He would conquer it, and he would win her. There could be no other end to it.

~o0o~

April 16, 1822

At twenty-three, rusticating in Yorkshire, I am halfway on the shelf. Today a handsome, wealthy, titled gentleman whose character I like very well asked me to marry him again—for the fifth time I daresay (as though I weren't counting!). He did not go to his knee, but, riding beside me along the lane, simply said he sincerely believed that we would suit.

I have made it as much of a habit to refuse him as he has made it to ask.

I, of course, have excellent justification.

Sylvia once told me that when some young man (I cannot recall who, precisely—there were always so many) begged for her hand, he first attempted to make violent love to her. Georgie is more discreet about such things. But one cannot help notice when she and Kievan visit that he touches her frequently—on the hand, the arm, the small of her back, sometimes even on her face. Of course he is a gentleman, and never offends propriety in the presence of others.

But, Diary, that day in Sir Jeremy's library, when they thought no one could see—days before they became betrothed—I saw Kievan kiss Georgie. He kissed her as though he could not prevent himself from doing so, as though (dare I say?) some passion within him—whether of the heart or otherwise—drove him to it. Once at an al fresco luncheon in the park, I saw Lord Marke kiss Nancy in that manner, too.

Although Peter Cheriot has offered me his title and name, he has never offered me that. That, however, is all I want of him. I am the greatest widgeon alive.

~o0o~

Chapter Six

Tip came to breakfast late, clearly just returned from riding. He wore breeches, top boots, and a deep blue coat that fit his lean, broad-shouldered frame to perfection. His hair looked dashingly tousled from the removal of a hat.

Bea was rising to leave, weary of watching Thomas cast calf's eyes at Lady Bronwyn and of Aunt Grace's stony silence.

"Ah, I see I am almost too late," Tip said, smiling beautifully at her as though he meant his comment for her in particular.

"We are obliged to serve ourselves." The dowager glowered at the sideboard. "The offerings are pitiful."

"Oh, Cook told me she must go to the village to fill the pantry." Lady Bronwyn's tone tinkled with light regret. "We so hoped visitors would come, but we did not expect any quite so promptly."

"I discovered the village this morning, in fact," Tip said, moving to the sideboard. "The locals were not inclined to speak overly much with a stranger. I hoped, Lady Bronwyn, that we could venture there together this morning." He gestured to include them all. "Perhaps we could encourage some of the more courageous souls to return to work at the castle."

"Oh, I do wish I could, my lord." The girl looked wan. "But the village is beyond the castle grounds. I cannot go there."

Tip's smile dimmed, but only slightly. His gaze shifted to Bea for a moment, then returned to their hostess.

"Have you attempted it, my lady?" he asked, his voice gentle.

"Of course she has." Thomas stood up, his chair clattering back. "What are you suggesting, Cheriot, that—"

Bronwyn's hand on his arm arrested him.

"Oh, goodness, Mr. Sinclaire," she said, "you must not chastise Lord Cheriot. You see, I have not attempted it. Lord Iversly simply told me I must not leave the grounds, so I have not."

Tip did not so much as blink.

"Did he tell you what the consequence would be if you defied his order?" he said.

"He said that I simply would not be able to leave, that the curse would hold me here."

"Let us take a stroll instead then, shall we?" he directed at Thomas. "The sun is bright this morning, the grounds extensive, and I suspect the ladies would enjoy the diversion."

"I should like that above all things, Peter dear," Aunt Julia said with a cockeyed twinkle. "How considerate you are. Beatrice, will you come along?"

"Of course, Aunt Julia."

Tip must intend to challenge the ghost's vague mandate concerning the borders of the castle grounds. If Iversly had any real power over holding Bronwyn here, he certainly would have said so. He didn't seem the sort to withhold threatening information. Bea would not miss this experiment for the world.

And Lady Bronwyn seemed brighter. She was such a vivacious girl, all alone for months but for her frail grandmother's companionship and two elderly servants.

The party dispersed, the ladies to don sturdy shoes, before they all gathered again near the rear gate. The fortress was not quite as large as Bea had at first imagined it, but sizable enough to require a thorough investigation. After lunch, while the others rested, she would go exploring.

A vast courtyard stretched from the pair of towers to either side of the main gate, accessed over a bridge crossing a waterless moat. The massive front battlement of the fortress ran along a ridge of the hill to a thick, round tower, even taller than the main towers. Another, much lower, rectangular edifice with two modest turrets completed the castle's rough-shaped triangle. It was a marvelously unusual construction and thoroughly menacing.

Thomas and Bronwyn led the way through the rear gate. It stood wide, a rotten portcullis wedged into the embrasure above. As propriety demanded, Tip offered his arm to Lady Marstowe, who came along with a frown. Bea linked elbows with her other great-aunt. The sun sparkled over the gray stone ramparts behind and the trees ahead that were gnarled with age.

The path from the castle ran alongside a gently rising hill. Sheep grazed above in velvet pastures bordered with low stone walls, clusters of evergreens and others with autumn-red and golden leaves stretching into a pine forest as the mountain rose steeply beyond. Nearby, a walkway paved in slate led to an ancient oak of broad branches scored with lichen. Beneath, a stone bench invited dalliance.

Bea stared at Tip's back, trying to imagine his scent. The night before, she had been far too preoccupied with feeling to fully appreciate the musky aroma of his cologne, but she knew it well enough. He had worn the same for years.

What would he say to her when they were again alone?

Upon rising, with the memory of his kiss still stirring in her senses, she concluded that he had been distracted. Her nerves were constantly tingling here. Perhaps his were too. After all, he had looked so odd the night before, and Bea's mother and Sylvia often said that men's lustful natures encouraged them to act impulsively on the merest provocation. The discovery of Lord Iversly was certainly cause for being overset. The close, dimly lit corridor probably helped.

Or, perhaps, he had just wanted to kiss her. Finally.

After seven years?

No. That seemed too remarkable. No man had ever wanted to kiss her.

They ascended the gradual incline beneath a canopy of grand old cherries with fallen leaves crackling underfoot. When they reached the bench under the oak, the great-aunts sat to rest.

"You young ones should not halt here on our account," Aunt Julia said brightly. "The view is lovely and Grace and I will be more than happy to await your return."

"A fine idea, Aunt Julia." Thomas eagerly led Lady Bronwyn farther up the path.

"Go along, Beatrice," Lady Marstowe ordered, gesturing after them, "and don't lose sight of them. That boy will ruin himself if he does not take care."

Bea was rather more concerned with Lady Bronwyn's ruination. Her brother was a careless fellow. He seemed enamored enough of Bronwyn, but he had seemed the same with at least a half dozen other girls in the past few years.

She continued along the path and Tip fell in beside her. As soon they passed out of earshot of the great-aunts, he spoke.

"Bea, I beg your pardon for my presumption last night. I hope you will forgive me."

Forgive him? She had never slept so peacefully, filled with sweet happiness and the pleasantest tinglings.

"You are very kind to apologize." She drew in a steadying breath and told the biggest lie of her life. "But it was nothing, really."

Silence followed. She could not bring herself to look at him. If she saw relief on his face, she might sink into the ground.

The formal path ended at a gate set in a wall, continuing as dirt and pebbles on the opposite side as it skirted the glade. Thomas and Bronwyn went ahead, her hand tucked into his elbow.

"Lady Marstowe seems concerned that your brother is in danger from Lady Bronwyn," Tip said, as though following her thoughts.

"They are obviously attached." Bea folded her hands into the pleats of her skirts.

"I understand she is an heiress. What could concern Lady Marstowe over such an alliance?"

Bea's heart thudded dully. He thought of marriage in such rational terms. But most everyone did, except foolish girls still in the schoolroom, and herself, of course. Her mother and father's marriage had been one of convenience, after all, although her father had adored his young, sparklingly beautiful wife. At first.

Bea cleared her throat.

"We know little of Lady Bronwyn's father. Only what Mr. Whitney told Thomas. I suppose Aunt Grace is worried about that. Thomas mustn't ally himself with a questionable family."

Another long pause ensued before he spoke again.

"I know nothing of Prescot except that he is a recluse and never takes his seat in Lords. But I have spent a great deal of time in the country these past few years, of course, so I am not acquainted with everyone in town. Would you like me to send to my man of business to inquire into him?"

Bea's steps faltered.

"Oh, that will not be necessary, but you are very ki—"

"Kind, yes," he finished. A muscle flexed in his jaw. "Nevertheless, to put Lady Marstowe at ease, I will write to London today."

Bea bit the inside of her cheek and started walking again, her feet sinking into the mossy ground cover like treading on pillows. A pair of black birds darted past, twisting about each other as they flew, and a gull cawed far overhead. The autumn breeze rose cool and salty off the hillside into the sunshine. But Bea's chest felt heavy.

"Papa should really do this sort of thing," she finally said.

"In his absence, I am happy to."

"Thank you, my lord."

"Thank you, Peter."

Her gaze shot up. He tilted his head to glance aside at her, his mouth curving into the barest suggestion of a smile.

"We have been friends for seven years, Bea. And now I have kissed you, as well. You sound perfectly antique calling me my lord, not to mention dreadfully prim."

Bea's pulse tripped. "That is a singularly ungallant thing to say," she replied to cover her shock of confused pleasure and irrational disappointment. *Friends?* But of course they were friends. They certainly were nothing else.

Before she could halt her increasingly unruly tongue, she blurted out, "Do you really think I am prim?"

He chuckled, a rich rumble of pleasure.

"You sound it, occasionally."

"When I behave as propriety demands?" Perhaps indignation would still the quivers in her belly.

"When you go on as though we are nearly strangers, when we are nothing of the sort." His voice continued light, but Bea's heart pounded.

Nothing of the sort.

"Not only ungallant, but ungrateful," she said as steadily as she could. "Calling you by your title is a mark of respect, of course."

He grasped her hand, encompassing it in his large, strong hold.

"Respect is all well and good, my girl, but I should think I deserve something more than that by now."

His emerald eyes above the slight smile looked intensely bright. Bea's heart wanted to explode. Her head chased after the excitement too. It spun. Stars danced before her vision, casting Tip in a aura of glittering light.

Good heavens, the dramatic aura of the castle must be affecting her. Seeing stars now?

She wavered on her feet, abruptly unsteady.

What on earth?

Heat flooded her cheeks, like a sudden fever. She tried to swallow but her mouth and throat crackled, her tongue thick. Her hand in Tip's flinched. As though he crushed her bones together, pain swiftly radiated into her arm, then her chest. She gulped air but could not seem to get enough.

"Dear me," she mumbled. This was perhaps more than natural agitation over his attentions.

"Bea." His grasp tightened and her hand erupted in agony. A soft yelp escaped her lips. Her head swam and the ground seemed to rush up to her, then back down again. Her legs gave way.

"Bea?" Tip's arms scooped behind her shoulders and knees to lift her into his embrace. But his touch became knives cutting her flesh. Her lungs seemed to compress, her chest too heavy to draw breath, as if she were being smashed by a huge press.

"I—" Her throat failed, closing.

"Dear God, what is happening?" He spoke close to her face. She tried to focus on him but her vision clouded, then blackened.

"Oh, Peter, I do wish . . ."

Then there was nothing.

~oOo~

Tip stared into Bea's white face, and against her inert body his heart ceased beating. *What was happening?*

He strode swiftly toward the castle, cradling her to his chest. She was light—too light.

"Cheriot!" Thomas shouted from a distance. The fort's rear gate seemed miles away.

Lady Marstowe and Miss Dews moved toward him. Thomas approached, breathing hard as he ran alongside Tip.

"What in the blazes—Oh, Lord, Tip. My sister never swoons."

Tip did not bother saying he knew that perfectly well, probably better than the cub did. He did not utter aloud that her sudden collapse frightened him more than anything ever had. He did not mention that everything he held dear in life was in his arms.

"Find smelling salts. Ask Lady Marstowe or Lady Bronwyn," he ordered. "Bring them to her bedchamber. I will take her there."

"Right." Thomas ran back and Tip swung through the rear portal toward the keep. He had brought this on. He had refused to believe Iversly's threat about the castle boundaries, and he had taken her beyond the acceptable border for a maiden. It had to be. Now she dangled limp in his embrace, horrifyingly still. Tip had dreamed thousands of times of having his arms around her, of holding her beautiful body, her living, breathing person—of her returning his embrace.

This was a nightmare. He was an arrogant ass, unwilling to believe what he could not see himself. When her eyes sparked in the breakfast room, he could have sworn she knew his purpose in suggesting the stroll. But it didn't matter. He should have protected her, not put her in the way of danger to test his theory.

Her sweet lips were gray, her eyelids translucent. Dear God, where had his lovely girl gone?

He took the steep stairs two at a time, accessing the landing quickly and pushing through the door.

In earlier years, when he was first infatuated with her, he had spent plenty of puerile imaginings on her bedchamber. Now her neatly made bed was not an invitation to pleasure but of grave necessity. He laid her down and sat beside her, taking her hands between his.

Her skin was cold, her breathing so shallow he could barely discern the rise and fall of her chest. He touched his fingertips to her neck. Her pulse beat slow and thin. A shiver of dread cut through his chest.

He had never imagined losing her. For years she had been his steady, stable reality. Even miles away from her for months on end, he had rested content in the knowledge that all he need do was ride a day or two to reach her, to see her smile and hear her voice, and all would be well. He would be well.

Blast it, where in the hell were those smelling salts?

He grabbed up a coverlet and spread it over her, then went to the hearth and relit the fire. Boot steps sounded at the threshold. Thomas entered, with Lady Bronwyn and the great-aunts.

"Smelling salts here!" Thomas brandished a glass vial. Lady Marstowe snatched it from him and marched to the bed.

"Beatrice," she said firmly, "you will not begin taking after your silly mother at this late date. You are far too sensible for that." She uncorked the vial and with a flick of her wrist passed it beneath Bea's nostrils.

Bea did not stir.

"Oh, Lord," Thomas uttered. "It's real. Iversly told us the truth." His horrified gaze went to Lady Bronwyn.

The dowager shook her head as though rejecting the evidence then jammed the smelling salts beneath Bea's nostrils, holding the bottle steady this time. Bea did not react.

Lady Marstowe turned her icy gaze on Tip.

"What happened, my lord?"

"They passed beyond the boundaries of the castle grounds," Lady Bronwyn whispered.

Tip could not look away from Bea. "I believe Lady Bronwyn is correct, but I cannot say for certain."

"Of course you can!" Thomas exploded. "We told you—"

"Thomas, that is enough," Lady Marstowe commanded. "What are we to do now?"

"Call for a doctor, I should say," Thomas spluttered.

"Speak to Iversly." Tip's gaze went to Lady Bronwyn. "Is he here? Now?"

Her agitated gaze rounded the chamber. She shook her head.

"I will find him." He strode toward the door.

"Lady Bronwyn," the dowager intoned, "remain here with my sister and see to Beatrice. If she moves or worsens, alert us immediately. Thomas, come. You are useless here, but you may help us root out Lord Iversly."

Tip went straight to the parlor, the other two following.

"Iversly," he called out, moving through the doorway.

No answer came.

"Well this is damnably inconvenient," Thomas cursed. "He ought to be here. Isn't this what he wants, after all?"

"He wants a living woman," Tip snapped, swallowing over the break in his voice.

Lady Marstowe cut him a swift glance then peered around the chamber.

"Lord Iversly," she said, "reveal yourself now."

"He won't come, Aunt Grace. Cheriot's right. He doesn't want Bea. He wants Lady Bronwyn."

"Then why—" Tip caught his tongue. He could not control the steadiness of his words. He pivoted toward the door.

"Where are you going, my lord?" the dowager demanded.

"Where I must," he growled and left them behind. If Iversly would not reveal himself here, Tip would try his bedchamber, where the ghost had spoken to him last night. Then every other crevice of the castle until he found him. He headed for the stairs.

"She may not recover."

The icy words hit him hard. Tip swung around.

"Where are you?" he ground out.

"Here."

The corridor shone with morning sunlight filtering through a trio of windows onto gray stone, softening the severe architecture.

"If I could see you, I would kill you."

"Endeavor not to become as foolish as that boy, my lord. I am already dead. You called. I came. You should be pleased. I am rarely so accommodating."

"What can be done?"

"Naught. She transgressed the terms of the curse. She now pays the price for it." His voice seemed harder than usual.

Panic sluiced through Tip.

"She does not deserve this."

"Perhaps not."

"How can I help her?"

"You cannot. You must simply wait."

"That is not acceptable!" The empty corridor reverberated with his anger. "Damn you, Iversly, tell me what to do."

"I am already damned, my friend," the ghost said evenly. "And I can only offer you consolation."

Silence stretched, long and hopeless.

"You might have had her." Iversly's voice was suggestive, man-to-man.

Bile rose in Tip's throat, his hands fisting.

"You have wasted your opportunity," Iversly continued. "You could have saved her."

"And you might yet burn in hell." Tip strode toward the stairs.

"You might still have her."

Tip swung around.

"She will recover from this?"

"Possibly," the ghost said slowly. "Probably."

"Which is the lie?"

"Neither. I never lie."

"Then you must not know for certain."

"Will you?"

Tip knew he should not respond, but the mingled fury and frustration in his blood urged him on.

"Will I what?"

"Take her. If she recovers."

"I have no words for you," he snarled.

"You could. You might." Iversly paused. "Unless I do first."

Tip made for the stairs.

"She is intrigued by me," the voice pursued. "She is . . . aroused."

Tip halted.

"How did you die, Iversly?"

Hollow hush filled the corridor.

"How did it happen?" Tip persisted. "At sword point? Cannon blast? Poison? A rope about your neck?"

Iversly waited a lengthy interval to reply.

"Much worse than all that you have suggested." His voice echoed.

"Since I cannot serve you as a man deserves for his roguery, do me a favor, if you will. Spend some time thinking on the details of that death today. Think on it and suffer it again." He turned and made his way up to Bea's bedchamber.

Chapter Seven

Bea awoke in her soft, musty bed, her face nestled in a damp feather pillow. She shifted and pain knocked through her head. She groaned but little sound came forth. Her mouth tasted wretched.

"Oh, she is awake. She is awake!" Lady Bronwyn's voice fluttered across the chamber. "Do you see, Miss Dews? Oh, Beatrice, you must have a sip of this. We were so worried about you. Oh, Cook, do go tell Mr. Sinclaire, Lord Cheriot, and Lady Marstowe that she is awake."

Cook? What on earth was the cook doing in her bedchamber?

Bea opened her eyes to a pretty face filled with distress. Lady Bronwyn hovered over her, twisting her hands together.

"Cook brought tea and soup, if you should wake. And you did! Would you like some? It is Grandmama's favorite." She held forth a spoon.

Bea struggled to clear her vision. Aunt Julia sat in a chair beside the bed, her face anxious.

"What happened?" Bea managed to mumble then fell into a fit of coughing.

"Oh, how dreadful it all was!" Lady Bronwyn exclaimed. "But I told you, Lord Iversly said not to leave the castle grounds, and you did and then this happened."

"This?" Bea repeated. She remembered Tip saying something that made her heart reel—she could not recall what precisely. But of course nearly everything he said made her giddy. Then she had begun to feel absolutely horrid. "I swooned?"

"Oh, yes. It was terrible." Lady Bronwyn nodded. "But

now you are awake and you will recover. Lord Iversly told Lord Cheriot that you would probably," Bronwyn added. "Now you have and all is well. How do you feel?"

"Shaky." But oddly better each moment. She sat up and as Bronwyn propped a pillow behind her shoulders, a fog lifted from her head. "I went beyond the castle grounds?"

"Oh, yes. Your brother and I thought you and Lord Cheriot were behind us as we entered the orchard. But you continued on the path when we left it, and through the gate to the village."

Bea did not remember any gate, only Tip's intent expression and his hand deliciously around hers.

"I called out to you," Bronwyn continued, frowning, "but you were both entirely heedless of my warning."

"Is Lord Cheriot all right?"

"Oh, yes. The curse only affects virginal women, of course. But he is very anxious for you. Shall I show him in?"

She shook her head, but Bronwyn had already hurried across the chamber. Bea lifted a heavy hand and smoothed her tangled hair.

"You look lovely, Beatrice dear." Aunt Julia smiled. "He will still admire you."

The door opened again. In two strides Tip came across the chamber to her bedside, knelt, and grasped her hand resting on the counterpane.

"How are you?" His voice seemed unusually taut.

"I am fine now. But I suppose we know now that Lord Iversly was not making empty threats, don't we?"

"What happened?"

"Well . . ." It was somewhat difficult to think clearly with his thumb caressing her knuckles. He probably didn't know he did it. "I think I began to grow ill. Rapidly. And," she paused, "perhaps, to die."

"Dear God," he uttered and his fingers tightened about hers.

"But I didn't. You must have brought me back within the castle grounds after I fell. Thank you." She ought to feel frightened, or at the very least a remnant of alarm. But she could not seem to summon unpleasant emotions beneath the blanket of his concerned gaze. "When did it happen?"

"Not twenty minutes ago."

"And you spoke to Lord Iversly about it already?"

He frowned. "Shouted, rather."

How lovely.

"Well, one cannot be too subtle about dealing with a ghost, I suppose," she murmured.

"You are taking this with too much good humor," Tip said. "I blame myself for putting you in danger. If something worse had happened to you, I—"

"You should not." She loved the feeling of his hand around hers, now that it was not causing her intense pain. His slightly rough palm and long, strong fingers felt so familiar. He had never held her hand for quite so long before, and only once or twice without gloves. But she had stared at his hands so often the sensation of his touch did not surprise her. Like everything about him, it felt right and good.

"I wanted to discover if Lord Iversly was telling the truth as much as you did," she said. "We simply should have paid closer attention to our direction." And she should not have lost focus simply because a wonderful, handsome man was saying confusing, delicious things.

"You are correct, as always," he said. "Practical to the core."

Bea did not think chasing after a ghost's threats was in the least bit practical, but she held her tongue. She glanced at Bronwyn, engaged in conversation with Aunt Julia, then back at Tip.

"What will we do next?" she whispered.

"We will not do anything. I will discover a way to nullify the curse, to free you and Lady Bronwyn from this place."

"I am not in any real danger. He intends to marry her."

"Let me be the judge of the danger, will you?"

"So, you believe it all?"

"I don't have any reason not to any longer."

Bea raced to think of an excuse to keep him by her side. She felt better with each moment that passed.

"I thought to——" She should not tell him. He would probably laugh at her.

"You thought to what?"

"I planned to explore the castle this afternoon. Perhaps a clue to the curse lies hidden somewhere and we have only to discover it."

He released her hand.

"You sound eager to do it," he said. "Haven't you had enough adventure already?"

"It is not adventure. It must be done."

"Then leave it to me. You should not be tangling with ghosts."

Bea folded her hands atop her lap. "No."

He stood up. "No, you agree not to involve yourself further?"

"No, I will pursue the matter as I wish. 'Two heads are better than one,' Georgie always used to tell me."

His hands flexed into fists at his sides. "Perhaps because she suspected you would get yourself in trouble if left to your own devices."

Tip had never before insulted her. This, coming alongside a compliment to her sister he so adored, was simply too much.

"If left to my own devices, I would not be recovering from a near-death experience now, would I?" she snapped—unfairly. But she hurt.

His jaw hardened. He looked extraordinarily handsome, so severe, his eyes intense. She wished she could be sufficiently piqued to be blind to it. But the spark in his gaze made her sluggish pulse jump.

"You may not pursue this matter further, Bea."

"Of course I may. Mama is not here to tell me what to do, and you cannot order me around either, Peter Cheriot. You haven't any authority over me."

"I don't. You have assured that rather successfully several times, haven't you?"

Bea sat speechless. It was a day for firsts, it seemed. Not once had he ever referred to his failed marriage proposals unless he was actually proffering another. And on only one occasion had he ever shown displeasure over the fact that she refused him: September 9, 1819. But then his mother had recently died, his father not even a year in the grave yet, and he had seemed very serious throughout, not only after she refused.

"Your mother placed you in my protection on this journey," he added. "I bear responsibility for your safety."

"Then you may investigate with me. That is your only option, I'm afraid."

"I begin to suspect you are not afraid of much, in fact." He looked surprised by that, and not particularly pleased.

"Perhaps I am not afraid of anything." Except never seeing him again. "As you know perfectly well, Mama is a gorgon. I have been trained to quiet courage."

Abruptly Tip's jaw relaxed and his mouth curved up at one side, but the smile seemed reluctant and his eyes remained sober. "You have, indeed."

"Beatrice, will you take some broth?" Lady Bronwyn came forward with a bowl.

Bea started to shake her head, but Tip's brow lowered menacingly. She accepted the bowl.

He left with Bronwyn to inform Lady Marstowe and Thomas of her recovery. But the memory of his concern lingered. His imperious attitude came as a surprise, but she supposed he felt guilty. Bea did not consider that all bad. At least he harbored some strong emotion because of her.

Chapter Eight

After lunch, they began their investigation in the corridor facing the north tower adjacent to the bedchambers. Lady Bronwyn visited her grandmother and the great-aunts rested, so Thomas came along.

After glancing at several rooms that seemed to be storage areas, cluttered with old furniture, building materials, and even a rusting suit of armor, Bea pushed open a thick door crossed with iron bars to reveal a sizeable chamber lined with bookshelves.

"A library," Thomas grunted.

"Ever been in one, Sinclaire?" Tip grinned. His mood seemed so much lighter than earlier, as though he had shaken off the accident, and his smile went straight to Bea's toes. She dragged her gaze away.

Thomas remained at the threshold. "I'll have you know, Cheriot, I received top marks at Eton."

"What about Christ Church, then, hm? Keep it up through university, did you?"

"Good heavens." Bea crossed the chamber to draw open heavy, sun-faded curtains. "If you two plan to continue this, I will be much happier investigating alone."

"Apologies, Bea," Thomas grumbled.

Tip moved beside her. "You won't be rid of me so easily, Miss Sinclaire," he said quietly, sending a shiver of warmth down her spine. "Ah, look here, *The Necromancer's Diary*. Perhaps that is what we need."

"A magician?" Thomas scoffed. "The curse is demonic. Mark my words. A man like Iversly is bound to have consorted with the devil."

"You don't know that, Tom," Bea said, rifling through a stack of dusty yellow papers. "Perhaps he stumbled into the curse accidentally. He seems reasonable enough for a man of his era."

Tip glanced at her.

"He is a monster," Thomas insisted. "Any man would be to demand marriage from a girl who doesn't want him."

At her side, Tip stiffened perceptibly. For a moment he remained perfectly still, then he spoke.

"Perhaps he has no choice but to marry," he said in unexceptionable tones. "Perhaps he must marry the first maiden to reside in the castle."

"In four hundred years there must have been maidens in this castle before Lady Bronwyn." Bea opened a slim, leather-bound volume.

"The local vicar might have a record of residents over the centuries. Tom, have you been to the village?"

"Not since the day we arrived. Charlie and I had a pint to fortify his courage, then we came up here. I haven't left the castle since I made Lady Bronwyn's acquaintance."

"So you have not asked the locals what they know about the curse?"

"No," the younger man replied rigidly. "After Charlie flew off, I didn't like to leave her alone with Iversly."

"We can begin with Cook and Dibin," Bea said. "But if they cannot help we really must investigate in the village."

"You cannot," Tip said.

She looked across the space separating them. He watched her steadily.

"I cannot, you are correct. Then you will have to do so instead. Thomas, won't you go, too?"

"I won't leave her, Bea. Iversly spoke to her again last evening. He means to force her to wed him by tomorrow night."

"Tomorrow night?" Bea jerked around. "Why didn't you mention this earlier?"

"He's been threatening to marry her for weeks already,"

he said in a rush, "and he only told her this last night. Though I don't know how a ghost plans to marry a living woman, especially without a vicar around."

"Had he ever mentioned a specific date before?" Tip asked.

"No." Thomas's face looked stormy. "Listen, the two of you cannot come prancing in here and think you know what's best for Lady Bronwyn, especially not after your fiasco at the castle boundaries. I've promised to protect her—"

"You don't seem to be doing a very practical job of it," Tip interjected.

"See here, Cheriot." His chest puffed out. "What business is it of yours?"

"You wrote asking for help," Bea said, impatience disguising her anxious excitement. Lord Iversly claimed he would fulfill the curse in less than thirty-six hours. "Lord Cheriot is gracious to offer his assistance. Now if you two will cease bickering perhaps we can discover something that will help us help Lady Bronwyn."

Neither replied.

"Good." She pulled a set of musty volumes from a shelf. "*Astral Projectivity Unbound.* Hm. There are a great many books here in French, and some in German. Do either of you read German?"

"A bit," Tip replied, coming to her side. His fingers brushed hers as he drew the book from her grasp. Bea smothered a sigh. It didn't matter that they had argued earlier. She could still feel the warmth from his hand around hers, deep down in her belly.

"This won't do us any good," Thomas muttered, still standing in the doorway. "I don't see the point of looking through a bunch of crumbling books."

"I am hoping to find a spell book, or even a diary or ledger of some sort, Tom. Perhaps someone who lived here might have something to tell us about Iversly or the curse."

"Spell book?" her brother said incredulously. "It would be better to talk with Iversly himself, I'll wager."

"That is unlikely to help us," Tip said, his voice odd.

"Perhaps I will go down to the village and have a look around, after all," Tom said. "Someone at the pub might have something useful to say." He disappeared into the corridor.

This time Bea allowed herself the sigh. Thomas was infatuated with Lady Bronwyn, devoted to protecting her, yet in the end a pint of ale won his attention more surely.

Tip flipped through the volume and laid it down on the table, taking up another.

"*Opus in Speculis*. Something about mirrors?" Bea smudged away encrusted grime from a gilt-edged binding. "*Conjuring Spirits*. Well that seems more to the point." She pulled the volume down and opened its stiff pages. "Hm. It seems to be about distilling whiskey." She chuckled and went for another.

Tip perused the shelves in silence. Alone with him again for the first time since the night before in the corridor, Bea could not halt her nerves from singing. She could still feel his lips on hers. She would remember it for the rest of her life.

"Here is one entitled *Six Hundred Sixty-Six Love Philtres*," she said. "How singular. Isn't six hundred sixty-six the number of the beast?"

"Perhaps the author had poor luck at love," he replied. "But how you know about the number of the beast, I cannot imagine."

"Thomas told me about it once when he was on holiday from school."

"Ah, so he did learn something. And shared it with his innocent sister, the rapscallion." His voice smiled.

"I daresay he tells me many things he should not. He is often tactless."

"One of these days Thomas should consider growing up." His attention was fixed on the book in his hands as he paged through the folios. A lock of dark hair tumbled over his brow like a schoolboy's, but his firm jaw and the serious set of his beautiful mouth were thoroughly man.

"He is not that much younger than you. Four years or so," she said.

He met her gaze. "Four years and the death of both of one's parents to violent accidents make the world of difference, I should say."

"I beg your pardon, Tip."

He set the book down and turned to her, a slight smile playing about his mouth.

"You are not at fault, of course. But even if you were, when you lay off calling me my lord I believe I could forgive you anything."

Bea's knees went weak. His emerald eyes held the expression that for years had kept her heart at his feet: warm, appreciative, as though they shared some wonderful secret. She opened her mouth to speak.

His gaze slipped to her lips.

Her breaths stalled. The night before, he had looked at her mouth that way.

She could not bear the silence.

"Why do they call you Tip?" she asked, barely above a whisper.

His gaze rose again to her eyes, he seemed to take a slow breath, then turned back to the shelf.

"My sister gave me the nickname when I was a child."

Bea forced herself to speak calmly.

"How did she come upon it? It is unusual."

"She overheard me speaking with my father."

"About what?"

A muscle contracted in his jaw.

"About a horse I was particularly fond of at the time. I wished to purchase it and my father suggested it was not a wise choice for a boy of fourteen. I was rather—" He paused. "Rather adamant about my feelings on the matter and refused to give way." The air in the chamber seemed to grow still.

"Really? But what did your sister overhear?"

"My father said that if I failed to control my emotions concerning a stupid beast, I was bound to tip beyond the acceptable point when someday it came to women."

Bea's heart turned over, leaving a sick sensation in the pit of her stomach.

"Elizabeth heard the chastisement," he continued, his features stony. "She thought it would be a great joke to tease me incessantly. My schoolmate visiting at the time adopted it. And so it goes." He shrugged.

"Oh."

"Oh, indeed. My father was clearly something of a hypocrite."

"I suspect he meant it for the best," she murmured. Everyone knew of Lord and Lady Cheriot's stormy marriage, so often entirely public. When Tip's father suffered the accident that led to his death, Bea and her mother had still lived in town. Gossip flew for days about how the couple fought openly at a ball, as usual over how he had taken up with another mistress. Lady Cheriot fled London and her husband sped after her, apparently to make it up to her as he always did. On the road he ran his horse lame, it stumbled, and he was thrown, breaking his back and paralyzing him from the waist down.

In a drawing room one afternoon shortly after the accident, Bea heard her mother say to a friend that even if her husband was not overly fond these days, at least he was not a madman. And what sort of woman complained publicly to her husband about his little peccadillos?

Bea had turned away from her mother in shame. A man and a woman ought to be allowed to love each other in any way they chose, though Bea couldn't like Lord Cheriot's dalliances, of course. Tip's story only confirmed that the baron was a conscientious father, if not a faithful husband. But he did not seem to have resembled his easy-natured son, or to have known his character very well.

Or perhaps he had known his son well enough? Perhaps it was Bea who knew Tip less well than she thought. He had been devoted to her sister, after all. Just because he showed *her* no excess of feeling certainly did not mean he was not capable of it. It only meant that she did not inspire it in him.

A dull ache lodged in her chest. But this time that ache

irritated her. She should not be moved by this. She had known the truth for years, reemphasized each time he proffered her yet another calm, emotionless proposal of marriage.

"You will not find what you seek in those books." The voice echoed through the chamber. Bea pivoted and met Lord Iversly's black gaze. He stood by the window, the light filtering through him in opalescent gloom. He wore a black cloak over a mail shirt, and his face looked more haggard than the previous day.

"Where is he, Bea?" Tip spoke quietly.

"By the window. Why won't we find what we are looking for here?" she directed to the ghost.

"It was never written."

"Not even in someone's diary? I cannot believe it."

"None ever remained here long enough to leave such a record. I frightened them all away." His low laughter sounded desolate. It seemed to hint at desperation.

Bea moved toward him. Tip's hand touched hers, as though he meant to stay her, but she went forward.

"You seem distressed, my lord," she said. "Are you unwell?"

"How could I be more unwell, my lady, than being dead?"

"Hmm. Point taken." But something about him seemed different today. Unsettled. Cold seemed to surround her.

"Have you come to tell us something, Iversly, or merely to frighten Miss Sinclaire?" Tip's voice sounded very deep. Threatening.

"She is not frightened by me. Are you, my lady?" Iversly's ebony gaze was unreadable. It scanned her slowly. "You would make an admirable bride. It is a shame you did not arrive here before the girl, or I would be claiming you tomorrow night instead."

A thrill of fear trickled through her, proving that the ghost did not know everything after all. Tip moved beside her, his stance undeniably protective. The combination of that and the specter's words set off a flower of heat in her middle. Her breaths came a bit short.

"What is this talk of tomorrow night?" Tip demanded. "Why then? Why not a sennight from now, or yesterday?"

Lord Iversly's face grew grimmer yet.

"The curse comes to an end on All Hallows' Eve."

"An end?" Bea said. "In what manner?"

"When the warlock cursed me, he allowed me one night each century to steal my fate back, if I should be so fortunate. One moment, at the stroke of midnight on All Hallows' Eve, during which I may claim my bride whether she agrees to it or not."

"What do you mean?"

"For four hundred years, dozens of maidens have lived in my castle, visited it, taunting me with freedom from this waking death, yet never once agreeing to give me the keys that would unbind me."

"Well, you cannot blame them," she said.

"But I can desire them. Desire what I want above all else."

"A living woman?" Tip growled.

"No." The ghost's voice was a sepulcher. "The freedom to die."

"To die?" Bea's heart sped. "You mean, when you finally marry a maiden you will—"

"Be no more. Travel to the bowels of Gehenna and cease to exist. At long last, blessed damnation will be mine."

Bea's hands trembled. It felt wonderful and awful at once. But being alive *should* feel just like that. It should be pleasure and pain, both of which she rarely ever felt. Like Lord Iversly, for years she had lived a sort of half-life. No wonder this journey seemed like an adventure. She had not really lived in so long, and it was glorious to finally feel something other than disparagement, dullness, and constant disappointment.

"And your wife?" she asked, a tremor in her voice. "What will become of her?"

"Bea." Tip's hand touched the small of her back, spreading warmth through her.

Abruptly, she hated her body's reaction to him. It felt like a betrayal. She did not want to feel alive from his touch. She wanted real life—heart and body together—not the same hopeless yearning she had nurtured for years.

With firm resolve, she stepped away from him toward the lord of the castle.

"What about your bride, Lord Iversly?" she repeated.

"She, unfortunately, will die."

Her breath failed. "Die?"

"You cannot do this to an innocent woman, Iversly," Tip said.

"I can, and I will. Spend four hundred years in lifeless exile, lad, watching warm bodies share their flesh like rutting animals, not knowing what true unity means, what they could have were they to understand, and then accuse me of villainy for wishing to be free of that torment. I dare you."

"But must she die, truly?" Bea said.

"Not if she comes to me willingly. If she awaits the midnight hour, however, she will suffer her fate." Light seemed to flicker in his coal-black eyes, almost like a spark. "Would you consent to becoming my bride, my lady?" His tone was thin again, laced with anguish.

"What would happen if I did consent?"

"Bea—"

"What would happen, Lord Iversly? To me?"

"We would both continue as I am now, never dying, but together. No longer alone." His voice seemed to plead, dark and deep and alluring in its danger, sending shivers from the soles of her feet to the crown of her head.

"Get out of here, Iversly," Tip ground out. "Now."

The ghost stared at him, the sunlight oozing through him like mist. His gaze returned to Bea.

"Consider it, my dear. We could get along well. With you, I think, I would not despise eternity."

He vanished.

Bea swallowed jerkily, and took a few quick breaths, but she felt astoundingly giddy and a bit dizzy. She clasped her shaking hands together.

"Is he gone?" Tip's voice grated.

She nodded.

He came to her side and grasped her shoulders firmly, pulling her around to face him.

"You wouldn't do it, Bea. Would you? To save Lady Bronwyn?"

Her eyes went wide. "Of course I wouldn't. What on earth—? Do you think me *mad?*"

His gaze swept across her face, his eyes bright and, it seemed, bewildered.

"You seemed so intrigued. And you— you—" He broke off.

Bea shook her head.

"Well, whatever you obviously do not wish to say, I am not out of my mind." She shrugged from his grasp, her feelings tangled. He could not look at her like this, with anxiety and intensity in his eyes, and not care for her a little. But she knew that already. They were friends, just as he had said earlier. *Friends*, and he did not wish to see his friend give herself to a ghost for eternity, of course. Just because his touch turned her joints to liquid did not mean a thing. Her longing for him was her curse, her own living death.

She tried to speak evenly. "I merely wish to learn as much as we can so we have more information to work with."

"Are you certain you don't wish for more than that?"

"Yes, I am certain. I don't want to be a ghost for eternity. What sort of person do you think I am?"

"One who seems extraordinarily interested in the details of this curse, not to mention in that scoundrel."

"Of course I am." She gave her indignation rein. "I intend to help Lady Bronwyn escape her fate."

Tip's cheeks were dark, his stance tense, as though he labored under powerful emotion too. Astonishment? Mounting anger, like hers?

Bea swallowed back the thickness rising in her throat. Here was proof. He could feel strong emotion, simply not the sort she yearned for him to feel for her.

"It is our best chance to ask as many questions as

possible," she said. "Then something useful might suggest itself to us. Lady Bronwyn's grandmother lived here for many years before Bronwyn came to be with her last summer. Perhaps she knows of the things Lord Iversly spoke of earlier, the maidens who have come through the castle but who have not been trapped here, and the—the warm bodies." Her cheeks burned, but she could not allow it to bother her. There was a mystery to be solved, a life to save, and it helped distract her from Tip's changeable mood now and the sense of hopelessness washing over her. "Perhaps there is some clue we can deduce from that." She moved toward the door.

"You are enjoying this drama, aren't you?" His voice halted her. It was strained and hard, entirely unlike him. "Playing the part of an amateur Bow Street Runner. Who will you question next, Bea? The milkmaid, or perhaps the vicar? Vicars always have a lot to say since they know everyone's business, I understand, although he might be somewhat put off by your line of questioning. Vicar, can you tell me how many virgins remain in the village, and if any of them have ever been to the castle?"

Bea's back stiffened.

"That is lovely, my lord. It is really no surprise that all those doting mamas and young ladies in town find you so charming."

"Perhaps they bring out the worst in me," he snapped.

Bea gaped. He had never spoken to her like this before. She clenched her teeth. "Do you think so?"

He shook his head, running a hand through his hair. "This conversation isn't going anywhere," he said tightly.

"Then I will. I have work to do."

Suspicion glinted in his emerald eyes.

"Off to have another chat with him?"

"With whom?"

"Your admirer."

Bea lifted her chin.

"I believe you are jealous, Peter Cheriot."

"That's ridiculous. Why would I be jealous?"

Her stomach was sick again.

"I thought I had left Mama behind on this trip. But I see she is here after all, though in clever disguise."

"Perhaps she ought to be here. At least she would recognize the impropriety in your salacious interest in the details of this curse."

"Salacious?"

"Would you prefer prurient?" His voice rose again.

"Because I wish to get to the heart of this?"

"Because you are clearly taking great pleasure in the minutiae of it."

"You sound like a prude."

"I beg your—" He blinked. "Blast it, I do." But his voice was still cool.

She tilted her head, energy pulsing through her now, anger surging ahead of helplessness.

"You are not a prude, are you, Tip?" Her words stung her tongue, but it felt good to finally give him back some of the teasing he had always served her.

"Bea," he warned.

"I cannot see why you would not answer me unless you are one. Are you, then?"

"Most certainly not," he said in strangled tones.

"You still sound like one."

"And you, missy, sound like a doxy."

"So? What does it matter how I sound, closeted in Yorkshire all the time as I am? Do you know what?" Her mouth formed words without thought. "I think you are displeased with me now because you are shocked to discover my true character—who I truly am."

He merely stared.

"You cannot disagree," she said. "See? It's true. You ride up to York when it pleases you to escape whatever concerns you have at Cheriot Manor or in London, or to see Nancy and Lord Marke. You amuse yourself, then you leave the moment you see or hear something you dislike. You never stay long enough to hear more. You might learn the unpalatable truth, then, mightn't you, Lord Cheriot?"

"For your information, Miss Sinclaire, I have never heard nor seen anything I dislike when I am in your company." His voice was very low. "Except of course for your repeated refusals of my requests for your hand, which by the way is no small reason for a man to decide it is high time he bring his visit to a close. You are speaking nonsense." But the peculiar gleam in his eyes suggested he knew perfectly well that she was not.

The truth hit Bea with the force of a storm. She stepped back and her words tumbled out.

"Why do you come to Hart House, Tip?"

He seemed taken aback, then his eyes darkened.

"I should think that would be perfectly obvious by now."

"It is obvious why you *believe* you come." She pulled in a harsh breath, screwing up her courage. "But now you may be relieved of your efforts, my lord. You needn't visit again. I pray you, do not. The girl that you believe would make a comfortable wife does not, in fact, exist. She never did. *I* do. A prurient, amateurish Bow Street Runner with the speech of a doxy who is thrilled, *thrilled* to be trapped in a dark castle with a bona fide ghost. I am terribly sorry to disappoint you." The words slid across her teeth, cold and metallic and horribly honest.

Shock suffused his handsome features.

Bea's heart felt like it imploded. It was true, what she had suspected for years but never wanted to believe entirely. Now, looking into his eyes, she saw that he realized his mistake.

She whirled around and fled.

~o0o~

November 3, 1821

Great character and sense.

Great CHARACTER and SENSE.

He thinks I am a girl of great character and sense.

I already knew he thought this of me. It is no surprise whatsoever. It is the very reason I could not accept him today, cannot ever accept the thing I want most in the world. He sees me submit to Mama, perhaps believes that I refuse him because of her dependency on me and my dedication to her happiness. He knows me to be generally content with my lot in this remote corner of England. Thus he concludes that I have great character and sense.

Sense—most certainly not.

Character—I am inclined to doubt.

He has no notion of who I am. No notion of the woman I would be if I could. No notion that I long to be loved the way Georgie is loved, the way Sylvia is loved, the way Nancy is loved. I am practical, sensible Beatrice, serving her mother quietly and steadfastly without complaint, who would serve a husband well in much the same manner.

To be entirely fair, he is not alone in holding that impression of me. Two other gentlemen have asked for my hand, assuming much the same of me. These pages record it, just as they record my refusals. Each professed his admiration. But they were not he.

Diary, he does not know me at all. He has no idea that I long for a towering castle, a wicked count, a dashing hero, and a happy ending. He has no idea that I long for him.

I could tell him, but it would not change him. That, of course, is my true weakness of character. Is this pride? Perhaps vanity?

No. It is an aching heart. Empty and longing to be loved, adored, and cherished. Not merely required.

~o0o~

Chapter Nine

Tip stood frozen in place, panic gripping him.

She was magnificent. Dark eyes flashing, cheeks crimson, lips dewy, perfect breasts heaving in indignation. As she'd spoken, he had barely been able to attend to her words. All his energies had gone toward restraining himself from hauling her to the couch and having his way with her.

But he had heard her order him to cease visiting Yorkshire.

He sucked in thick breaths, trying to still the chaos in his chest and the voice—actually inside his head this time—telling him he was the greatest fool alive.

He had always known all that she had just said about herself. He had tried to pretend otherwise, but it was useless. She did not often reveal her passion, but it always simmered beneath her demure surface, glimmering in her warm eyes, ready to break free. The very night he fell in love with her he had seen it. In an instant he had lost both his mind and heart.

But he had not lost his will, and for four years he had pretended he had complete control over the part of him that responded to her secret ardor for life like gunpowder to a spark. He wanted her so much he willfully blinded himself to who she had always been. Practical, sensible, clearheaded— yes. But also vibrant, ardent, and deeply feeling.

An image came to him of her beloved garden, a riotous mass of roses, a tumult of rich color and heady fragrance, with her at the center of it.

She was correct. She was not what he wanted in a wife. He wanted agreeable companionship, pleasant conversation, and a bedmate he would enjoy looking at in the morning with her hair in disarray and circles beneath her eyes because he had kept her busy all night.

He did not want impassioned speeches, hurled accusations, or wide eyes sparkling with unshed tears. He certainly did not want to be called ridiculous names and have his masculinity questioned, or to share his woman with a damned impertinent ghost. He emphatically did not want this tangled tumult in his midsection, this difficulty drawing breath, this crushing sensation in his chest, this wild need to find her now, take her in his arms, and make love to her so that her shouts of anger became cries of pleasure.

He dragged a hand through his hair, gripping the back of his neck, his arm unsteady.

Dear God, he was shaking.

Once he had come upon his parents after a particularly nasty row. He had only been about ten at the time, and miserable over their screaming match though he hadn't understood much of its content.

His father had been kneeling on the ground, his mother bent over him, stroking his hair and kissing his brow. The baron wrapped his arms around her waist and murmured soft words in a broken voice, and she cried, "My darling, you are trembling!" She had cradled his head to her, and Tip found he could no longer watch. He went straight to the stable, mounted his father's fastest horse, and rode until the sun disappeared.

Years later he came to understand why they fought: his philandering ways, her intolerance of it; his pleading, her threats of leaving. It made no difference to Tip. Seeing his father weeping, a great man cowed by passion, and his mother, a gentle soul in such pain, he vowed he would go a different route. That sort of unbridled mania of the heart would never control him. He would choose a wife wisely, a woman he could admire and who would respond to his affections with measure.

He had apparently chosen poorly.

He had never simply admired Beatrice Sinclaire. He adored her from the start. At that Christmas gathering at her great-uncle Sir Jeremy's home seven years earlier, she had bedazzled him—not even sixteen, yet already with the grace and self-possession of a lady. Her eyes had captured him, their thick, black lashes fanning down when she caught him staring at her, then lifting again so she could cast him a sparkling, irrepressibly honest smile.

The realization that his adoration was love had taken him three more years. In that time she had only grown more beautiful.

He did know her. He simply did not know now if he could live with her.

The trouble was, he was certain he could not live without her.

~o0o~

Bea tucked herself into a ball on her bed and cried. She could not remember the last time she had wept so thoroughly or at such length. All the hurt poured out, the misery from the constant unkindnesses her mother practiced on her, the ache of her father's negligence, and the pain over finally losing Tip.

He must already be packing to return to Derbyshire.

Then good riddance to him. Perhaps if she did not see him every several months, her heart could recover from him. In a few dozen years.

A scratch sounded at the door.

"Beatrice?" Lady Bronwyn whispered. "May I enter?"

Bea uncurled, straightened her gown, swiped a hand across her cheeks, and went to the door.

Late afternoon sunlight came through the window, dust motes scampering about in the pale glow. Wearing a simple frock of white muslin, her black curls bound in a knot and her gentian eyes wide, Lady Bronwyn looked like a faery, the sort Bea remembered from childhood stories—the sort she had always wished she could be, free and unfettered from everyone's dispiriting opinions of her.

"How is your grandmother?"

"Oh, she sleeps much of the time now. But, oh! Beatrice, have you been crying?"

Bea turned her back and went to fluff the pillow on her bed.

"I have been napping. I am a bit weary after all the excitement, you see," she lied.

Bronwyn perched on the dressing table chair and worried her cherry lip between her teeth.

"My grandmother insists she is weary of life." She paused. "Lord Iversly says he is weary of death."

"Yes, he mentioned something like that to me, as well."

"Your brother—" Bronwyn halted, took a breath, and began again with greater certainty. "I think he does not fully understand the danger I face."

"I believe he does, Bronwyn. He was just speaking of it. He has gone into the village to search for information about the curse."

"Oh, he has?" The girl's face brightened. "Beatrice, is he spoken for?"

"Spoken for?"

Lady Bronwyn continued, head bent but her words quick.

"Oh, what I mean to say is, I admire him very much. My father arranged for my betrothal to Mr. Whitney, but the contract was never signed." She peeked up sweetly through sooty lashes.

Bea could not wonder that her brother had lost his head to this girl. Privately she agreed with Tip that her twin required time to mature. At twenty-three he was still a boy. Yet she herself was already on the shelf. "I do not know that Thomas has any plans to marry soon."

"Oh." Lady Bronwyn's pretty face fell.

"If he did have plans," Bea offered, "I am certain you would be the first to know."

Hope spilled from Bronwyn's glittering eyes.

"Bronwyn?" The pallid whisper came from the doorway.

"Grandmama, what are you doing out of bed? How brave you are!" Bronwyn hurried to her. Though Mrs. Canon seemed

of an age with Bea's great-aunts, she shared none of the
cherubic health of Aunt Julia or steely energy of Aunt Grace.
Instead she was thin as a waif and frail, her eyes wan. She
seemed more like a ghost than Iversly.

"Grandmama, this is Miss Beatrice Sinclaire, Mr.
Sinclaire's sister. I told you about her last night. She and her
friends have come to help us scare away Lord Iversly."

A tremor shook the elderly lady's insubstantial frame.

"The fiend," she rasped, then coughed. Bronwyn hovered
around her, looking helpless.

Bea took Mrs. Canon's arm and led her to a chair. When
she was settled, shrunk back into a corner of the cushion like
a child, Bea asked, "Mrs. Canon, do you know anything of the
curse that might help us solve this trouble? I understand that
you lived here for quite some time before your granddaughter
arrived."

"Oh, she never heard the ghost before I arrived,"
Bronwyn supplied.

"You did not? But he spoke with us nearly the moment
we came here."

"Iversly does not show himself unless a maiden resides in
the castle." Mrs. Canon's voice quavered, from age or perhaps
fear.

Bea's attention prickled. "How do you know that? Did
one of the servants tell you?"

"The woman did."

"The woman?"

"Oh." Bronwyn's delicate brow creased. "She must be
speaking of Miss Minturn."

"Who is Miss Minturn?"

"My old governess. She lives in the village, but I have not
seen her in an age. She is sickly, you know. Much worse than
Grandmama."

"This Miss Minturn told you about the terms of the curse,
Mrs. Canon? And about Lord Iversly's habits?" Bea's nerves
stirred with renewed eagerness. "How does she come to know
about them?"

The grandmother shrank further back into the chair.

"I suspect everyone around here knows about him," Bronwyn replied.

Bea had already asked Cook and Dibin to tell her all they could. Either they were not interested in sharing information, or they truly knew little beyond what Bea had already learned. It seemed remarkable that this Miss Minturn would have more information, unless she had been personally involved with Lord Iversly.

"Mrs. Canon, would you like to return to your chamber and rest?" Bea gently helped her to stand. Bronwyn followed them through the keep to the grandmother's room and they deposited her in bed.

"I will send up Cook with a posset for you." Bea closed the door and turned to Bronwyn. "Was Miss Minturn ever married, Bronwyn?"

"Oh, no, of course."

"I must ask you something indelicate now."

Bronwyn's lashes fanned outward.

"Do you know if your former governess ever had a gentleman admirer? A particular one?"

Bronwyn's face went blank, then comprehension filled her eyes.

"Oh, I am fairly certain she did not. She is very plain."

"I see." Bea chewed on her lip, impressed at the depth of Bronwyn's naïveté. "Do you think that if my brother goes to see her she would be likely to speak with him openly about the time she lived at the castle?"

"Oh, no. Gentlemen frighten her."

Bea nodded. She would find a solution. Perhaps Aunts Grace and Julia would go down to the village and interview Miss Minturn. She could hope.

~oOo~

Lady Marstowe refused. She stared from behind her

lorgnette with hauteur and announced that she would not step
foot out of the fortress until Beatrice was gone from it.

"Aunt Grace, unless we learn more about the curse, I may
never be able to leave."

"Iversly intends to take the chit as his bride tomorrow
night. Let him do so and then we will leave."

"Aunt Grace!" Bea exclaimed at the same moment Julia
warbled, "Gracie."

"I will not be party to further foolishness." The dowager
glowered. "You are your family's bedrock, Beatrice. However
much I despise most everything Harriet demands, your duty is
to her, not to this girl or her ghost."

Something tugged at Bea's attention, and she turned
toward the parlor door. Tip had entered, handsomer than ever
in evening garb.

A treacly discomfort stole through her. But it didn't matter
if he had heard her great-aunt's comment. To him she was an
unruly, sharp-tongued miscreant.

He was welcome to his opinion. She wished he had already
left Gwynedd.

But his gaze upon her now was warm and she could not
help thinking he stayed for her. It was simply odious. *And
wonderful.*

"Gracie dear, perhaps one of our party could make a trip
down to the village after breakfast tomorrow," Julia suggested.
"I am in need of red thread, and Cook tells me there is a fine
sewing shop along the street." She reached into her embroidery
bag and pulled out a handful of tangled yarns.

"I will be glad to accompany you, Miss Dews," Tip said
with a bow.

Thomas and Bronwyn appeared in the doorway.

"Oh, Dibin tells me dinner is served," Bronwyn said,
glancing shyly at Bea's brother. He took her arm and moved
toward the dining room. Tip approached Lady Marstowe and
held out his arm, and she laid her hand upon it, her thin lips
pursed.

Dinner consisted of several remarkably tasty dishes served

all at once. Bea wished she could stomach it, but Tip sat beside her and her entire attention wrapped around him.

It could not be helped, she supposed. She could rant and rave all she wished about the true woman within, but she could not force her heart to give him up so quickly after loving him for so long, especially not with him sitting two feet away, so gorgeously wonderful in every way. Except one.

When the meal ended, he drew out her chair and took her hand onto his arm, stalling her as the others left for the parlor.

"I would like to speak with you in private before you retire tonight, if you would allow it." No anger or displeasure colored his candid eyes.

Bea took a steadying breath. She should say no. Adamantly no. What good could come of more tête-à-têtes with him? More teasing? More accusations?

More heartache.

She must be strong.

"All right."

She could be strong starting in the morning.

He escorted her into the parlor and seated her beside Aunt Julia. Julia gave him a twinkling smile, he winked in response, and Bea's heart made an uncomfortable pilgrimage around her chest cavity.

"I wonder if this governess, Miss Minturn, will come now," Thomas said. "Lady Bronwyn says she hasn't been to the castle in an age."

"She sounds like an imbecile," the dowager remarked with a frown. "Is this Miss Minturn an imbecile, Lady Bronwyn?"

"Oh, no. I do not believe so. She taught me everything I know."

Lady Marstowe's lips tightened.

Bea stifled a grin. Bronwyn was a sweet girl, and Bea herself was an absolute ninny to feel so giddy, especially when danger loomed so near. They should be doing something about it.

Tip stood by the mantle, his hand tucked at the back of his neck and head bent in an attitude of thought. As though he felt her regard, he looked up and across the chamber at her. He smiled. Bea's legs went watery.

This *would not do*. She had been in love with him for years, friends for the same time, yet it only required one little kiss and a shouting match to thrust her emotions back to her first months of infatuation. *Ridiculous*. Especially given what he must think of her now.

What on earth must he say to her in private? And how would she go on, now that she had convinced herself she must not love him any longer?

No, she could not meet him tonight. She was determined to be a new person. Her own person. The old Beatrice Sinclaire wasted away in hopeless attachment to Lord Peter Cheriot. Well, not precisely. In fact she ate and drank and enjoyed walks and read books and gardened and saw to her mother's needs. But the new Beatrice Sinclaire would do all of that with a lighter heart, free of pathetic yearnings. If she were to live life the way she wished, she could not hang on to unproductive imaginings.

Let him think whatever he liked, and do whatever he did. She would resist his enticements, and maintain a firm stance.

A new life awaited her. It did not include Peter Cheriot.

~o0o~

June 29, 1821

He has never asked me why I refuse him. Today he only smiled and shook his head.

If he continues in this pattern, Diary, I shall be obliged to invent an excuse in the event that someday he requires an explanation.

I doubt he ever will.

~o0o~

Chapter Ten

Tip strode along the corridor, his mouth set in a grim line, his jaw tight. She had escaped him. Willfully. Despite her promise to meet him.

Not exactly a promise, of course. Never a promise. But not a refusal this time, either.

Clearly she did not wish to speak with him. But he had something to say. So she could just listen. And he was not above going to her bedchamber to make it so. A man did not come to an important realization in the course of an afternoon and let it sit without acting on it. Gentlemanly behavior, be damned. He'd had just about enough of it at this point.

He rounded a corner and nearly slammed into Thomas.

"Odd's blood! Watch your step, Cheriot."

"Watch your own," Tip growled.

Thomas frowned. "What's the matter? You don't look well."

"Good of you to notice." Tip took a hard breath, anger and impatience boiling beneath his skin. But he couldn't very well tell Sinclaire he needed to hurry off to interrupt his sister at bedtime.

A picture of Bea preparing for bed sliced through his imagination, staggering him momentarily.

"Is there something I should know?" Thomas's frown deepened. "Have you had news since I left the parlor? Did Iversly appear again?"

"No." Tip shook his head. "No news. I will escort Lady Marstowe and Miss Dews to the village tomorrow to speak with Lady Bronwyn's governess, as planned. Hopefully she will tell us something we can put to use."

"But you don't think she will." Thomas peered at him the way younger men often did, especially when it came to horseflesh—seeking guidance, answers.

"I don't know. But Iversly did not hoax when he said he is determined to end the curse at midnight tomorrow." Tip had never heard a man sound the way Iversly did when he spoke to Bea: desperate, with an undertone of despair so acute it dug into Tip's conscience.

He was not about to allow Lady Bronwyn or Bea to be sacrificed for Iversly's eternal contentment, but he could not help feeling sympathy for the fellow. The ghost's misery was the very thing that now drove him to speak to Bea. Iversly's fate was sealed, but he still had a chance.

He wanted Beatrice Sinclaire, for better and apparently for worse as well. One argument would not turn him into his father, and a single outburst did not make her his mother. He had been cross with her in the first place because all that talk of warm bodies had him hotter than he had been in months. *Years.* To prevent himself from grabbing her, he had criticized her instead. Not very gallant, admittedly, but now that he realized what he had done he could avoid it in the future.

Yes. They would get along fine.

"Tip," Thomas said hesitantly. "I've been thinking . . ."

"About what?" He struggled to bank his impatience. Control. Calm. Reason. His imagination conjured Bea in a diaphanous nightgown. Her bedchamber was just ahead along the corridor. He nearly groaned aloud. "What, Tom?" he pressed.

"Iversly can marry only a maiden. He's said so any number of times. Only a maiden is able to break the curse."

"Yes."

"Well . . ." Thomas's brows slanted to a point. "It's only that—"

"Tomorrow we will discover a solution," Tip said quickly, suspecting where Thomas's thoughts had gone and not blaming him at all for it. He gripped the younger man's shoulder. The gesture seemed to comfort Thomas.

"Right then. Good night, Tip."

"Good night, Tom." Tip watched him continue down the corridor toward his chamber. When he heard Thomas's bolt clank in place, he pivoted around and went the rest of the way to Bea's door.

No answer met his knock. He set his shoulders back and turned the handle.

Moonlight crept through partially drawn curtains, but no woman sat at the dressing table or reclined on the bed. He drew the door closed and started up the corridor again.

He found her in the dining chamber. She stood before a window, looking out onto the dry moat and hill sloping out from the side of the castle. Bluish-silver light illuminated her hair caught up in a knot, glinting off the satiny tresses like river water at night and caressing her lovely neck and graceful collarbone. The moonlight defined her figure in silhouette, tracing each gentle curve, her gown a mere glove upon her intoxicating body.

Tip drew a long breath.

She looked over her shoulder, hesitating before turning to him fully.

"I thought you meant to avoid me after all," he managed to say in what sounded to him like an unremarkable tone. She remained perfectly placid, entirely unlike earlier when her eyes sparkled with emotion and he had to struggle not to drag her into his arms.

Good. Her return to normalcy would make this easier.

"I did. But then I changed my mind," she replied.

"I'm glad." He crossed the chamber, folding his hands behind his back. Better to trap them than use them impulsively. He did not entirely trust himself. "I hoped we could speak. Actually, I hoped I could speak, if you will hear me out."

Her brow furrowed, but she nodded.

"We have never quarreled before, in my recollection," he began, winning a twitch of her lovely lashes. "Frankly, I didn't believe it was possible. No, wait—" He held up a palm as her lips parted. "I am many unenviable things, but intractable is not one of them. At least concerning most matters," he added.

She looked wary. "What do you mean?"

"You expressed yourself very clearly this afternoon, and I was a boor about it. I apologize for that."

She took her soft lower lip between her teeth. Tip's temperature inched a notch higher.

"Thank you, I think," she said. "I can tell you are about to add 'but,' aren't you?"

"Not in the least. I have no intention of backtracking on that apology."

"Unintentional backtracks do occur occasionally."

"Then let them, if you will. They will not come in the way of our friendship."

She blinked but did not speak. Her eyes were luminous and rich in the moonlight. He could lose himself in those lucent eyes and never wish to find his way out again.

"I realize it has been barely a sennight since I last requested your hand in marriage," he said, tightening his fingers together behind his back. "This evening, however, I understand matters between us somewhat differently."

"I should hope so," she said, her voice unusually thin.

"I believe more firmly than ever that we should suit, Bea."

He had to unbind his hands to get on one knee, but he trusted in his newfound sense of measured calm that he would be able to restrain himself from employing them inappropriately. If they could speak civilly so soon after a tremendous row, he could contain his lust. At least for a while. "Will you marry me?"

Her entrancing eyes popped wide and her delectable mouth fell open.

"Are you *insane*, Peter Cheriot?"

"Not yet." He hoped she meant the question rhetorically. His heart lodged in his throat. "And I fully intend never to be. Marry me, Bea."

Her expression grew if possible more astonished.

"Didn't you hear a word I said this afternoon?"

"Every one of them." Except perhaps a few. He had been

excessively distracted by the pressing need to throw her on the floor and make passionate love to her.

"Then to whom, exactly, do you think you are proposing?" Her breasts rose on a hard breath.

Tip stood up so as not to be quite so dead-on with the entrancing sight.

"You. There is no one else in the room that I can see, ghosts notwithstanding." This was not going so well. "Say yes, Bea."

"No." She looked pained. Her eyes closed tight for an instant. When she opened them again, they were bright with unshed tears. "No, I will not marry you. I will not."

"You will not?" He had not anticipated this. He should have. He was, perhaps, the greatest idiot alive. "Again?"

"Nothing has changed since last week, has it?" She obviously meant this question rhetorically.

He shook his head to clear it of confusion. It *had* changed. They had quarreled like lovers, yet hours later they could sit through a perfectly pleasant dinner conversing on various topics, and all was well again. That ought to count for something. His parents had never moved from passionate anger to benign companionship so quickly and easily. They cried for days, moped for another week, then finally fell back into each other's arms as enamored as they'd been before, despite broken furniture, carriages, and horses, and the wagging tongues of society in their wake.

Bea's impassioned speech roused his desire more than ever. But he could control that. He had been controlling it for years already, like this afternoon when he had controlled it by calling her a doxy.

Good God.

"No?" he offered, uncertain.

"Of course something has changed." Her voice pitched on a peculiar note. "*I* have changed. You are not now offering marriage to the same woman you did seven days ago." She lifted a hand and swept back a twist of dark hair that had slipped over her cheek. Tip ached to do it for her, to stroke the satiny tress and caress her soft skin. Dear God, if he couldn't have her soon, he might actually go mad.

"Then will this new woman marry me?"

"No! Oh sweet heaven. No," she insisted. "No." Her eyes were fraught with distress.

He swallowed hard. He had caused this. Her unhappiness.

"So, that is a refusal," he heard himself utter.

"You are insane." Her voice broke. "Or suddenly an imbecile."

She was entirely correct. Only a complete fool would continue asking the same woman for her hand after she refused it so many times. Only a buffoon of the lowest order would put his heart on the line again and again to have it crushed, and rather savagely this time.

He was indeed a fool for this woman. A hopeless imbecile. But he never wanted to hurt her. Yet somehow he clearly had. He deserved to be horsewhipped.

"All right," he said, taking a deep breath. "You have made your point. I regret to have distressed you."

She nodded, dashing the back of a slender hand across her damp eyes.

They stood like that for a handful of seconds, a minute perhaps. Tip didn't know. He didn't care. The only thing he truly cared about, it seemed, was entirely out of his reach. And this time—this blasted out-of-control, emotional, tear-dashing time—it must end. Each time she had refused him in the past he had held out hope that someday she would accept. But he could not deceive himself any longer. Her response now, so unlike her previous measured demurrals, made it perfectly clear.

"Do you know, Peter Cheriot," she said, her voice quiet and uneven, "all these times you have offered marriage to me, you have not once asked why I refuse you."

The words blindsided him.

He floundered for a response.

"It is not my place to ask."

"It is, if you insist on offering again."

Abruptly, Tip's crushed heart made way for his neglected temper.

"That is absurd."

"I think you don't want to know."

"What?"

"You do not want to know why I won't marry you. It is safer for you that way."

"What in the devil's name are you talking about? There is nothing whatsoever safe about offering marriage to a woman."

"Precisely my point." She breathed hard, her eyes bright again. "You do not wish to marry. You ask me again and again in the certainty that I will refuse you, so that you can feel satisfied you have made the effort and never be obliged to admit to yourself that you do not actually want a wife."

"I do so want a wife. I want you." Dear God, he sounded like a child. Worse yet, like his father.

"I don't believe you," she countered. "If you truly wished to marry me, you would ask me why I refuse you each time."

No, he wouldn't, for the single reason that he feared her response.

Everyone knew what a profligate his father had been, and the shame of his parents' public battles and reconciliations. His own beautiful sister, a noblewoman, had married a country curate to escape the ton's gossip. He did not want to hear Bea confess that she could not be with him because she did not trust him not to carry on in his parents' mode. So he kept asking, hoping his constancy would prove to her that he was not cut from that cloth.

"You see?" She backed away, blinking rapidly. "You cannot bring yourself to ask me why."

His hands fisted at his sides, his jaw tight enough to break his teeth. If it meant even the slightest chance of winning this woman, he would force himself to ask her. And finally he would hear the answer that would smash his hopes once and for all.

His tongue struggled to find words.

A tear spilled over the cusp of her dark eye, slipping down

her cheek in a silvery trail and catching at the edge of her lips. Tip stared at those lips, sensuous and ripe, and desire gripped him so hard and fast he rocked on his feet. Wild with it, he gulped in air, every mote of his being focused on her beautiful mouth.

He grasped her shoulders and captured her mouth beneath his.

Her lips were as warm and supple as when he had kissed her before. But this time they did not remain motionless. Instead, they moved against his, gently parting and tasting his with soft, tentative touches that sent Tip's pulse careening.

He gripped her beneath the arms and pulled her close. She grasped his coat sleeves and released a little sigh of pleasure.

His world spun. His thumbs brushed the sides of her breasts, and he delved deeper into her mouth, caressing with the tip of his tongue until her grip on his arms tightened and she leaned into him, parting her lips. She was sweet and hot and *willing*.

Sweeping his hands around her waist, he dragged her against his body. Her curves tucked cozily to him, her breasts and thighs yielding. Her hands moved to his back and her lips opened wider.

He was in flames everywhere she touched him, everywhere their chests and thighs and hips collided he could feel her. He needed to touch her *everywhere*, to feel her closer. He slipped a hand over her soft behind and cupped.

"*Peter*," she sighed against his lips.

He pressed into her, letting her feel his desire. *Dear God*, she was an innocent, but he needed her. He had needed her for years and she responded to him so eagerly.

"You want this, Bea," he murmured, nipping at her bewitching lower lip, filling his hands with her. "You want me. Admit it."

"I do." She breathed brokenly, sliding her arms around his shoulders.

He kissed her deep and hard, and she responded with hunger, her tongue venturing to touch his, awkward but intoxicating, her hands clutching his neck. He trailed caresses along her jaw to the fragrant tenderness just beneath her ear, weaving his fingers through her hair. She tilted her head, allowing him freedom on the silken skin of her throat where her pulse came heavy and fast.

He couldn't get enough of her—her eager mouth, her captivating scent of roses and honeysuckle, her clinging hands and perfect, shell-like ears. Why hadn't he ever noticed before how perfect her ears were? How slender her wrists? How delicate her collarbone? He had adored her and still remained blind. But now he saw her with perfect clarity, and he was ravenous.

His hand sought her breast. Bea stiffened, then relaxed into his touch. The fabric of her gown was fine and thin, the satin swell of her breasts teetering at the edge of her bodice with each deep breath she drew. So beautiful. *Temptation.*

He reveled in the shape of her, and her warmth, and his cock throbbed harder against her. A soft moan escaped her lips. He took her mouth again, drinking in her flavor, and slid his thumb up and across her skin. Then he dipped it beneath the fabric.

She gasped, a sound of complete pleasure and he felt her supple, velvety skin and the rough, beautiful texture of her swollen nipple. She breathed hard against his mouth, her fingers gripping to hold him near as he caressed. Her knees parted and he spread his hand on her behind and moved against her. She moaned, this time fully. He pressed his mouth to her neck, tasting her, adoring her, aching with need he had controlled for far too long.

He must have more of her.

He freed her breasts of the bodice.

"*Bea.*" His voice was hoarse.

Sublime beauty. All pink and white perfection. With absolute reverence he touched her breast, the full curve of woman. She sighed. Drawing upward, he passed his fingertip ever so lightly over her peaked nipple and she gasped.

He stroked, gently at first, then more firmly until she

whimpered her pleasure. Forever he had longed to touch her like this, to feast his senses on her. The reality flew far beyond his fantasies.

He bent and ran his tongue along the column of her throat, into the tender gully of her collar, then beyond, licking the valley between her breasts, her softness brushing his cheek. Her tight, rosy nipples begged to be tasted. Savored. In his mouth.

She gripped the back of his neck, her breaths coming hard and fast.

"Peter?" She whispered her plea. An invitation he could not refuse.

He covered a peak. She shuddered, her body trembling. He circled her exquisite arousal with his tongue, and stroked it gently. He licked, sucked, and brushed his teeth across her flesh. She clutched him tighter and her gasps became a desperate moan.

"Oh, *Peter*."

His cock was so hot, so hard. So hungry. And she was *allowing this*. Welcoming it. He needed her. His hand slipped over her sweet, soft abdomen, seeking the intoxicating junction of her thighs.

No.

A frisson of sanity wound through him.

He could not do this.

He wanted her more than air, more than life and breath. But after so many years of waiting, he refused to make her his in a dining room.

He thrust her to arm's length and dragged in a gulp of clarifying control.

"You will marry me as soon as the banns can be read, Bea. I'll be damned if you don't."

Her hair was in disarray, lips swollen from his kisses, eyes hazy with desire, the tips of her breasts damp and taut. She was more beautiful than he had ever imagined.

The dining table would do well enough.

Good God.

He locked his elbows.

"From nonchalant to insistent." She released a shaky sigh. "You have never insisted before."

"Of course I am insisting." With enormous effort he released her, and raked his fingers through his hair. "I have any number of inestimable reasons for doing so, only one of which is currently at the fore."

"That being?" Her voice was thick.

"Blast it, Beatrice Sinclaire, are you a simpleton not to know it? I want you in my bed."

He hadn't thought it possible, but her dark lashes spread yet further, and her eyes grew wider than he had ever seen them. A pink flush rushed from the edge of the gown he had nearly torn from her, across her breasts and up her delectable neck, filling her cheeks with flame.

Tip's throat caught.

"Good Lord, Bea. I didn't mean to say that. Not in that manner." He reached forward with one hand, then dropped it again sharply. "Say you will marry me."

Her eyes flooded with emotion.

"I-I am so confused," she said in barely a whisper, blinking rapidly. She turned her face away, strapping her arms across her breasts protectively.

Tip sucked in a choking breath. She really didn't want him. Her body might, but the rest of her fought it.

The reason she had refused him so many times now seemed so clear. His parents were not to blame. She simply did not want *him*. Perhaps she thought of him like a brother, as her mother always said. Or perhaps there was another man, someone she wanted as much as he wanted her.

Now she must feel trapped, as though she hadn't a choice. He had never wanted that. Never. Only her happiness mattered.

"I will not force you to it, Bea. No one need know of this." He sounded like a complete scoundrel. Felt like one too.

Her gaze returned to his, stunned. But she did not speak. Clearly, he was not alone in thinking he was a scoundrel.

He stepped back, shutting out the voice in his head shouting that he was making the greatest mistake of his life to retreat now.

"I will not renew my suit. When we return to England, I promise you will not see me again in York." He turned and strode from the chamber swiftly. To go throw himself off a parapet.

~oOo~

September 9, 1819

Mr. Cheriot—Lord Cheriot, now—renewed his suit yesterday.

He was in the area advising Lord Marke on a purchase for his stables, still wearing mourning for his father, of course. He came only for tea, seemed distracted, then begged my company on the terrace, remarkable in such inclement weather, although I understood afterward why he desired privacy.

He said that when the year of mourning is out he wishes to marry. He understood that a year ago he had perhaps taken me by surprise with his addresses, but, although we had seen little of each other in the intervening months due to responsibilities that held him in Derbyshire, he now wished to restate his case. He hoped I would reconsider. He then departed so that I might have time to consider it before responding.

This morning he returned, and I refused him. He did not inquire as to the reason.

As he took his leave, Mama asked why his visit was so brief. He bowed over her hand, spoke a few gallantries, and said that as his business was complete in Yorkshire, Cheriot Manor required his presence at once—the harvest, etc. After he left, Mama criticized me for displeasing him. If she only knew. But I will never tell her, and he clearly never requested her permission or my father's to pay his addresses to me.

Business. His business was complete.

My heart is a useless organ, Diary. I must be the most foolish woman in England, perhaps in all of Great Britain. I could live quite comfortably as Lady Cheriot, with no Mama throwing barbs at me on the hour and no Papa forgetting that I exist.

But I could not bear to love him every day so greatly and not be loved in return. I have become accustomed to it with Mama and Papa. With him, I never could.

~oOo~

Chapter Eleven

Bea did not appear for breakfast. Tip surprised himself with his anger over her unusual cowardice. For years she had silently accepted her lot as unpaid companion to her demanding mother, but she had never been a milksop.

Thomas was absent as well. Lady Bronwyn nibbled on a piece of toast, her cheeks glowing, as usual. She dimpled when she greeted Tip. She was a taking little thing, and thoroughly aware of it. Exactly the sort of girl a man with porridge-for-brains would admire.

Lady Marstowe rose from the table.

"Well, are we to do this or not, Lord Cheriot?"

"I am at your disposal, ma'am."

"Peter dear," Miss Dews said to her muffin and jam, "I will remain here while you and Grace visit Miss Minturn."

Lady Marstowe cast her sister a low glance before leaving the dining room.

The village was no more than a dozen or so buildings, with dwellings above shop fronts mostly. The former governess's cottage stood slightly apart from the rest, unremarkable in gray stone and wattle. They knocked and were admitted.

In her youth Miss Minturn might have been comely. Intelligence winked in a pair of fine pale eyes set in an oval face. Now, however, those eyes shifted restlessly back and forth between them, and her fingers twitched on her lap.

"We are here to learn about this curse," Lady Marstowe began without preamble. "Speak up, woman, and tell us what we must know to depress Iversly's intentions toward Lady Bronwyn."

At the sound of the ghost's name, Miss Minturn's wan

cheeks went chalky.

Tip leaned forward.

"Ma'am, are you unwell?"

She flinched back from him.

"I cannot help you," she uttered. "I know nothing."

"You must know something," the dowager stated. "You appear as though you are looking at a ghost this very moment." Distress churned in Miss Minturn's eyes.

"I cannot see him. I cannot."

"Well of course you cannot," Lady Marstowe said. "He is at the castle. But you may tell us what you know of him and the curse, and we will manage it after that."

"I cannot see him."

Lady Marstowe's lips pinched, her eyes narrowing.

They left the cottage shortly.

"She is not a simpleton, that much is clear," the dowager said as Tip handed her up into the carriage.

"No."

"There is a history there. He did something to her."

Tip nodded, admiration for the old termagant getting the better of his frustration.

"It seems so."

Her uncompromising gaze fixed in his.

"You must not allow him to harm our Beatrice."

Tip returned her regard steadily.

"I will not."

When they arrived at the castle, Bea had not yet arisen. Miss Dews and Lady Marstowe took their young hostess to stroll in the garden. Tip stood in the middle of the courtyard, watching them pass beneath the open portcullis. Lady Bronwyn smiled and laughed. For a girl anticipating a horrible fate, she seemed peculiarly high-spirited.

Unease passed across Tip's shoulders.

He needed his horse. His brain functioned best from the saddle. He headed toward the stable.

He was sliding the headpiece over his stallion's ears when Thomas appeared in the doorway.

"No groom, I suppose?"

"Nor stable boy. But I am not so high on the instep that I cannot saddle my own mount, Tom. You know that." He stroked the horse's dark neck, the precise shade of Beatrice Sinclaire's hair. He was an equine expert, yet he had bought the beast for that feature alone. That the stallion turned out to be a prime goer was only his luck.

"I'll wager you prefer it." Thomas's voice seemed edgy.

Tip laid his arm across his mount's back and studied the younger man.

"Aunt Grace said that the governess would not give you the time of day." Thomas's face was oddly flushed.

"She was unforthcoming, it's true."

"It's all right, though. Iversly won't be marrying Lady Bronwyn tonight."

Tip's unease returned.

"He won't? Have you spoken with him?"

"No. But—What I mean to say is—Well, a gentleman shouldn't tell, but all things considered, you came here to help and—I daresay I can trust you to—"

"Have it over, Sinclaire."

"Lady Bronwyn is no longer a maiden."

Tip stared. Anger and a violent wash of choked, hamstrung lust built up in him quick. He stepped away from his horse.

"So, you see," Thomas continued, much more at ease now that he had unburdened himself, "the danger is past and—"

Tip's fist connected with Thomas's jaw with a satisfying crack. Thomas reeled back on his heels against a stall door.

"That is for placing your sister in danger by satisfying your own needs." Tip swung again more forcefully. The whelp crashed to the straw-strewn floor. "And that is for years of expecting her to wrest you out of scrapes of your own making, this one the worst of all." He rubbed his knuckles and glared.

Thomas's eyes and mouth gaped, blood trickling over his lower lip.

"I—" he began, flinched, and cupped his jaw in one hand.

He grunted, then his gaze flickered up. "I didn't think of Bea. I cannot believe I didn't."

"Too busy thinking of yourself, as usual." Tip stepped back, flexing his hand. Hitting Thomas had not relieved his anger.

"Guess I've botched matters badly this time, haven't I? Bea is in danger. What should I do?"

"If I knew that, would I still be here, or have allowed your sister to remain?"

"I won't leave," Thomas said stoutly, sitting up straight.

"Go find your future bride and take her to the village. She must speak with Miss Minturn."

Thomas remained silent for a moment.

"Will you tell Bea?"

"I knew you to be a scapegrace, Tom Sinclaire, but until now I hadn't realized how much of a coward you are as well."

Thomas's face reddened. He jerked to his feet.

"You're right. It's not your place, of course. What was I thinking? I'll go now." He started toward the stable door.

Tip took a deep breath.

"Don't frighten her," he said.

Thomas halted. His gaze slung back, regret on his features. He nodded, wiped the blood from his nose and lip with a handkerchief, and left.

Tip turned to his horse, his heart beating faster than it had since the first time he had proposed to Bea. Thomas was an immature, self-centered boy and something of a cad. But for all her dimples, Lady Bronwyn Prescot was no wilting lily. Tip had little doubt that the lady had encouraged her eager admirer to free her of danger. They were a perfect pair.

He mounted and rode out the front gate.

~oOo~

August 9, 1818

Mama and I attended the Assembly tonight in Aldborough. It was dreadfully hot and I had no wish to go, but Mama insisted. She has thoroughly despaired of finding a husband for me, but she enjoys going about to see her friends. She intends, I think, to show a brave face to the world despite Papa's defection.

My card filled with the autographs of timid second sons and gloomy former soldiers. None of them were Peter Cheriot, whom I believed to be still attending his declining father in Derbyshire. It did not matter to me with whom I danced.

Then he appeared.

Imagine the leap of my heart, Diary, the smile I could not suppress as he approached, as handsome as the last time we met, before Mama and I departed London. He kissed my knuckles and asked after my health. I hardly knew what to say, but I must have replied suitably since his warm smile did not diminish. What on earth was he doing there? The place was astir; young, handsome heirs to baronies do not typically attend the public ball at Aldborough. I had not even heard he was in the district. Certainly Nancy would have told Mama had she known he intended to come. He must have arrived only tonight.

He requested the next set, I regretted that it was already spoken for, as well as all others. He heard me without any show of disappointment, then stood by Mama's side like a chaperone for the remainder of the evening, pleasantly conversing with all but not dancing (to the dismay of any number of ladies present).

Afterward, he rode alongside our carriage to Hart House and Mama invited him inside for tea.

Tea at midnight. In the countryside. She will seek company whenever she can, she is so weary of mine.

We conversed about many things, including Georgie, in whose activities and interests he was predictably interested. He seemed reluctant *to speak of his father's ill health. Mama fell asleep on the divan and began to snore lightly. With barely a break in the conversation he said, "Bea, I admire you greatly and believe we would suit. Would you do me the honor of accepting my hand?"*

I said, "No, thank you."

I could hardly have replied otherwise.

At first he appeared surprised. Shortly, however, he spoke easily again, proof enough, Diary, that I was justified in refusing him. A man in love does not recover from such a rejection in fewer than two minutes. Or so I understand it.

I could probably marry any other gentleman under such circumstances, but not Peter Cheriot. Never him. I would rather die.

~o0o~

Chapter Twelve

Bea's eyelids cracked open to the unfamiliar sight of midday sun creeping through her bedchamber curtains. Typically she rose before dawn, stealing an hour in peace before Mama's demands and complaints began.

She could have left that behind.

He had kissed her, touched her, made her mad with longing, and asked her to marry him again. Astonished, confused, awash in sensations wholly unfamiliar and deliciously shocking, she had not quite comprehended what was happening.

She rested a shaky hand on her brow.

He wanted her in his bed.

It seemed incredible. All those years of teasing, brotherly attention, and now he wanted her *that way*.

He cared for her as a friend, and he desired her. Wasn't that love?

But now he had promised to do exactly as she insisted. He was leaving her life. He would not abandon the castle yet, of course. He had made it clear that he considered it his responsibility to make certain of Bronwyn's and her own safety.

Bea dragged herself out of bed and went to her traveling trunk. All her gowns were hopelessly wrinkled. She wished she had the enthusiasm to put an iron to them. She wondered if Cook was ironing her great-aunts' clothing. In any case, they would be gone the following day, having abandoned Bronwyn to her horrible fate this very night.

Bea shivered, opening the trunk. The contents seemed to have shrunken. She reached in and pulled out her prettiest gown, spring green with emerald-colored ribbons she had woven through the bodice and sleeves, chosen because they reminded her of Tip's eyes.

She stalled, her hand hovering over the trunk.

Then, with firm intention, she shook out the gown and reached for her undergarments. Her hand met more gowns, stockings, and shoes. She dug into the trunk, but it was empty of shifts and petticoats. No stays in sight, either.

She went to the warped garderobe.

"You will not find them there."

Bea started, then grabbed up the green gown and covered the front of her thin nightgown.

"Lord Iversly," she said, "it is unseemly for you to enter a lady's bedchamber without invitation."

"Yet there is another in this castle to whom you would offer an invitation to this bedchamber with alacrity."

Bea sucked in a quick breath.

"Why do you stand by windows? Don't you know the light comes right through you?"

"I have not bothered musing upon such insignificancies for centuries."

The door swung open and Lady Marstowe entered.

"You should have been up hours ago, Beatrice. What would your mother think?"

"Mother is not here, Aunt Grace. Lord Iversly is, however."

The ghost's gaze shifted to Lady Marstowe, and Bea hastily slipped the green gown over her nightgown.

"That cannot be helped, I suppose." The dowager snapped her fingers and Bea turned to allow her great-aunt to button her up. "What does he want?"

"My bride," Lord Iversly intoned.

"Then go find her, my lord. I must speak with my great-niece in private. This gown fits atrociously. Where are your stays, Beatrice? Have you lost all sense of propriety in this uncivilized place?"

"I cannot find them, Aunt Grace."

Lord Iversly caught her eye. Bea's stomach flip-flopped. He looked very dark today, but shockingly attractive, his black hair swept back from the harsh planes of his face. He smiled, a slow curving slash of his mouth. His gaze slipped down her body, lingering on her unconfined breasts, then her hips.

Bea's eyes went wide.

"You have taken them, haven't you? Why on earth would you do such a thing?"

"What are you talking about?" Lady Marstowe demanded.

"Women in my day did not wear such ridiculous garments." Iversly chuckled, a wicked glimmer in his ebony eyes. "Modest women did not need to pretend modesty by layering themselves in unnecessary cloth."

Bea frowned. "Well I am dreadfully cold without them." Heroines in ghost novels were complete ninnies, it seemed. She was not about to be the same, not even if her spine was tingling in the presence of the large, slightly translucent man. Today he wore a shirt of mail over lean leggings and a black tunic with a gold eagle emblazoned on the chest. "It should not matter to you what I wear, whether my hat upon my feet or my stockings around my neck."

"Beatrice," the dowager hissed.

"Aunt Grace, he is a ghost, and he is a horrible man for taking my stays. He has not stolen your petticoats, has he?"

"He would not dare."

"No, of course not." Bea swung back to Iversly. "Have you left off harassing only your intended bride, Lord Iversly, in favor of every virgin in the castle now?"

"Only the one." His mouth set in a dangerous smile.

"Bea?" Thomas's bumpy voice came from the doorway. Aunt Julia stood behind him, her eyes dancing.

He came forward, anger on his face as he looked toward the window where Bea's gaze fixed.

"He's here, isn't he?"

"Yes. Thomas—"

"Aunt Grace, Aunt Julia, I would like to speak to my sister alone, if I may."

"Of course, dear." Julia took Lady Marstowe's arm. "Grace and I were just going to meet Bronwyn's grandmother, weren't we, Gracie?"

"No. But it is about time I had an interview with that useless invalid. Thomas, where is Lady Bronwyn?"

"I don't quite know, Aunt Grace." He looked uncharacteristically abashed.

Lady Marstowe frowned, then followed her sister from the chamber.

"Bea, you are in trouble."

"Greater trouble than being trapped in a crumbling castle by a miserable wretch of a specter?" She shot Iversly a glare.

He lifted a thick brow.

"It is best not to cast insults at your bridegroom upon your wedding day, my dear. When you are finally his, he may repay you in a manner you cannot like." His words slithered through her.

"This is not my wedding day. And for Lady Bronwyn's sake we will discover the weak place in your foolish curse and beat you at your own game, my lord."

"Bea," Thomas said. "He's speaking the truth of it. You are the only maiden in the castle now."

Bea's breath caught.

"Where has Bronwyn gone? Did she manage to escape? Oh, I am so relieved for her! How did she do it?"

Thomas shook his head.

"She's still here, Bea, though I suppose she can leave now since she cannot serve his purposes any longer."

"She is still here? Then . . ." Understanding dawned swiftly. Her shoulders fell. "Tom, how *could* you?"

He shrugged and had the decency to redden up.

"Did you at least engage her hand before the deed was done?"

Shame crossed his face, then acute discomfort. His lip was bleeding.

"What happened to you? Have you been injured?"

"Bea." He came toward her. "Here you are, thinking first

about Lady Bronwyn's honor and my injuries, before you ever think of yourself. You are a jewel of a girl. I'm proud to call you my sister." He clasped her hands warmly.

"How touching. Brotherly love at its finest," the ghost murmured, his voice echoing through the chamber in eerie accents. Thomas's hands tightened.

"I am so sorry, Bea. I didn't even think of what it would mean to you. You must be horrified."

She pulled away.

"I don't see the purpose in being horrified, not when there is work to be done. We will best this curse, I tell you. I will not be forced to marry this heathenish brute."

"The heathens were before my time, my lady," the apparition said.

"I am not your lady."

"You will be."

She struggled to ignore him, but fear scampered through her.

"Thomas, long before midnight tonight we will have worked this out and tomorrow we will all be far from this wretched castle, no doubt laughing about the whole episode. What did Miss Minturn have to say, or haven't they gone yet? They really must, right away."

"Cheriot and Aunt Grace went, but she wouldn't speak to them. I'm going now to escort Lady Bronwyn to the village. Cheriot thinks the woman might speak more freely with her."

"He knows Bronwyn can leave the castle?" Her heart sped up. She didn't know why it should race, except perhaps that her mind ran to precisely the same conclusion that Thomas and Bronwyn's had the previous night.

Thomas frowned, looking uncomfortable again.

"I told him. Of course."

"Of course." Bea's stomach clenched.

"I should go," he said hesitantly. "We haven't much time."

"Yes. Return quickly and let me know what Miss Minturn says."

"Will you be all right with him?" He gestured in the

direction of the window.

"I will. He cannot force me to wed him until midnight. If it reaches that point, then I will be happy for all the company I can get." She pasted an untroubled smile on her lips.

Thomas squeezed her hands then hurried from the chamber.

Bea turned to Iversly.

"I do not wish to die tonight."

"And I do not wish to spend eternity haunting this castle. It seems we are at an impasse. Unfortunately for you, the curse has already decided."

"I don't believe it. This is a ridiculous curse. No one in his right mind would have contrived it. It penalizes the innocent along with the guilty."

"I believe that was the intent." Iversly's voice was hollower than usual.

"Really?" Bea stepped toward him. Chill swirled around her, cooling her face. She tucked her hands into her skirt. "Why would the warlock have done that?"

"He did not deign to share his rationale with me. But if you should like, when we are able to leave the castle, we can search for his shade and ask him."

"You will be able to leave it, even as a ghost?"

"If my bride comes willingly." Despair rippled upon Lord Iversly's words. "I regret you must take part in this, my dear. But I am glad it is you rather than that empty-headed child."

She pursed her lips.

"I suppose I should consider that a compliment."

"I admire your poetic passion."

"My what?"

"Your heart seeks with such abandoned hope. Hidden from the world, yet still it seeks. We will make a fine pair, forsooth."

Bea took a sharp breath.

"I am not anything like you, my lord. And I will not marry you."

"You are more like me than you imagine, my lady. And

you will become my bride tonight."

She broke his gaze and, grabbing up a shawl, ran from the chamber.

Halfway down the winding stairwell she met Tip. Light filtered through a slit aperture, casting his features in stark angles.

He halted several steps below her.

"Are you all right?"

Of course she wasn't.

"Yes."

"Your brother told you?"

She nodded, certain he could hear her heart's pounding in the confined space.

"What did you learn in the village?" she said. "Aunt Grace came to me earlier, to tell me news in private I think, but Lord Iversly interrupted us."

"Iversly spoke to you today?" Tip's jaw hardened. Bea's stomach did an uncomfortable tumble.

"Just now. What did Miss Minturn say?"

He stared at her steadily, the silence stretching between them.

"Peter, tell me." Her voice whispered across damp stone. She gripped the rotting rope that snaked up the center of the spiral stairwell.

"Lady Marstowe and I received the impression that Miss Minturn at one time suffered an encounter with Iversly."

"What sort of encounter?"

"She said little."

"What little, exactly?"

"She repeated several times that she could not see him."

So, the spinster governess was not a virgin.

"Then she cannot help us," Bea concluded.

"For a woman who will not step foot on the castle grounds, she is peculiarly nervous of him."

"Who wouldn't be?"

He moved up a step toward her, his brilliant eyes thrown into shadow.

"You aren't," he said.

Bea's throat tightened.

"Do you intend that as another criticism?"

"A statement of fact. Deny it, otherwise."

"I do not wish to argue semantics with you." She wished to be in his arms, surrounded by him, his warm skin beneath her hands and his hands on her, everywhere, as they had been the night before. "Have Thomas and Lady Bronwyn left to interview her?"

"A few minutes ago, duly chastened."

"You *reprimanded* Lady Bronwyn? You cannot be such a hypocrite."

Anger crossed his face. Bea instinctively backed up a step.

"Yes, you had better retreat, Beatrice Sinclaire," he said, with nearly as much menace as Lord Iversly, "or I may teach you to give as good as you got. Then who would the hypocrite be?"

Heat flooded Bea. She must redirect the conversation. Or escape. But he stood below her so broad-shouldered, his stance rigid, entirely blocking the narrow staircase.

"Bronwyn was frightened," she said hastily. "And she likes my brother very much. Yesterday she asked me about his marital prospects."

"She saw opportunity. So did he, although not in the same vein as she, I'll merit."

"Oh, no." Bea lifted a hand to her mouth. "Do you think he won't marry her?"

"He will, or he will have another lesson from my fist."

The vision of Thomas's swelling cheek and bloody lip came back to Bea.

"You *struck* him?"

"He deserved it."

"For trying to save Lady Bronwyn's life?"

"For putting you in danger," he snapped.

Bea's lips shut tight. "He could not have been expected to consider that," she finally said.

"He should have. He should have thought of you before

Lady Bronwyn. You are his sister, for God's sake."

She swallowed over the thickness in her throat.

"He wasn't thinking," she said. "He is enamored of her. I am sure he cannot spare a thought for anything more."

"You know, Bea, if you are so intent on proving that you're not the retiring, obedient girl everyone thinks you are, you might consider no longer putting yourself on the line for your jackanapes twin who hasn't given a thought to your needs or wishes since I can recall."

Prickly indignation spiked in her, and hurt so deep it whisked her breath away. He spoke the truth. Thomas never thought of her except when he needed her.

"You are a wretch for throwing that in my face," she said. "I did not think you could be so cruel."

"Not cruel, merely honest." But his eyes suggested something entirely different. He scanned her face, lingering on her mouth as he had the night before. But this time struggle shone in his eyes, and the spark of anger had not receded.

She gripped the rope harder.

"I don't need you telling me what to do," she said.

"Yes, you have made that perfectly clear. But someone needs to straighten out the tangle of half-truths you're feeding yourself."

"That is rich, coming from you."

"More insults. We haven't quarreled in our entire acquaintance, yet now constantly these past few days." He looked so stiff and unyielding, so different from the man she thought she knew.

"Forced proximity," she uttered from a place of hopelessness.

His eyes narrowed.

"You have never been obliged to spend so much time with me," she explained, "nor I with you."

"We have returned to that accusation now, have we?" His voice sounded rough, at odds with the inflexible set of his shoulders.

"I was merely pointing out—"

"That you grow increasingly impatient with me the more hours you must endure of my company. I don't think I need to ask why you will not marry me, Bea. I am compiling a perfectly good list on my own."

"I didn't say that I don't like your company." *What was she doing?* "I like it very much. After last night that ought to be obvious to you." *Her double-crossing tongue.*

His gaze sharpened.

"It seems to me that very little of what I once considered obvious, in fact, is," he said in a low voice. "Now come here."

"What? Where?" Bea quivered.

"Three steps down. Come here."

"No." *Yes.* "What for?"

"I do not intend to beg you to marry me, if that is your concern. I told you I would not." His words suited his appearance. He looked entirely un-lover-like. Rather, about ready to do murder.

She bit the inside of her lip.

"Then what do you want?"

"For you to stop talking." His arm cinched her waist and he pulled her off the step, trapping her to his chest. "Like so," he growled over her mouth, and covered it.

Chapter Thirteen

Bea sank into him and Tip's hands swept down her back and over her behind, dragging her body against his muscular length.

Sweet, powerful aching invaded her. She gripped his coat and opened her mouth to allow his tongue entrance. She could not help herself. She belonged in his arms—nature and feeling and need all bound into one. He cupped her in his hands and wild, wet heat surged through her where his hard need pressed, igniting a craving so intense she trembled. She yearned for him in a secret place deep inside her that was primal and shockingly physical. It could be so easy: succumb, and save herself from danger.

His hand scooped the base of her skull, his lips traveling a hot path down her throat. Then his fingers slid through her hair and along her neck and down to cover her bodice and Bea's breath caught upon a moan. His touch was perfect pleasure, rousing all the need inside her. He caressed her through gown and nightgown, and without the stays now she felt him completely, as she had when he had stroked her naked breasts. She wanted him to kiss her breasts again, to use his lips and tongue on her and make her weak with need. She moved into his touch, wanting more, needing him.

Her heart screamed at her to stop.

"Please," she whispered, caught within the delectable torture. *Please, no.* No more teasing. No more attentions. No more bringing her so close to what she wanted without giving it to her. "No," she whispered.

He broke away, his eyes a flood of desire.

Swiftly, alarm stole into the emerald depths.

Then panic.

"No?" His voice was rough.

She wrenched out of his hold, tripping back up a step.

"No," she panted, dashing a hand across her mouth. "*No*. I don't—" Her voice broke. "I don't want this."

"Then what do you want?" he said, breathing hard. "Iversly? Because he is what you are going to get."

"I don't want *this*. What is wrong with you? You kiss me and then look as though you hate it."

His hands fisted.

"A man is not always able to choose as he likes."

Bea's heart stopped, her lungs abruptly empty. He was doing this only to save her? It couldn't be.

"There must be another way," she uttered. "The village. Miss Minturn." Her gaze darted over his shoulder down the stairs. "Let me past."

He shifted aside.

"Your escape, my dear."

"My dear? You sound like him now."

"Perhaps I am beginning to understand him." His voice sounded as cold as the stone.

She pushed past him. He gripped her arm and spoke low by her cheek.

"Do not mistake it, Bea. There is no other way."

She pulled free and stumbled down the steps. Smudging tears away, she emerged beneath the gate and hurried toward the bridge. The day hung gray with pending rain, a heavy cover of clouds above, and unusually warm for the season. A woman wrapped in a cloak stood at the opposite end of the drawbridge.

"Aunt Julia?"

"Dear Beatrice. You may not go any farther. The castle grounds end here. I can feel it in my bones. A bit shaky, you know." Her eyes danced.

A shock of understanding went through Bea.

"Aunt Julia, you are a maiden."

The elderly lady twinkled.

"Pure as new-fallen snow."

"Then you are trapped here too."

"Oh yes, until the curse lifts." she smiled, crinkles deepening at the corners of her eyes. "How is your young man today?"

"My young man?"

"Darling Peter."

"He is not my young man, Aunt Julia." Bea's gaze shifted over the misty slope descending to the village. "I came to wait for Thomas and Lady Bronwyn's return. What are you doing out here? Where is Aunt Grace?"

"Resting. The trip to the village this morning wearied her."

"Of course, you did not go."

"Oh, no. But it was terribly exciting awaiting their return."

"Exciting? Aunt Julia, are you enjoying this?"

"I enjoy everything, I daresay." She smiled, adjusted her cloak so that it fell halfway over her shoulder and the remainder upon the damp ground. She tilted her head aside. "Save yourself, my dear. I won't mind it."

Bea gaped.

"Aunt Julia?"

Her great-aunt's skewed gaze fixed as stably as Bea had ever seen.

"Choose a warm, breathing man who cares for you, over a specter."

"I—" She didn't know quite what to say. "You would be trapped here. Wouldn't you?"

"I daresay, yes."

Or Iversly would . . .

Bea could not bear to think of it.

But could he? She did not believe he would. Unless he truly was that desperate. In desperation, a man might do anything.

She gripped her frigid hands together.

"When will they return?"

"I rather think a great while from now. You would be more comfortable inside."

But Bea doubted that she would ever be comfortable

again.

~o0o~

They hadn't long to wait before the carriage returned with Thomas and Lady Bronwyn. He handed her out, then offered his arm for another lady descending the steps. Tall, slender and pale-haired, she had the appearance of someone who had been ill for some time, grayer and older than her years.

"Oh, Beatrice, this is my governess," Lady Bronwyn drew the woman forward and placed her hand in Bea's. Miss Minturn's fingers were icy.

"How do you do, Miss Minturn?"

"I understand that Iversly wants you."

Bronwyn's hand fluttered over her throat.

"Our Beatrice is very clever," Aunt Julia chimed in. "He will have to think quickly to win her."

"He will not win me, Aunt Julia. Miss Minturn, please come inside and have some tea. It is starting to rain."

As they entered the parlor, Miss Minturn's eyes searched the corners.

"Is he here?" the governess whispered.

"He is not," Bea replied, tugging her shawl more firmly about her ill-fitting bodice that Tip's hands had been all over in the stairwell. "Miss Minturn, please have a seat. Will you tell us what you know of the curse and Lord Iversly? Perhaps it could help us." She skipped a glance at Julia, but her great-aunt seemed content rummaging around the tea tray.

"The curse," Miss Minturn said in throaty accents, "is a maiden's damnation. And he is the most glorious lover a woman could ever have."

Bronwyn released a little squeak. Thomas blanched. Bea's gaze went to the door. Tip stood there, wearing riding clothes and studying their visitor.

She dragged her attention back to the governess.

"Miss Minturn, could you tell us precisely what you mean

by those comments?"

The woman's pale gaze slewed about the chamber and her chest heaved with emotion. She closed her eyes.

"I loved him, and he betrayed me," she said.

Lady Bronwyn gasped.

"You *loved* him?"

"How did he betray you?" Bea asked.

"He absconded with my heart." Miss Minturn's brow folded. "Then he crushed it like an insect beneath his boot."

"Good heavens, woman," Lady Marstowe snapped. "He is a specter. He has no real boots to speak of. Now tell us something of use."

"Miss Minturn, did you offer him your hand?" Tip asked, moving to her side.

She opened eyes full of anguish.

"I did," she whispered.

"Did he accept it?"

"He led me to believe he would. He made love to me with his words, then—"

"Then I put another man in her bed."

Miss Minturn sprang up, casting her gaze wildly about the chamber.

"Iversly?" she exclaimed. "Oh, Iversly, have you come to torment me anew? Oh, sweet sorrow! Oh, honeyed grief!"

"Woman, take hold of yourself," the dowager ordered.

"Did you do as she said, Iversly?" Thomas demanded.

"I gave her what she deserved."

"You said you loved me and would keep me, then you gave me to *him*."

"Who is him?" Lady Bronwyn's crystal eyes were round as saucers.

"A convenient, lustful knave," the ghost said, "who knew not the boundaries between master and servant."

Tears seeped from Miss Minturn's eyes.

"It was dark!" she cried. "I thought he was you. I did not love him."

"Rather to the point, you did not marry him, did you?"

Lady Marstowe commented.

"Obviously she didn't, Aunt Grace," Thomas said.

Bea caught Iversly's black gaze. "Why did you do it?"

The Welshman tilted his head. Then, slowly, he shifted his gaze to Tip.

Bea held her breath.

Iversly returned his regard to her.

"It is a game I sometimes play." His voice was a lion's forbidding purr.

"A *game*." Miss Minturn wept. "I gave him my heart."

"But Minnie," Bronwyn said, "you did not wish to become a ghost, did you?"

"To be with him, I would have," she declared upon a weak wail.

"Miss Minturn, cease this drama," Lady Marstowe insisted. "Lady Bronwyn, take her away and calm her. We cannot converse rationally with all that noise."

Tip escorted them to the door, then closed it when they had gone.

"Now, Lord Iversly," the dowager said, "tell us why you used that woman so dreadfully."

"She imagined herself in love with me."

The parlor fell silent. Bea's gaze slipped to Tip. He seemed to be studying the ground at his feet.

"Seems rather churlish of you, Iversly," he commented, his gaze rising to her. He frowned.

Bea forced her attention to the ghost.

"She loved you," she said, "so you hurt her."

"Love was invented by fools," the ghost said.

"But you allowed her to believe you returned her feelings."

"She believed what she wished to believe. Women often do."

Bea swallowed around the ache in her throat.

"Not all women."

"Aye? For four hundred years, foolish maids have come here imagining they could comfort me. They seek adventure."

He laughed derisively. Then his tone dipped. "And I provide them with it."

Seeking adventure. *Just as she.*

"You have done this before," she said. "That is, before Miss Minturn?"

"She was not the first. So many come, with no notion of what they promise. No notion of the horror of this existence. They disgust me beyond endurance."

"But they offer love." Bea's voice was not steady. The others stood transfixed, staring into nothingness where they could not see the ghost. Only Tip's pensive gaze rested upon her. She felt it like a caress. "You could have that affection," she said to Iversly. "You would not be alone any longer."

"I do not wish to spend eternity with a woman who loves me. I would rather rot in the bowels of hell."

Tip turned and looked at precisely the spot where Iversly stood by the window.

"You may rot yet," he growled. "How do you know Miss Sinclaire will not also succumb to your charms?"

"Because, my fine noble friend," Iversly spoke slowly, "her heart lies firmly with another."

Bea's nails dug into the seat of her chair.

"What does that mean?" Thomas demanded. "Bea?"

"Foolish boy." The ghost turned his perceptive gaze upon her. "Your sister is already in love."

~oOo~

May 1, 1817

Mama and I encountered Mr. Cheriot today while shopping. Mama instantly launched into recounting Lady Ashford's ball, which he listened to with all appearance of sincere interest. He responded with polite sounds when she told him how four eligible gentlemen had already paid calls that morning, naming them particularly. He smiled at me as though pleased for me, which made my stomach queasy.

When Mama stopped to converse with an acquaintance, Mr. Cheriot took my hand and placed it upon his arm, and we strolled a bit further to look in the window at Lumley's. We spoke of various matters, then he said, 'You know, Bea, I am very glad for all the attention you are receiving, but don't lead on those poor fellows, will you?' I was nonplused. I responded, 'Mr. Cheriot, are you flattering or quizzing me?' 'Neither,' he replied. 'It's only that you don't want to disappoint them, since you are already intended elsewhere.' I could not have been more astonished. 'To whom?' I asked. 'Why, to me, of course.' He grinned as though we shared a joke.

Diary, after months in town, I imagined I had finally got the hang of it. I said to him, 'Tease all you will, sir, but I am wearing a new bonnet today and nothing can overset me.' He smiled and only said, 'Those poor fellows, indeed.'

He wishes to amuse me. Another woman might, I suspect, find such a flirtation diverting. I think he is odiously familiar.

His groom then appeared, bearing a message on a slip of paper. Mr. Cheriot begged my forgiveness, returned me to my mother swiftly though without any less kindness than usual, and went off after only a brief good-bye. I nearly wept, but did not. Weeping is for silly girls, not girls who know better.

Tonight at dinner Papa told me Mr. Cheriot sent a note to explain his hasty departure this morning. It seems that Lord Cheriot fell from a maddened horse and broke his back, and his son was at once required at home. How horrible! My heart aches for his family—his mother and sister. For him.

And yet, I cannot deny it, I continue to refine upon his teasing comment. When he has such significant concerns, it seems an unpardonably silly preoccupation.

But oh, Diary, the trouble is, I am very much in love with him.

~o0o~

Chapter Fourteen

Tip's universe stilled.

"Is it true, Bea?" Thomas demanded. "Or is this merely another of this blackguard's lies?"

"Temper, temper, boy," the ghost murmured.

She sat rigid, arms straight, fists clenched at her sides, her color high. As though reluctantly, her gaze met Tip's across the chamber. Guilt shone in her rich eyes.

"It is true, Tom," she uttered.

Tip swallowed hard, his chest so tight his lungs seemed not to function. She loved another man. By the pain on her face, it had to be a man she should not love.

"Who is he?" Thomas asked hurriedly. "If he's within a few hours, Cheriot or I can ride fast—"

"Be quiet, Thomas." Tip wondered that he possessed the power to speak.

"Why haven't you told me before this, Bea?" her brother pressed. "We could have sent for him right away."

"It was not possible." Her voice sounded strangled.

"Well, why not?" Thomas demanded. "Who is he? Has he—"

"He is . . . ineligible," she whispered, her eyes bright with unshed tears.

Silence descended on the chamber once more.

Iversly chuckled mirthlessly.

"See what you have done, young fool?" He laughed outright. "You have brought your sister extraordinary distress. Perfect for me, of course. The more pain she brings to our marriage bed, the greater my pleasure will be."

"Leave, Iversly," Tip said. "Or I vow I will find a way to

make you pay for this, beyond the grave, if I must."

"Ah, chivalrous to the very core," the ghost murmured.

"He has gone," Miss Dews chirped, but her gaze rested on Bea with quiet compassion.

Tip stared at the woman he had loved for years, who had loved another man possibly all that time. A man, no doubt, whose passions did not goad him into kissing her to within an inch of her innocence in a stairwell against her will.

Perhaps the man lived close to Hart House. Then she might endure her mother's demands in order to remain near him. Perhaps he was a member of the local gentry, a married man with a family. Did the cad know he had won her affections? Did he tease her with what she could not have? Or was he beneath her station, a servant?

Filled with shame, her face now admitted everything.

Tip's heart burned.

"Well, that is that." Lady Marstowe's voice was less than steady. "Beatrice, that ghost will not relent." She stood. "You are in grave danger."

"I believe he is bluffing." She sounded calm, and very certain.

"Nonsense. His threats are perfectly sincere," the dowager stated. "What will you do?"

"I cannot leave Aunt Julia to her fate."

"Aunt Julia?" Thomas exclaimed, gaping at Miss Dews. "Oh, good Lord, I hadn't even thought!"

"Of course you did not, Thomas dear," Miss Dews tittered. "But Iversly will not harm me, and perhaps Beatrice is correct." A dollop of cream attached to her lower lip wiggled as she shrugged.

"He is playing a game," Bea stated. "He wishes to harm the living, and so we must not play to his wishes. We must simply ignore him."

"Ignore him?" Thomas exploded. "That is preposter—"

"Sinclaire, that is enough," Tip said. "Go find Lady Bronwyn and escort her and Miss Minturn back to the village."

Thomas set his jaw like a mule.

"I will stay and help my sister."

"Tom," Bea said. "Your responsibility now is to your betrothed. And I will be fine, truly."

"But Iversly will——"

"I am persuaded he means me no harm. Now, go. They are both overset and need you."

He approached, crouched before her, and grasped her hands with a nervous shake.

"You are an excellent sister, Bea, and I am a dashed poor excuse for a brother."

She touched her fingers to his cheek.

"I love you, Tom."

He blinked rapidly, pulled away, and hurried from the chamber. She gazed after him, eyes troubled.

Tip moved toward her. "What do you intend?"

"I will wait out the night," she said to her palms upturned on her lap. "And tomorrow we will determine how Aunt Julia and I might leave the castle grounds without mishap." She stood. "I will look again in the library and see if I can find something there that we missed."

"You will voluntarily put yourself in the way of danger?"

Her gaze fixed on his neckcloth.

"If he is telling the truth, I am already in the way of danger. If he is not, which I believe, I have nothing to fear."

"It is not that simple."

"It seems so to me."

He moved closer, her beguiling scent and the determined tilt of her chin tangling his thoughts.

"Bea, don't do this."

"Do what?" she said in barely a whisper. "Save my aunt?"

"Sacrifice yourself."

Finally, her gaze rose to his.

"Perhaps it is the lesser of two evils."

Tip stepped back, his heart thudding.

"Then you have made your decision and I cannot alter it."

She shook her head.

Panic washed through him. The woman of his dreams was

slipping away, and he had never truly had her.

"Do you expect me to remain here and watch you damn yourself?" His voice was unsteady.

"No. I expect you to depart before it becomes too difficult, as usual. You have heard something you do not like." Her gaze was firm, her voice resolute. "I give you leave to go now."

Tip fought for composure.

"Bea—"

"Go to the village. Ask if anyone knows a thing to help us escape this place." Her eyes challenged him to refuse. "We will see you tomorrow."

He could not draw breath and he feared that every one of his emotions showed clear on his face.

"Tomorrow, then," he said, but his feet would not move.

He grasped her hand and drew it to his lips. Her lashes fluttered and she looked away. He released her, bowed to the dowager and her sister, and left.

~oOo~

Tip spent the next four hours scouring the village and surrounding farms for information that could thwart Iversly's plan. He found nothing except, finally, a pint of ale between his palms and the cold, hard realization that Bea was justified to accuse him of fleeing. Only a coward would run from life in the fear that it would be too difficult to handle.

He pushed away the glass.

This was not about his life. It was about hers. He could not allow her to remain in danger. She might not let him give her his name, but he would give her what he could. If it meant tackling his own ghosts to do it, then so be it.

~oOo~

"Well, Beatrice, you have made your bed," Lady Marstowe said apparently without irony. "But dinner must still be eaten, even at this late hour. Where is that foolish cook?" She strode from the chamber.

"You should not have sent dear Peter away, Beatrice dear. I told you, poor Rhys will not harm me."

"Rhys?" Bea started. "Do you mean Lord Iversly?"

Aunt Julia nodded, her eyes prancing in different directions.

"How do you know his name?"

"We have had a number of lovely chats."

"Lovely chats? Aunt Julia, he is evil."

Julia smiled and dug in her embroidery bag.

"Now, what did I do with that lace? I must finish this cap before you leave so that you can deliver it to Harriet. She will look fetching in it, I daresay. It is such a shame dear Alfred will never see her wearing it. Silly man."

"Aunt Julia," Bea sat forward in her chair, "I am not leaving here, except perhaps in a different form than I have now."

"That's all well and good, my dear."

"What did you and Iversly speak of?"

She waved her hand about vaguely.

"He is a regular ghost, I daresay."

"Yes, I know, Aunt Julia. But did he say anything about—about you?"

"He promised he would be very good to me. They always are, you see."

They? Aunt Julia's mind worked differently from most people's, but she was not mad. Bea almost wished she were.

"Have you known other ghosts?"

"Several, to be sure," Julia chirped, fishing around in her bag and pulling out a tangle of fabric swatches.

"Are they like Iversly?"

"Oh, no. He is much more unhappy." She plucked up a pink silk and pinned it to the edge of the cap.

Bea grasped her great-aunt's hands.

"Aunt Julia, did he say anything to you that might help us here tonight? Is he sincere in his threats?"

"Perfectly, I should say." She laid a wrinkled palm on Bea's cheek. "Dear, dear Beatrice. We will miss you when you are gone. And Harriet will be so cross. She has always considered you the best of her children, however she goes on about Sylvia's beauty. And of course your father will grieve. He admires dear Georgianna so, but he depends on you."

"They will not miss me." The words popped out. They felt good and awful at once. "I suspect they will barely know I am gone." Except, of course, that Mama would have to find someone new to order around.

But even if she somehow did return to Hart House, those days were over. At least, she wanted them to be. At present, with her dreams of Peter Cheriot finally destroyed, she didn't know if she had the strength to make any lifetime decisions.

"Of course they will know, and they will miss you," Aunt Julia patted her knee and returned to her sewing. "And poor darling Peter will be devastated."

Lady Marstowe marched into the room.

"Come, Beatrice. Dinner is served and you must maintain your strength for tonight. Perhaps Iversly will make a mistake."

Bea didn't have stomach for the meal. Aunt Julia ate heartily, and Aunt Grace commented on the village and Miss Minturn's ridiculous behavior. When they returned to the parlor, the dowager called for tea as though it were a typical night. Bea appreciated the pretense, but still she could not eat. She nursed a cup until it grew cold, then poured herself another.

She met Lady Marstowe's gaze across the table.

"You should go to bed, Aunt Grace."

"I will when I am ready."

Bea cast her gaze to Aunt Julia, who was scooping spoonful after spoonful of sugar into her cup. Clearly they intended to wait with her for midnight.

She took up a book and tried to read, but remembered

nothing at the end of each page. Tip's words from the stairwell kept returning to her, that he was not able to choose as he liked. But not only his words. His touch, his desire, his eager possession of her. Her body filled with yearnings and despair. She hardly knew how to think of his departure now.

When the great-aunts fell asleep on the couch, Bea fled the chamber, trying to escape her thoughts.

In the library she rifled through piles of scrolls and loose papers, and studied the shelves again. Halfway through a stack of books she came upon a small, leather-bound book with gilt edges. It appeared to be a diary of sorts. Heartbeats quick, she opened it. The entries dated to 1770 and recounted the daily life of an elderly widowed gentleman residing at the castle. She read through it, flipping pages swiftly. It said nothing of Iversly.

She sighed.

"You are a coward." Iversly's voice sounded distant.

"I don't care what you think of me."

"You will shortly."

A shiver slithered up her back. She shook it off.

"What time is it?"

"Nearly too late for you, my dear."

"Do you still think I will come to you willingly?"

"As the hour nears, panic will get the better of you. You will come before midnight."

"Perhaps I would prefer death."

"I know what you would prefer. But that is not to be your lot, is it?"

Bea turned. Iversly stood before the closed window shutter.

Her breaths stalled.

"You are desperate to be free of this castle, aren't you? It must be the reason you so often stand before windows. They offer you tantalizing glimpses of what you cannot have."

"Mayhap I prefer the dramatic effect." His voice sounded gravelly.

"You said earlier that you didn't care about such things

any longer."

He was silent for a moment.

"In my day, my dear, they described that as the pot calling the kettle black."

Bea shook her head.

"You think you are very clever, don't you? Earlier, you said those things to shame me. But you are not clever. You are simply cruel."

"I am desperate, as you say. You foolishly discarded the only chance I will give you. I am somewhat disappointed. But alas, it cannot be helped now." His face looked almost too impassive.

Bea's stomach churned. He could not be trusted. She could not put Aunt Julia in danger.

"Would you have hurt her?" she made herself ask.

"We will never know, will we?"

Dread trickled through her veins.

"You are disgusting. Horrid. Sufficient words do not exist for you."

"You warm my heart, dear lady."

"You have no heart."

"Better that than your pitiful condition. Forsooth, I am relieved you have failed to come to terms with your young lord. The foolish boy and silly girl proved wearying enough to observe."

"You *watched* them?"

"I had a particular interest in the matter."

Sticky loathing wrapped around her insides. A chill descended on her skin, seeping beneath the surface in icy fingers. She pulled her shawl tighter around her shoulders, but the cold seemed to come from beneath her clothing. A cool breath of air wafted through the library chamber, stirring the tiny hairs about her brow and cheeks against her skin.

She glanced at the door. It was closed.

Her gaze went to Iversly. He was no longer there.

A frigid hand spread upon the nape of her neck. Bea gasped. Another seemed to stroke her thigh, heavy and cold.

She leaped up and away, slamming her back into a bookcase.

"Is it you?" she breathed. "What are you doing?"

"Touching you."

"But you said you do not have the sense of touch."

"The hour draws near."

"How dare you?" she hurled into the lamplight.

The caress came again, icy upon her arm. She jerked aside.

"But I cannot see you!"

"Over the centuries I have learned a few useful tricks." He chuckled, a wicked snarl of pleasure.

"You cannot do it. You will not," she insisted.

"I can and I will," he countered. "Even now I feel blood in my veins. Warmth. After a century, it intoxicates."

"No. You are bluffing."

"I am not." His voice seemed very near, in a single location for the first time.

Bea pivoted. He stood a yard away. The lamp burning on the table behind him did not seep through him. Instead it cast his body in an aura of gold, silhouetting him. Pale gray, almost ephemeral, his shadow stretched on the ground.

Lord Rhys Iversly stood before her. The ghost of Gwynedd Castle was a man.

Chapter Fifteen

Tremors seized Bea.

"What is happening? You look—" She choked. "You look real."

He tilted his head, and the light flickered around him.

"I must be, briefly, to consummate our union."

"It is not yet midnight."

"It will be in minutes, my dear. Then we will both be free."

"I do not want to be free of anything."

"Are you certain of that?" he challenged.

"Yes. No!" She wrung her hands. "If you know so much, than you must know I no longer wish to be servant to my mother. But I will not trade that for servitude to you."

"Not servitude. Partnership."

"Why are you so eager to continue as a ghost?" she demanded. "Do you wish to be freed of that existence or not?"

"A man becomes accustomed to life in whatever form he is allowed it. I suspect your young lord would have something to say to that, were he here." His black gaze bored into hers.

Bea shook her head, backing to the door.

"Are you speaking in riddles to confuse me? To make me agree to go with you or refuse you?"

"I do not offer riddles, only truth. You are, however, too late to grasp its bounty."

"I don't understand."

"It matters not. You have but moments now."

"No!" Bea grabbed the lamp, yanked the door open, and ran down the corridor. She found the door to the courtyard and bolted through it, her feet slipping on the grass in the courtyard, rain blinding her as she threw herself through the darkness. The eastern tower rose up before her, black, solid, enormous in the downpour. She wrenched up the door handle and stumbled in.

The space was empty, a long cylinder of thick stone stretching up three stories into complete darkness. In the center of the round chamber, a rope hung lifeless from the void above.

A bell tower? Dear Lord, it was like a mockery.

But it could not be real. It simply could not.

"Did you think to escape me?"

This time his voice came from above, echoing from the belfry. No interior staircase circled the walls. Access to the bell had to be from the parapets. But he could not possibly have climbed that distance in such a short time.

"Are you corporeal yet?"

"Nearly," came the ominous reply.

"Then why aren't you down here? How can you still move from place to place like a spirit?" Bea spoke to prevent herself from screaming. Her lips and fingers were numb. Straw littered the floor, dry and crackling beneath her feet. She set down the lamp, her hands shaking so hard she feared to drop it and set the whole aflame.

He did not reply. Wind moaned through the belfry, drowning the sound of the spattering rain. In its cage, the bell wheel creaked into motion. The rope began to swish across the dirt floor.

"But no one is ringing it!"

"Do you think such a curse requires a human hand to put it into motion?" Iversly's voice was horrible. "You cannot trick destiny, my dear."

"This is not *my* destiny!"

"But it is the one you have chosen."

The sound of the bell heaving into position drove dread down her back.

"So it begins," Iversly's voice cascaded through the tower, reverberations of hope in it that she did not want to hear.

A cold wind wrapped around Bea, her arms prickling.

"What will happen?"

"Choose now, and discover that for yourself."

"That is not what I mean."

"Then what, my dear?" he echoed.

Bea's insides twisted.

"What will you do?"

"After the final stroke of midnight, I will take full corporeal form long enough to take your body." He paused. "Then I will take your soul."

"Not if I can prevent it." Tip's voice cut across the tower like a summer wind, strong and warm. Bea whirled around, a sob clogging her throat.

"Ah, the champion arrives," Iversly uttered. "Barely in time, it seems."

"Peter," Bea breathed. "But Aunt Julia—"

"I have just spoken with her. She is in no danger from Iversly. He told her so. He wants you."

The giant clapper tapped against the iron mass, the rope hanging from the darkness above beginning to dance.

Iversly laughed from high up in the belfry, the sound rolling along the stone walls like icy water.

"Twelve chimes, my dear, then your fate will be sealed and freedom mine," he called out.

"But—"

"Bea," Tip moved toward her, the lamplight casting him in shadows. "You have no choice now." He halted within reach. "I am sorry I cannot be the man you want, but I am here."

The bell's clang split the torch-lit dark, pounding into her blood and bones. His beautiful eyes were filled with compassion. He looked again like the man she had always loved.

"No," her voice broke. "It is my fault. I am sorry."

"It will be all right." He stepped forward, his body brushing hers, and his hands slid into her hair. The pad of his thumb stroked her trembling lower lip. "Trust me."

Wide-eyed, she nodded. The huge bell chimed mercilessly

again and a laugh as deep and horrible as the pit of hell sounded from above. *Two.*

Tip's gaze moved swiftly across her features, then locked with hers.

"Do you know what happens when a man and woman make love, Bea?"

"What do you mean, what happens?" she croaked.

"How it is done."

She nodded. Sylvia had told her, and teased her that she would be lucky if she ever experienced it. The awful iron clang came again, its echo spreading through the tower like evil. *Three.*

Tip took a fast, deep breath.

"There isn't time—" He ran his hand through his hair. "There isn't time for anything."

"For what?" Her words trembled.

"To prepare you."

"Prepare me?"

"There will be pain. Possibly a lot." The bell tolled, as though to emphasize his hurried words, a fourth hated chime.

"All right." She bit her lip, her heart leaping unsteadily, breaths coming short. "Peter," she whispered, "time is running out."

He swallowed hard, the movement clearly visible above his cravat.

"Bea," he spoke quickly, "when I kissed you, did you feel anything? In your body, any stirrings of heat or dampness?"

How could this get worse? She had felt *everything*. But how on earth could she say it aloud, to him, now, here? Why did he need to know?

"This cannot be real," she whispered, her voice a mere rasp.

The ghost's hard laughter careened through the blackness above, the bell's thunder following. *Five.*

Tip's hands tightened.

"Did you?"

She nodded.

"Yes, a lot of stirring."

His eyes seemed to darken. He bent his head and captured her mouth with his. Without delay his tongue swept across the seam of her lips, urging hers open and filling her with a delectable ache. Her hands found his arms, grasping at hard muscles. Her lips parted and heat flared below her belly. His tongue caressed her mouth, urging her to obey, to return his kiss and she did, desperately, her body growing hotter with each throb of her needy heart. She sank into his kiss with a sigh.

The bell clanged and Bea's sigh became a gasp. *Six.*

"Don't listen to it," Tip ordered against her mouth, his voice low. "Put your arms around my neck, and hold on tight."

Hold on tight? *Hold on?* The man she had loved without ceasing for years was commanding her to hold on to him tightly?

She slipped her hands around his shoulders and clasped them behind his neck. He was wonderfully tall, and her breasts pressed against his firm chest, her nipples taut, sending delectable sensations downward through her body. Tip's hand left her face, moving between them, against her abdomen, but he kept kissing her, his mouth more urgent now. She gave back eagerly, wanting more and needing to *not* think about how he must be unfastening his breeches. It was too alarming. Too real. She wanted him. She had wanted him for years. But her nerves battled between desperate need and thorough fear.

His palm slid over her breast.

Yes. This was what she wanted. Peter Cheriot touching her, intimately caressing her.

Thunder boomed through the tower, or was that the bell? Tip pushed her gently to the wall, and chill air swished around her stockinged calves, then up, slipping across her bare thighs. She pressed her mouth against his as his hands gripped her hips, lifting her onto her tiptoes effortlessly it seemed. His thigh shifted between hers. She knew what came next, but her knees locked together and her hands shook clasping his neck.

"Now, my girl. Don't be afraid." His voice came deep

against her cheek beneath the toll of the bell, his breaths moving his chest hard against hers.

"I am not afraid," she uttered. "It's only—"

He covered her mouth again, hungrily, needy too it seemed, urging away all hesitation, all doubt. She had wanted him since before she was even a woman, and she would have him now, as she had dreamed. Not in a dungeon tower, flickering lamplight casting his handsome features into sharp relief. But in her body where she yearned for him.

She unlocked her knees, and his hands swept beneath her thighs, parting her so he could move close. Fingers twining through his hair, she held his mouth to hers, never so certain of anything in her life.

The tower erupted in sound. *Nine.*

"I'm ready now," she whispered against his mouth, and he pressed intimately to her, hard and hot against her flesh. She ached, wildly, deeply. But he didn't move, only kissed her again and again.

Ten.

He stretched her open and pushed inside. She gasped, then she only felt, his unyielding hardness, her body's resistance. He was so big, much bigger than she would have imagined. And thick. Too thick? He pressed forward and she gulped in breath, gripping his shoulders. She tried to focus on his mouth, the thrilling friction of his chest against her breasts, and ignore the odd, *not* comfortable stretching of her body.

The bell exploded above and all around them. *Eleven.*

"Bea," Tip moaned, and thrust deep into her.

"Ow!" The cry erupted from the very bottom of her lungs. "Ouch! Oh—" she gasped. "I—ouch!"

He held her tight, his brow pressed to hers, his warm body surrounding her, perfectly still now. The tower shook with the bell's final ring, the ghost's cry of anger and misery careening through the rafters, ululating with abandoned hope. A shout of eternal despair.

Abruptly, the tower fell silent except for the lash of rain against the walls without and Bea's own labored breathing.

"Are you all right?" Tip's voice was low and strangely taut.

Bea could not speak. She could hardly breathe. Her body had closed around his somehow, and it throbbed, seeming to want more. But the act was complete, successful. She was no longer a virgin. It would end now.

It was too soon.

She tilted her head and pressed her lips to his. They were so delicious, soft and firm at once, tasting of ale and heat and something ineffably male and entirely him. He opened them over hers, then took her lower lip between his and traced it, lingering, then nipped lightly. It felt good. *So* good. She never would have thought having her lip bitten by a man could feel good. But this was Peter Cheriot, her love. Now, her lover.

She curved her arms more fully around his shoulders, breathing in his scent. As an experiment, she shifted her hips.

A low rumble sounded in his chest. He pressed her more securely against the wall and his hand slipped between them, beneath the bunched up fabric of her skirt. Before she understood what he meant to do, he touched her there.

"Oh!" she gasped. "What are you—?"

"It's all right," he murmured against her cheek as his fingertips began a thoroughly improper exploration of her most sensitive parts. "Let yourself feel me touching you."

She could do nothing *but* feel. She was drunk with it. In an instant the pulsing inside her turned to need. Then *desperation.* His caress centered, gentle yet with such perfect rhythm Bea could not remain still. She pressed her hips forward, gasping as sweet, hot sensation scurried through her. Gripping his shoulders, she opened her mouth to his kiss and pushed tighter to him.

A sound of pleasure rose from Tip's chest, and she moved on him again, his fingers and his rigidness inside her driving the tight pleasure higher, harder. Soft cries she could not prevent rent the silence of the tower. The pleasure was so intense, so pure. It felt so right. But she needed more.

Tip gripped her hips and pulled her to him hard, driving up into her. She cried aloud, gasping as he thrust into her again, then again, dragging her closer each time, and she struggled against him, *to* him, needing something—anything—*more*.

More came, hard and shocking, sweet, scandalous and *everywhere*, pleasure from him and pleasure within. She couldn't breathe. She was weak in a fabulous ecstasy that shimmered through her and entirely alive at once.

"Peter," she whispered.

Beneath her hands his neck grew taut, then inside her, mingled with her, he seemed to change. He pressed into her, hard, and groaned.

He went still.

In the silence of the cold tower, their fast, rough breaths were louder now than the diminished storm on the other side of the massive walls. Beneath her hands his shoulders rose and fell heavily.

Bea trembled, her limbs and insides like jelly. She slid her cheek against Tip's, adoring the touch of his skin, holding on to him for a few precious seconds more. A mischievous sprite inside her insisted that if she did not let go of this fantasy moment, perhaps it would never end.

"Bea." His breath stirred the tendrils of hair at her ear. "I am going to release you now."

The words came like a dash of icy water. She didn't know what she had hoped he would say. Certainly not immediate dismissal. Somehow her no-longer-maidenly imagination had conjured the possibility that he might kiss her again. It was ridiculous, of course.

She nodded and he drew out of her. Bea's heels met the stone floor, an empty sensation of loss shivering through her, and her trembling increased. She had dropped her slippers at some point, but she tried not to feel foolish about that and hastily rearranged her skirts. The gown and her sheer nightgown beneath were barely thick enough to merit smoothing. She stared at the damp, hopelessly wrinkled fabric.

Tip bent and retrieved her slippers, then her shawl. She flinched when his hand slid around hers, warm and large. He went still, then dropped to one knee. Her heart leaped into her throat.

"Come. Sit and put these on," he said, pulling her to his knee.

Hot prickles jumped behind her eyes. He was not going to propose to her again. How silly of her. Nothing had changed.

Except now she knew how it felt to love him with her body as well as her heart. Her entire world had changed.

She balanced on his makeshift seat and tugged on her slippers, then stood. He followed, drawing her shawl around her shoulders. She remained perfectly immobile, trying to rein in her raucously beating heart. Tip stepped back, away from her, and the air seemed colder yet.

"You will marry me now, Beatrice Sinclaire." He looked rigid, like earlier in the stairwell, severe and grim.

"What?" she uttered, all pleasure dashed to pieces despite the hot aftermath still simmering in her body.

"Which word didn't you understand? They ought to be familiar enough to you; I've said the same so many times, albeit not in the imperative until yesterday. But this time you will agree to it."

Bea's entire body shook; he must see it. But his hard gaze was locked in hers. He could not possibly appear less like a man pleased with his prospects.

"You cannot mean to marry me simply because of this." She could barely push the words past her throat.

"There is no *simply* about it. And yes, of course I can and I mean to. What sort of cad do you think I am?"

"But you were forced into it. You did not have any choice."

"You are perfectly correct. Making love to a beautiful woman rather than allowing her to die does not constitute a choice."

She drew in a deep breath.

"And now I am the one without the choice in the matter."

Tip's eyes shone flinty in the flickering gold light.

"That is not precisely what a man wishes to hear at a

moment like this."

"There are no moments like this!" Tears thickened her
voice. "At least there should not be."

"What is done is done."

An invisible fist tightened around Bea's heart. How could
the warm, laughing man she had known be looking at her this
way now, sounding like this?

She had done it to him. She had brought him here and got
him into this mess. She should have insisted more forcefully
that he not come. She should have left Thomas to fend for
himself. Now Tip would suffer for a lifetime, unable to find
another woman he could love as much as he had loved Georgie
because he would be trapped with her.

"Very well," she said. "I will go tell Aunt Grace and Aunt
Julia."

"As you wish."

Bea longed to reach up and smooth out the lines in his
brow. Perhaps someday she could. Wives did that sort of thing
if their husbands allowed it, she thought.

Would he ever welcome such a touch from her? Would it
always be with benign tolerance, or at best easy natured grace?
Or would she sometimes spy that glimmer in his eyes she had
seen yesterday before he kissed her? Would he at least want her
in his bed as he had said?

"Thank you for saving my life, Peter. I am sorry it had to
be like this."

"You are sorry," he repeated without inflection. "Good
night, Bea."

He left without another word.

~o0o~

December 21, 1816

    Despite the chilly weather, Mr. Cheriot invited me to ride in the Park this morning. It is the first invitation he has formally offered. We went out at an unfashionably early hour with my maid. He arrived at the house at quarter past ten, helped me to mount, and gave me a pat on the back of my glove once I was in the saddle.

    His mount is magnificent. Everyone says he is a noted horseman. He told me he will complete his final term at university next spring. I replied that by then I will have had my second season and be thoroughly replete with Town Bronze. He smiled and said that when he is finished he will have a great deal more time to court me properly.

    Naturally, I had no rational response to that. Sylvia would have batted her lashes and encouraged him to pursue the matter. Georgie would have said something clever, which no doubt he expected of me too. But my mind became a whitewashed wall.

    Fortunately, he soon began to speak of other things, the theater, I think. I barely attended. It was all very disconcerting. And thrilling. And confusing.

    If this is how gentlemen in town flirt, I will be obliged to develop a thicker skin. At least if this particular gentleman continues in this vein.

~o0o~

Chapter Sixteen

Bea lay atop her mattress, eyes wide open, staring into blackness. The rain continued to fall, but gentler now, pattering on her window, its quick rhythm matching the rush of blood through her veins.

Three doors down the corridor, Tip slept. At least she supposed he slept. She must be the only one foolish enough to still be awake.

Alone, wet and bedraggled, she had gone from the tower to the parlor to show her great-aunts that she was safe. She had not explained exactly how that came about, although certainly her ramshackle appearance told its own story. Aunt Grace pursed her lips and remained silent. Aunt Julia wished her a good night's rest and said a bowl of porridge for breakfast would make her right as rain again.

Bea doubted it. The man she was now betrothed to was a stone's throw away. And she wanted him.

She ought to be exhausted, but her heart and body overflowed, drowning in the need to be close to him again, to feel him and assure herself that it had not all been a dream. Her skin still tingled everywhere he had touched her.

She turned over and slid her feet to the floor.

"Sleepless, even now?" the ghost said softly.

Bea drew in a slow breath.

"You sound weary."

"It has been a long day, forsooth."

"I know what you did."

"What did I do, my dear?"

"You did all you could to assure this result." She stared at the window. The curtains were open, and she saw nothing but silvery drops sparkling on the pane against the night without. Yet she knew he stood there. "You taunted me in the parlor so that I would confess my feelings for him. When I did not oblige you in that, you frightened me so that I would accept him."

"You are wondrously clever, my dear, but regrettably softhearted. I fully intended to make you mine."

"I don't know that I believe you."

"It matters not. But I do regret that our betrothal should have been so brief."

"Why did you do it?" She tilted her head. "Don't you want to be free?"

"I want peace."

"But not love."

"Never." His voice sliced the stillness.

"Again."

Silence met her.

"You meant to say never again," she said.

"Wondrously clever," the ghost murmured, his tone smiling now. "Now go as you wish, and find your young lord. I will remain here, unmolested by human passions."

"Did you—" She must know. "Were you there the entire time?"

A moment's pause.

"I found that I could not be."

Bea drew her wrapper around her shoulders. Casting a final glance toward the window, she stole out of her chamber. A dozen steps took her to Tip's door. Heart pounding, she grasped the handle and turned it. The door was unlocked. It creaked inward.

Across the chamber, Tip stood by the hearth. He wore only trousers and a deep green satin dressing gown tied loosely with a belt. Bea's heart climbed up her neck.

He seemed surprised to see her. An interminable moment passed before he turned fully from the fire to face her.

"Bea." His voice sounded very deep, the single syllable a question.

She took a fortifying breath, screwing up her courage.

"I would like to do it again," she said.

His gaze grew wary.

"Do it?"

"Make love. Again. Now," she added to make certain he understood.

He stepped back.

"Bea, as a gentleman of at least a modicum of remaining honor—"

"I would say a great deal of honor, given what you have sacrificed to save me."

He seemed to recoil. Bea's heart lurched into her stomach. He regretted it all. Why had she come? What could she hope to accomplish with this, except, perhaps, extraordinary pleasure with the man of her dreams?

"Be that as it may," he said tightly, "I would be taking advantage of you if I allowed it to be repeated before we are wed." His eyes seemed strange, evasive even as he looked straight at her, as though he weren't quite convinced of his own words.

Hope tingled in her.

"But you do wish to repeat it?"

His brow creased.

"How many times must I tell you—*show* you that I desire you for it to register in your thick head, Beatrice Sinclaire?"

"Perhaps several more," she whispered. "May we do it again now? Please?" Dear Lord, she was begging. But she could not stop. She wanted him to touch her, to hold her and move inside her. His words sent thick heat and a soft insistent throbbing between her legs.

He swallowed visibly, his throat jerking. Bea did not know why the action should act upon her midsection like a torch. Perhaps it was because she had never seen his entire sinew-corded neck, his man's collarbone, and the tantalizing glimpse of his chest revealed where the dressing gown parted at the top.

She stepped forward.

He did not retreat.

"You won't make this easy for me, will you?" His voice sounded deliciously husky. Bea recognized that tone now. He wanted to do it again too.

"Why should I?" She moved toward him. "You haven't made it easy for me for years."

He obviously didn't like that. His gaze intensified, like the day before when they had quarreled. But instead of backing away as he had done then, he loosened the belt of his dressing gown and removed the garment.

"Allow me to apologize for that now," he said, draping it over a chair arm.

Bea had only seen a few men partially unclothed, mostly farmers, and none of them looked at all like Tip—like a carved marble statue, but warm and alive, lean and powerful, with coiled muscle and smooth skin.

"My Lord," she said on a weak breath.

"That is what they call me, yes."

Her gaze shot to his face. Was he laughing at her? He was not smiling, yet his tone recalled the teasing friend she had known for years.

But her agitation would not be calmed. He was half-undressed and wholly breathtaking. She stood paralyzed.

"Before tonight, Bea, with me, had you ever touched a man?" His eyes retained that dark vibrancy.

Her mouth was incredibly dry. She had to moisten her lips to speak.

"Don't be silly," she barely managed. "Of course I had. Gentlemen have lent me their arms, helped me to mount my horse, taken my hand. Once I twisted my ankle by the Serpentine and my escort put his arm around my shoulders to assist me to a bench. And naturally I have danced with plenty of men. I have danced with *you*." Oh, Lord, she was babbling.

Tip gazed at her steadily.

She tried to swallow around the lump in her throat, without much success.

"You mean, have I touched a naked man, don't you?" she croaked. She couldn't believe her foolishness. She had given her virginity to him mere hours earlier, pressed against a stone wall for pity's sake, and now she could not speak ten rational words. She was hopeless. From babbling to tongue-tied. What an exceptionally talented seductress she was turning out to be.

Amazingly, he seemed to be withholding a smile.

"You have not answered my question," he said.

"No. Of course not," she replied promptly. "Well, only hands," she amended.

His eyes shone like gemstones held before a candle. He moved to her, halting less than a foot away. The heat from his body dragged her senses deeper into delicious chaos. He had bathed, and his hair was still damp. He smelled of soap and musky cologne that stole into her blood, intoxicating, weakening her with longing.

"Hands are a start," he said in a low voice. He grasped one of hers gently and drew it up between them. Holding her gaze, he turned it over and placed his mouth against the center of her palm.

Heat soaked her within. It spun up her arm and all through her middle. She released a trembling breath. How could such a small caress affect her so thoroughly? Her fingertips curled, scraping across his whiskered jaw, driving the pleasure deeper.

"Touch me, Bea," he whispered against her sensitive skin. Then, as though he would taste her, he traced her palm with his tongue in slow, delectable circles. She felt it between her legs.

"I don't know how," she gulped. Her gaze skidded over his shoulders and chest. "Or where." She wanted to touch him every surface of his beautifully taut skin and every curve of muscle.

Gently he turned her hand and kissed the soft inside of her wrist.

"However you wish," he said. His lips trailed a path of tingling delight along the soft flesh of her arm to the tender depression of her elbow. "Wherever you wish."

She loved the way his hair curled behind his ears to his neck, a little too long to be truly fashionable. She wanted to touch him there too. Everywhere.

"Really?" Her voice wavered.

He straightened, and he gave her a perfect half smile. "Really."

She lifted her free hand, hesitating. He took in a breath, the pad of his thumb stroking her palm. She reached to the side of his face, slipping her fingers through his hair and around to his neck. The textures were satiny and thick and so sublimely *him*.

His chest expanded on another tight breath.

She slipped to the depression at the base of his throat, then lower.

"Is this all right?" she said.

"More than all right."

His skin was so hot and smooth over hard muscle. She spread her fingers, her palm flattening, and shivers of need darted through her. Soft hair tickled the base of her hand. She slipped her fingertips lightly down until she covered his heart. It beat strong and remarkably fast. Like hers.

Her thumb sought.

"You are so—" Her words caught as his nipple hardened beneath her touch. She stared. "Handsome." Male. Enthralling. *Perfect*.

"Thank you."

"I would like to kiss you like you kissed me yesterday." Her thumb stroked, and his hand gripped hers tighter. "It felt so good. May I?"

"Be my guest." His voice, rough and deep, rumbled in his chest against her palm.

Bea leaned forward and pressed her lips to his firm flesh. He seemed to shudder. A thrill of purely feminine satisfaction skittered through her. She opened her mouth. He was hot and hard-muscled and he tasted wonderful—clean skin and perfect man. The man she had wanted forever. Her tongue stroked more boldly, and a sound of pleasure sounded from his chest.

She slid her hand along his ribs, under his arm and back. Muscles flexed beneath her touch.

Tip released her hand, sank his fingers into her hair and
drew her up, ducking his head and taking her mouth with such
sudden force Bea lost balance. His arm clamped around her
and she grabbed at him, the strength of his body washing
through her as his kiss devoured. His arousal was already
obvious against her. She smoothed her hands along his corded
arms, to his chest again, then around to his back, feeling,
memorizing, making herself drunk on him.

His lips moved to her neck, freeing her to gulp in air.

"I want to keep touching you," she said.

"Never stop." His hands swept down her back. He
scooped her up and Bea threw her arms around his neck.

He carried her to the bed, laid her down, and kissed her
until she could no longer breathe. Her fingers tangled in his
hair, holding him to her, but her body ached with need.

She broke free.

"Peter, make love to me now. I want to," she whispered,
astounded at her brazenness.

But he didn't seem to mind it. His eyes were like a forest
at midnight. She reached up to smooth back his hair, and he
caught her hand, pressed his mouth into her palm again, then
bit down lightly. Bea gasped, her body clenching as though he
touched her below. She wanted him to.

Her fingers curled around his hand.

"Feel me, too," she said. "Please. Caress me."

He smiled.

"Yes."

"Everywhere?" she said upon a breath.

His hand cupped her breast.

"Everywhere."

Her nipple was tight beneath his touch. Hot coils of need
curled inside her, descending, making her ache with need. She
reached for his waist, but he grasped her hands and pressed
them into the mattress at her sides, and took the peak of her
breast into his mouth. Through the thin fabric of her
nightgown, he lapped her.

"Oh—" She gasped. "*Ohh.*"

He sucked, and she was lost—lost to propriety, to inhibition, to all forms of reticence. Her hand pulled free, sought the thick bulge beneath his trousers and closed around it. Tip moaned and drew on her nipple harder. Her back arched and he tugged at the laces confining her breasts. Fabric ripped.

He went still, then pulled back.

"No!" She grabbed the torn nightgown and tore it down the center, exposing herself entirely.

Tip seemed to choke, then his eyes flared as he stared at her breasts, then traveled lower. White linen lay in tatters, her skin quivering. For moments that seemed like forever his gaze scanned her body. Her nipples strained for his mouth, points of desperate want nearly as strong as the craving below.

"Bea."

His hands surrounded her hips and he bent to her.

He kissed her navel.

She groaned in frustration. Then in ecstasy. His thumbs stroked inward, skirting her throbbing need. His tongue traced wet anticipation down her abdomen. He could not possibly intend what she imagined, but she wanted it. *She wanted it.* She shifted her hips, parting her thighs, and he covered her with his mouth.

A long, low moan erupted from her throat, and deeper, as elemental as earth as he caressed her. His tongue was soft and hot and moving so perfectly. Stroking. Teasing. Her knees fell to either side and she let him take her, nothing of shame in the shockingly intimate kiss, this beauty, this revelation.

She slid into delirium to the rhythm of his tongue, firm, and giving until she could not see, hear—could only feel. He grasped her buttocks and tilted her down, releasing a shower of heat across her thighs. Then he did it again, more, drawing her need forth, liquid and scalding, so quickly aching with such intensity it was nearly pain. She thrust forward, crying out, and he was there, his mouth controlling her, driving her higher as she gasped for breath, reaching, tightening in agonized coils. His tongue thrust inside her and her body erupted.

Sweeping shudders rolled through her, gripping, folding

within one another, tumbling in a race to reach every part of her at once. She gasped, her pleasure sounding in deep, hard sighs.

She struggled to sit and threw herself into Tip's arms.

"I want to do that to you." She sank her face against his neck, kissing him, breathing him in, reaching for him. Her hand encircled his thick male part and he drew in a sudden breath.

"I would be more than happy to oblige you," he said huskily. "But not now." He rolled her onto her back, pushed her thighs apart, and came down on her, pressing her hard into the mattress. "Now, I must be inside you."

She nodded frantically, wordless beneath his ravenous gaze. Her fingers plucked at his trousers, the fabric brushing against her flushed feminine parts with rousing roughness. He lifted himself away, off the bed, and removed the garment.

Bea had only a moment to stare in astonishment and some alarm before he covered her again, wrapping her in his arms, and capturing her mouth. His tongue stroked hers, and she wanted him again. Wanted the pleasure so acutely. Against her he was so hard and hot. She shifted and lifted her knees, bringing him closer. He drew back, his eyes dark and hungry.

"There should not be pain this time."

"I know," she said quickly, running her hands down his spine and pressing into his lower back. She wanted to feel him inside her again. To have him. "Please, now. Please."

He reached between them and pressed into her entrance. There was only a slight soreness, and the odd stretching, and deeper a quivering, stirring sensation. Her body accommodated swiftly to him, cradling, pulling him in.

"Sweet woman," he breathed as though in relief, "Bea," and sank into her completely.

There was no waiting this time. He moved in her, his hands circling her face, fingers tangling in her hair as he served her body. Slowly, tantalizing, his thrusts grew faster. She gripped his arms, opening to him. Again and again he came into her, and she met him eagerly, her neck arching. His hand came around her throat, his thumb atop it.

"Peter," she whispered, the pressure of his touch a sweet danger, the building tension in her a wonderful torment. She moved against him, needing, seeking. "Make me yours."

It didn't make sense. She didn't know where the words came from. But he understood. She grasped his hips and he kissed her, long and deep, his body slowing, stilling, grounding his possession of her in time, in a single immutable moment.

Then, drawing away from her lips, he thrust hard, harder the second time, then again until the fierce pleasure twined, built, and rose again. She gripped him, his sinews taut and his gorgeous face averted as he filled her, over and over, faster, firmer, so steady, and then not steady but desperate, reckless.

"Sweet Jesus, Bea."

"*Peter.*"

She convulsed, crying aloud and gripping him hard. He moaned, and they came together, entwined in one another, and clinging.

His arms surrounded her and he buried his face in her neck. With her arms she encircled his back, slick with sweat, and held him tight, wanting to never let go. Beneath her hands, between her thighs, and against her he trembled.

Her heartbeat stumbled.

He pulled back and she loosened her grip on him. He cupped her face in his hand and brushed damp hair from her cheek. His eyes shone with wonderment. A sob caught in her throat—improbable, foolish. She swallowed it down.

He shifted to lie beside her. Taking her in his arms, he rested his cheek against her hair. He held her until she slept.

Chapter Seventeen

Tip watched her in slumber. Her lips softened into a gentle curve, as though she dreamed pleasant dreams. Her breaths rose and fell, slow and shallow.

His heart pounded, faster and harder than when she had first entered his bedchamber, even greater than when she had touched him. His body was satisfied for the moment. Yet still he craved her, with a power beyond anything he had known.

He had thought he knew what it was to love her, but he had been a fool. Now he was truly lost, consumed, needing her with every fiber of his body and every corner of his soul.

He didn't want to sleep. He only wanted to look at her, to trace the lines and curves of her face, her creamy shoulder and arm tucked into the coverlet, resting so trustingly. If she only knew the damage he could inflict on her, the pain he could cause simply by being himself. By loving her.

His feelings were too raw. Somehow he must wrest control of them before she woke.

A night years earlier came back to him, when he had been close to leaving for university. That evening his father left the house after a row with his mother, ravaged like a man broken. Before he walked out the door he warned Tip in a hollow voice never to allow love to weaken him. Hell was preferable, he had said.

But Tip did not feel weak now. Gazing at the woman he loved, who had given herself to him so thoroughly, strength resonated in his limbs and chest—strength as he had never felt before. Perhaps his father had been wrong.

But perhaps not.

Bending, he gently kissed Bea's closed eyes. Then her

brow. Her neck. Her rose-hued lips. Until she stirred.

He turned her onto her back and without foreplay came into her. She arched to him, sighing her pleasure, her lashes fluttering. He moved in her, stroking her need, satisfying his, slowly building her pleasure. She whimpered, begging him for release. He gave it to her, and took it, sinking his soul deeper, giving away the last remnants of his heart. She had owned most of it for so long, the remainder did not resist going.

After, with her slender body curled around his, her hand rested lightly on his chest branding him as hers forever. Like the ghost within stone walls, Tip was trapped, in a heavenly prison whose walls he might shatter himself.

~oOo~

"Cheriot? Cheriot, wake up, damn you!" The door handle rattled.

Reluctantly Tip loosed his arm from around Bea, climbed from the bed, and pulled on his trousers. She rustled in her sleep, releasing a soft sigh and turning her cheek to the pillow. The coverlet exposed one smooth, pale shoulder and slender arm, and the swell of her breast.

Tip tugged the bed curtain closed, drew a steadying breath, and went to the door.

"Blast it, Tip, what business do you have sleeping so late? It's nearly noon."

"I was under the impression that you were at the village with Lady Bronwyn, Tom."

"I was, of course, but I hurried over as soon as—" He broke off, his face a study in agitation. "Listen, I can't find Bea anywhere, but Aunt Grace said she saw her last night after midnight. She's nowhere now, and I've looked everywhere but—*Good God*." His mouth hung open.

"Tom?" Bea said at Tip's shoulder. She wore his dressing gown cinched about her waist. It draped almost to her knees, revealing shapely legs that Tip had discovered held surprising strength. "Is everything all right?"

Thomas swallowed a few jerky times, his eyes shifting

back and forth between them.

"Well, I say," he stammered, "Aunt Grace didn't mention anything about—What I mean to say is, she told me Iversly bluffed the whole thing, as you predicted, Bea, and that you were right as rain after all. I had no idea—I was always under the impression that—" He stiffened and shot a hard glare at Tip. "Do you mean to make an honest woman of my sister, Cheriot?"

"She is already honest, as you should know. I do intend to marry her, though," he said, "as soon as she will have me." Warmth suffused his chest, a cool trickle of apprehension chasing in its wake.

"Well, I daresay you ought to have—"

"What do you need, Tom?" Bea asked with extraordinary composure. If she could see her rich eyes sparkling, her face aglow amidst tangles of satiny hair, she might not be so sanguine, standing before her brother now. And if she knew what Tip wished to do now to the body beneath that dressing gown, she would be even less so.

Thomas seemed to recall himself to his earlier distress.

"It's Aunt Julia, Bea. She's ill."

Bea clutched the dressing gown over her breasts.

"When? How?"

"I don't know. Aunt Grace said Julia wouldn't wake this morning, and when she did, she went all dizzy and weak. Lady Bronwyn has just sent Dibin to the next town over for the sawbones."

"Is Lord Iversly about? Has anyone spoken to him?"

Thomas looked taken aback. "No. I don't believe so." He shook his head. "Whatever would we want him for?"

"Don't be a complete idiot, Sinclaire," Tip said, pulling on his shirt.

"O-oh," Thomas stuttered. "I hadn't thought—"

"You never do."

"He said he would not hurt her," Bea said firmly, but her eyes swam with guilt. "I believe it."

"She seems terribly bad off, Bea," Thomas said, "and he's

a nasty fellow."

"Perhaps the effects of the curse are not entirely within his control," Tip said, wishing Thomas to perdition so he could speak with Bea alone. She would not meet his gaze.

Thomas stuffed his hands in his coat pockets. "But that's not all, Bea. There's more."

"More? Is it Aunt Grace? Or Lady Bronwyn? Tell me, Tom."

"You won't like it." Thomas's gaze flickered between them again, growing more anxious. "It's our parents, Bea. They're here."

Chapter Eighteen

Mama and Papa? Here? Now? It wasn't possible.

More importantly, *why*? They had come all the way to Wales *for her*? No. That could not be. They must be worried about Thomas.

"What do you mean by here, Tom? In the village?"

"Here in the castle. Downstairs."

"Oh, good heavens," Bea muttered, clasping Tip's dressing gown tighter to her skin. She was entirely bare, all the way above her knees. No wonder Thomas had gaped. But the satin was marvelously soft and it still held Tip's scent. And of course her own nightclothes were a wicked shambles. Heat filled her cheeks at the memory of how they had become a shambles.

She nudged past Tip's solid frame into the corridor, darting a glance both ways.

"I will see Aunt Julia immediately, after I dress."

"I would go right down to the parents after dressing if I were you," Thomas warned after her. "Mama's brought at least five servants and they'll all be on their way up here in a heartbeat, with Mama in their wake. You'd better face her and our father head-on and get it over with."

Bea cast him an exasperated glance before dashing down the corridor. She could not manage to look at Tip.

Inside her bedchamber, she braced herself against the inside of the door, breathing fast. She knew she should be constricted with alarm and confusion. But all she felt was languorous, perfect happiness.

Except for Aunt Julia's illness.

She went quickly to her traveling trunk.

"Iversly, I hope you returned my underclothes," she spoke aloud. "I don't think Mama would understand that little joke at all."

Had Thomas told them everything? Was Lady Bronwyn down in the parlor right now introducing herself as Tom's betrothed? Would Tom tell them about her and Tip?

No. Not the last. He couldn't. But he was heedless, and he had said she should get it over with. Oh, Lord. Why couldn't she be allowed to revel in bliss for even a single morning?

She rang for Aunt Grace's maid. Within minutes Peg had buttoned her into a jonquil muslin, regrettably wrinkled, but at least Iversly had returned her undergarments and she wore a clean shift, stays, and petticoat beneath. Bea wrapped her hair in a hopeless knot and threaded a red ribbon through it, her single admission to her newly fallen state.

How lovely it had been to fall.

She hurried to the great-aunts' bedchamber.

Lady Marstowe raised lofty silver brows.

"Good afternoon, Beatrice. How did you sleep?"

"Well, thank you," for the two hours she actually slept. Chin high, she ducked into the bedchamber. "Thomas told me about Aunt Julia." The bed curtains were drawn around the massive four-poster. "Is she very ill?"

"Groggy, rather. She is asleep now, and seems not to have a fever, but complains of aches in her joints and a megrim. She believes it is rheumatism."

"Rheumatism," Bea said thoughtfully. "Do you think this is Iversly's doing?"

"Do you?"

"No. Although . . ." She could not hide it from her great-aunt. "It could be."

"I assumed as much last night."

"But Thomas said you—"

"Thomas hasn't half your brains or a quarter of your character. I felt it was your news to share if you wished."

"Well, he knows now. But thank you."

"I presume Lord Cheriot means to marry you?"

"Yes."

"You don't appear happy about it." The dowager frowned. "Perhaps you haven't as many brains as I thought."

The trouble did not at all reside in Bea's brain.

"I am happy, Aunt Grace. It is only that Aunt Julia has fallen ill, and now Mama and Papa . . ."

"Harriet always knows precisely when she is least wanted."

Bea went to the door.

"Will you send Peg to fetch me when Aunt Julia wakes?"

Lady Marstowe nodded, perusing Bea's hair and gown.

"You will do. And in any case it does not matter whether you please them. You have only one person to please now."

She wanted it to be true, but not as Aunt Grace meant it. Once and for all she wanted to please herself.

She descended the spiral stair with a firm step, drawing in fortifying breaths until she reached the open parlor door. Her mother's voice trailed out to her. She paused in the corridor.

"Good heavens, doesn't anyone in this horrid place know how to make a reasonable tisane? I should have brought my chef along, after all," Lady Harriet sighed. "You there, Claude, is that your name? Go tell that Cook person this beverage simply will not do."

"You should be thankful you've got that at least, Harriet," Bea's father said in a stern tone. "I have never heard of such a thing—an old woman and a girl barely out of the schoolroom setting up house together in a castle in the middle of nowhere. How did my son get mixed up in this business?"

A footstep sounded behind Bea.

"Will you go in, or do you imagine they will come out here to meet you?" Tip's voice washed over her like honey, smoothing out the kinks in her stomach with warmth.

She looked over her shoulder. He wore a dark cutaway coat, waistcoat, and pristine white shirt and cravat. He had shaved, and he looked as breathtakingly handsome now as he had hours earlier in his bed with a shadow of whiskers and no clothing whatsoever.

"I'm hoping that if I wait here long enough they will simply disappear."

"Come now. It cannot be all that horrid." He touched the small of her back, sending delectable awareness through her exhausted body, and urged her forward.

She let the sensation of his hand make her smile.

Within the parlor, Lady Harriet held her habitual position, reclining on a sofa, swathed in exquisite fabrics of azure and cobalt to reflect her eyes and complement the gold in her shining hair. She enhanced the color of her coiffure with chamomile leaves and lemon juice, and Bea herself had ordered the gown and shawl in York according to her mother's exact specifications.

Bea's father stood at the window, his back to his estranged wife. At sixty years of age, Alfred Sinclaire was a robust, handsome man, with an almost military bearing. But Bea detected an extra rigidity to his stance now.

Thomas was nowhere to be seen.

"Good day, Mama, Papa." She curtseyed. Tip no longer touched her, but his presence behind gave a tangible memory of how lovely life could be sometimes, if not entirely at this moment. Bea moved toward her father.

"Afternoon, Cheriot." He nodded to Tip.

"How do you do, sir?"

"Beatrice." Her father took her hand and allowed her to kiss him on the cheek as she had since she was a girl. "It's been too many months since I last saw you. You look well. A little peaked, though. Have you been sleeping?"

"Papa," Bea said, warmth crawling into her cheeks, "you sound like my mother."

"And where is your kiss for me, Beatrice?" Lady Harriet cooed from the other side of the chamber. She and her husband were as far apart from each other as they could be in the space.

Bea obeyed her mother's summons. "What brings you here, Mama?"

"The carriage was horrid, not nearly as well sprung as I

would imagine he would keep it. I have the most tiresome aches and fidgets from—"

"I brought her here," Mr. Sinclaire said ominously. "When I arrived in York the other day to discover that you had gone on this harebrained chase after your brother, I demanded we set off to find you at once. Of course that was after your mother waited nearly all afternoon to tell me where you were." He cast his wife a glower.

Bea clasped her hands tightly. Tip had seen her parents' unpleasantness with one another before. She could not fathom why it should make her feel especially ashamed now.

"Papa, I did not need to chase Tom anywhere. He wrote to me exactly where he was staying, and before I left home I gave the direction to Mama, which is how you come to be here as well."

"How have you embroiled yourself in this business?" He scowled. "You shouldn't be chasing about the countryside after Thomas's doxies. You will tarnish your reputation, and your mother depends on you. She needs you at home."

"Lady Bronwyn is not a doxy, Papa. She is a fine girl. Haven't you met her yet? Where has Tom gone?"

"He went upstairs to fetch you nearly an hour ago."

Her brother was a wretched coward.

"No doubt he will return soon," she said, affecting serenity. "May I get you something, Mama? Freshen your tea?" Anything to be gone swiftly.

"Beatrice, you are withholding information from me." Her father's eyes narrowed. "What is happening in this place?"

Bea's stomach churned.

"We are all quite well except for Aunt Julia, which I suspect you know. She is ill. I would like to go see her right now, in fact." She did not dare edge toward the door yet. Her father's face was too dark.

"Has your brother compromised this Miss Nobody?"

"Lady Bronwyn, Papa."

"Is that what this is all about?"

"I am sure you should speak with him on that matter."

"He *has* compromised her!" Lady Harriet wailed, draping the back of an ivory hand over her mouth.

"Has he?" Mr. Sinclaire fixed Bea with an accusing glare.

"How could you allow him to do such a thing, Beatrice—to throw himself away on a *nobody*? Has she even made her bow to society? Good heavens, she must be Welsh. How dreadful." She shook her head. "Oh, you are a faithless girl not to care for your brother more dearly, and to protect my sensibilities with greater care, my third and most thankless daughter."

Bea clasped her hands together. They were clammy.

"I don't know that—"

"You don't know by now that your brother depends on your good sense?" her father interrupted. "That without your guidance he is unable to make rational decisions? I hold you responsible for this mishap, Beatrice. I only hope I can find a way out of it before it is too late."

"I suspect it is already too late, Papa." Bea could not manage to raise her voice above a whisper. "Thomas is quite taken with her, and I believe he has asked her to marry him. But I am not certain." Her last words were swallowed by her father's exclamation and mother's renewed wailing.

"Sylvia could have prevented him from making such a foolish match," her mother declared. "She always knew precisely a gentleman's worth and how to gage his position in society. I gave you all the advantages of town for two full seasons, yet you did not learn anything! Wretched failures, both of them." She waved a contemptuous hand.

Bea's breath shortened. Her eldest sister, Sylvia, had married a man who once hired himself out as a lover to wealthy women at the French court. Sylvia had told this to Bea in private, and she had kept her sister's confidence.

Now the tip of Bea's tongue itched to tell her mother the truth and dim some of the shine of her eldest sister's perfection. She swallowed back the impulse, ducking her chin.

"You have proven a disappointment to your mother in this, Beatrice," her father said with a shake of his head. "And to me. You should not have allowed him to do this."

"I don't know that I could have halted him from it, Papa," she said, knowing that Tip watched her too. Her parents must be truly distressed to speak to her like this in his presence. "But I ought to have tried, I realize." Instead of flinging herself into adventure at the castle, she could have written Thomas a strong letter from the safe distance of the village, encouraging him to come home. Georgie would have done that sort of intelligent thing. Her father was probably thinking that right now.

Of course, she hadn't known about the curse or that she would be trapped in the castle. But she might have thought ahead rather than spending hours worrying about her own imprudent infatuation—an attachment that until a few minutes ago finally seemed so lovely, perhaps even not entirely wrong.

Now her hopes all seemed foolish beyond measure. She stood completely immobile, hands cold and face hot, stunned at how swiftly all sense of freedom and happiness had deserted her.

"Perhaps, sir," Tip's voice came behind her, particularly deep, "I might be of use in searching out Thomas so that you can speak to him directly."

Bea's pulse quickened. Her parents could not mistake his mild chastisement. But they would not heed it. Tip did not understand anything about the situation. How could he?

"Oh, dear me, yes, Lord Cheriot. We are a family lost and abandoned, and you are more than gracious to offer your assistance," her mother trilled. She still called him by his title after so many years of familiarity. Abruptly, the formality seemed very silly to Bea, yet until a few days earlier she had insisted upon it too—not out of respect for his consequence, she now realized, but to keep him at a distance. To keep her heart safe.

But it had never been safe from the moment she met him.

"That is very good of you, Cheriot," her father said. "Harriet mentioned that you have business in the region. How do your interests go along here?"

"Quite well, thank you," he said lightly. But he had not yet gone to Porthmadog. A dull ache lodged in Bea's middle.

"You have no doubt had a great deal of bother here," her father said tightly. "I wish my son had the integrity that you do." He shook his head.

"It wasn't too many years ago that I was stirring up trouble as well," Tip replied.

"Your parents never despaired of you. Your father, I know, was always very proud."

"And your beautiful mother so fond. And your sister, poor, sweet Elizabeth," Lady Harriet sighed. "Left without her mother at such a tender age. My Georgianna was such a comfort to her, although I suppose she was already in Ireland with Kievan then, wasn't she?" she said, as though the effort of piecing together the chronology of the past three years proved too onerous.

"Fortunately, my sister had already married by the time my mother passed away. She had two children of her own in whom to take solace."

"But, of course." Lady Harriet laid a languid hand upon her brow. "How time slips away when one is closeted in the country with no pleasant company, no diversions, nothing but tedious gray days and disobedient servants that never attend to one's wishes suitably."

Bea's cheeks burned.

"Miss Sinclaire," Tip said. "Would you care to accompany me to the village in search of your brother? We might prevail upon Lady Bronwyn to return to the castle as well so that she can become acquainted with your parents." He turned to them again. "Lady Bronwyn's former governess took poorly yesterday. Our hostess generously spent yesterday evening at Miss Minturn's cottage in the village."

"I should remain here and see to the settling in of the servants," Bea mumbled. She didn't think she could bear the sharp sweetness of his company, not as she felt now.

"I suspect they will do well enough on their own, and Cook is here to assist." He moved to her side and she could not avoid looking at him.

On the surface, he seemed perfectly at ease, but a message

glinted in his emerald eyes. He would not allow her to evade him; that much was clear.

She took his arm.

"Ma'am," he tilted his head to her mother. "Mr. Sinclaire, we depart in hopes of returning shortly with Thomas and Lady Bronwyn."

"Do be quick about it, Beatrice," Lady Harriet instructed with a heavy breath. "You are the only one who knows just how I like my wardrobe arranged. I shan't have a decent gown to wear to dinner this evening if you tarry long in that wretched village."

"Yes, Mama."

"Do as your mother requests, Beatrice," her father said. "The sooner we find him, the sooner we can be gone from here and return you home where you belong."

They went toward the door.

As soon as they were in the corridor, she tried to pull away, but his arm pinned her to his side.

"Oh, no you don't," he said, his voice as firm as his grip, and dragged her through a door near the stairs.

"I thought we were going to the village." Her gaze darted around the tiny space. It was no more than six feet square, dust on the floor, and a bucket, mop, broom and dustpan the sole occupants. A tiny, deep aperture window provided very little light.

"Not just yet," he said behind her, shutting the door.

Bea's heartbeats skipped. The last time he had said those words, he kissed her.

She turned to face him, and all hope of a lovely dalliance in the broom closet vanished. His face was hard, his stare incredulous.

"What in God's name just happened in there?"

~o0o~

April 18, 1816

   Mr. Peter Cheriot proposed marriage to me today.
   Actually, he did not precisely make a formal offer. He simply said (as we strolled past the tennis players on the green, with Mama and two of her friends), 'When we are married, Bea, we must have a tennis court put in the yard, don't you think?' He waved his hand toward the players, smiled, and immediately spoke of something else. I hardly knew what to say, in any case.
   I do like him, Diary. I do not even mind it that he teases me.
   I like him very much.
   Very much.

~o0o~

Chapter Nineteen

Bea released a miserable breath and it seemed to Tip that she bit the inside of her cheek.

"It's obvious, I should think," she said, her voice dull. "Mama and Papa are unhappy about Thomas's situation."

"Of course they are unhappy. Any sane parent would be."

"It is truly remarkable that they came. I didn't even know Papa planned to visit York this month. But Mama sometimes forgets to tell me of such things." She clasped her hands together. "It is good to see him. It is nearly two years since he visited York, and four since that last time in London when he told Mama he would no longer hire the house there for her."

Tip remembered the day like it was yesterday. Between his father's declining health and finishing university, he had barely had time enough to call on Bea in town. With her removal north, he often had to arrange his schedule in labyrinthine twists to manage to see her. And the months between his visits to Yorkshire lasted far too long.

"Your mother is, as ever, entirely insensible of your feelings." He raked his fingers through his hair.

Her gaze followed the movement of his arm and grew abruptly warm.

His hand stalled at the back of his neck. He tried to remember what he'd been haranguing her about. It was difficult to think straight when she looked at him in quite that manner, like she had the night before when she first touched him.

Dropping his arm, he cleared his throat to recapture his indignation.

"Why are you allowing them to treat you in this manner?

Your damn fool inconsiderate brother got you into this and you didn't say a blasted word about it."

"You needn't use such language." The glimmer of arousal left her eyes.

Tip's frustration redoubled.

"I will damn well use whatever language I choose. Why didn't you tell them the truth and defend yourself?"

"The truth? You mean, about Iversly and Bronwyn?"

"The truth about how your brother got himself into this muddle."

"You know how it is with Mama. She becomes very agitated when I suggest she hasn't the right of it. And Papa is so disappointed with how poorly Thomas has turned out—in his estimation, of course."

"Not only his."

Bea's slender brows lowered.

"He is my brother, and if you choose to insult him again, or my loyalty to him, I will walk straight out of this room, Peter Cheriot."

"Then what about your father, accusing you of being at fault?"

"I believe it is easier for him to fault me instead of his only son."

"So you accept wrongful blame from both your parents because of their delicate sensibilities?"

"They are merely acting as good parents should."

"To whom? And no doubt your brother welcomes your championship, so he can avoid responsibility for his own misdeeds."

She glared at him, her lush lips clamped tight now.

"What of the other matter, Bea? Why didn't you tell them about us?"

"Us?" Her dark eyes glinted with alarm.

"That you are marrying me," he clarified, a hard stone of discomfort gathering in his chest.

She did not wish to answer. He could see it clearly.

"Why not?" he prodded, when she remained silent.

She turned her face away.

"I could not bear to," she finally whispered.

Tip's heart thudded hard.

"The fact of it is so abhorrent to you?"

Her eyes opened wide.

"Oh, no," she said hurriedly. "It's just that I know how they will respond."

"How?"

"Not well," she muttered.

Tip's spine stiffened.

"They require more than a title and ten thousand a year for their daughter?"

Her pretty lips fell open.

"*Ten* thousand?"

"Thereabouts."

"But I thought your father ran the estate nearly to ground."

"Yes, well, I remedied that."

"So quickly? It has only been four years!"

"I have been very busy," he snapped, then regretted it when her gaze shuttered. He took a steadying breath. "Is that insufficient for your parents? Do they expect more for you?"

"For me?" She seemed to choke, then shook her head vigorously.

"Then what?" It must be something more significant. Something he would not want to hear.

"It's only that," she began slowly, "They will say . . ." Her voice faded, her eyes again distressed.

Tip stepped toward her, wanting to touch her but restraining himself.

"What will they say?" he said.

"They will not believe me." Her gaze remained upon the floor. "Papa will be irritated that I cannot speak rationally, and Mama will prose on about what a considerate brother you have been to me all these years, and say what a feeble joke I am playing."

Tip struggled with his warring emotions—anger and a

peculiar sort of nausea.

"What we did last night, Bea, was hardly brother-and-sisterly."

Her glittering gaze darted to his and her breasts rose on a tight breath.

"I cannot very well tell them that, can I?"

Anger won out.

"Why not? This is absurd. Speak the truth and make them accept it."

"I am not absurd, and it is not as simple as it seems. You don't understand the way of it."

"I did not say you are absurd. I said the situation is absurd. And it is simple. You are merely afraid to put yourself forward."

"I-I am not."

"You're stammering, for God's sake. When do you ever stammer? Are you afraid of them? Of your own parents?"

"They are difficult to speak with." She swallowed the words.

"Then pretend they are me and tell them off," he said, hoping she would grin in response and dissipate the burning inside him. Instead, her eyes lit with vexation, which he supposed was better than misery. And it suited his ill humor perfectly.

"This is not amusing, Peter," she said between clenched teeth.

"It is to me," he countered unwisely, but the words spilled out. "Your father must listen to you if you insist on it, Bea. And your mother, while admittedly unpleasant, is somewhat rational when not complaining. At least they are able to have calm, measured conversations with one another, however infrequently. Try having a pair of untrammeled dramatists for parents and then tell me you know what it is to be afraid."

"You don't know anything about my family." Her brow was dark. "You have no idea what it is like to live in the shadow of—"

"People who behaved with such a thorough lack of

modesty that you spend every day of your life endeavoring to make up for it? Parents who allowed passion to so thoroughly overcome them that they died because of it? Who bequeathed to their son the same unruly sensibilities so that sometimes each moment is a struggle to withstand it, like now, when I am so angry that you won't simply go in there and tell them what they need to hear that I nearly wish to shake you?"

Her mouth formed a perfect O.

Tip gulped in air. Dear God, what had he said? He reached for her, but she backed to the wall.

"Oh, Lord, Bea, my cursed tongue."

"I can withstand their criticisms. I have been doing it for two decades. But I cannot bear this censure from you too."

Panic gripped him. With her eyes flashing in anger, she was exquisite, and he wanted her. Here. Now. *Immediately.*

"I don't mean to censure you," he insisted.

"Then why are you shouting at me?" she hurled back.

"Because I only wish them *and you* to regard you as highly as I do."

"So highly that you never once asked my father, or even my mother, for permission to court me?"

He blinked, clearly stunned. It had simply never occurred to him to show her that sign of respect.

The last bit of Bea's hope collapsed.

"I don't wish to do this. I cannot do this." She went to the door.

"Cannot do what?" His voice was unyielding. "Speak your mind to them? What does it matter how they respond? Who cares?"

"I do."

"Why, dammit?"

"Because they are my parents!"

"And they have made you feel worthless for your entire life, your mother lavishing Sylvia with attention and your father always overly impressed with Georgianna."

Bea halted before the closed door. Tip had never before spoken of Georgie critically. But for all that she had longed for a sign that he no longer cared for her sister in that manner, she could not like it. Georgie had done nothing to merit blame.

She turned to face him.

"It was not my sisters' fault."

"Then whose was it?"

Her throat closed.

"Mine," she forced out.

"Then it is yours to remedy. Go in there and speak to them, Bea, or I will do it for you."

"No, you will not. It is not your business."

"You will be my wife. It bloody well is my business now."

Her misery flashed into temper.

"Stay out of this, Peter. I will speak to them on my own terms when I am ready. I cannot be expected to be thinking straight when Aunt Julia is so ill and—" And she'd had so little sleep because she had spent the whole night making love with the man of her dreams. "And I—" And all she truly wanted now was to curl up in his arms until her parents vanished.

He looked so angry, so disapproving. She could not bear it.

"I wish to help," he said between tight teeth.

"Well, you don't sound like it." Her cheeks felt damp. "Or even look like it." She dashed the tears away with the back of her hand and whirled toward the door.

He grasped her arm, staying her. His eyes were over-bright.

"Have I done this? Have I made you cry?" He sounded horrified.

"No. Yes. I don't know!"

He took the side of her face in one large hand and brushed a tear from her cheek with his thumb. He bent to her mouth.

His kiss was sweet and hot, the perfection of it soaking into her raw senses. She leaned into him, welcoming his arm cinching her waist and drawing her against him. She opened her lips and drank in his warmth and his desire.

It amazed her that he still wanted her, just as she had always wanted him. His hands holding her were so strong and

certain, filling her with that fire she couldn't escape now. He
had awakened the spark of it in her so many years ago, stoked
it to a blaze the night before, and now it could only be fed by
him. Still new, it was wonderful.

A murmur of voices came through the thick wooden door
at her back. Tip drew away from her mouth, but he did not
release her from his arms.

"She has already gone to find her brother," her father said,
his boots scuffing on the corridor's stone floor.

"She ought to have remained here to assist me. No doubt
Lord Cheriot would be better off without her making a
nuisance of herself while he searches for our son."

"You say he visits Hart House regularly?" They seemed to
have paused at the base of the stairway.

"Three or four times a year. He comes to see Lord Marke,
of course, and makes his bow to me when he is in the country,
like a true gentleman," she said in a slanted tone, as though she
expected her husband to do the same. "Marke is collecting a
fine stable and dear Lord Cheriot counsels him, you know. But
of course you would know that if you had not abandoned me
to my fate, all alone in the horrid wilds of Yorkshire."

"He does not have any intentions toward Beatrice, does
he?" He sounded skeptical.

"Lord Cheriot? Heavens, no! He used to be so fond of
Georgianna, of course, before Kievan returned from Ireland.
But Beatrice? Whatever would a gentleman such as he see of
interest in her?"

"She's pretty, Harriet. Doesn't have Sylvia's beauty,
naturally, or Georgie's mind. But she looks something like my
Aunt Mabel did in her youth."

"And now Mabel is eighteen stone if she is an ounce,"
Lady Harriet tittered. "But there is no point in refining upon
it. Our third daughter is regrettably very foolish, entirely unable
to appreciate the attentions of fine gentlemen. Even when
several did court her during her first seasons, she never showed
any interest." A pause. "Do you know, Alfred, I have long
suspected that she developed a tendre for some inappropriate

man while I lived in town, before you exiled me. Perhaps a footman or a groom."

"And you failed to mention this to me at the time?"

"What would it have mattered? Beatrice is too much of a mouse to act on that sort of infatuation. And since then, she has showed such little enthusiasm over any gentleman, it simply never crosses my mind to worry about it."

"Mm. You must have the right of it."

"A compliment? Dear me, Alfred, it must be years since we have agreed on anything."

"No doubt it will be years again before the next occasion."

"Now where is that wretched Claude with my bandboxes? I will ring a peal over Beatrice's head for abandoning me to my fate with these careless servants. It was horrid enough on the road."

Their voices receded within the stairwell.

Bea's heart beat so swiftly she could barely breathe, a thick knot twisting her stomach. She drew out of Tip's arms and turned to the door.

"You must make yourself plain to them," he said.

"You don't understand? Even now?"

"I understand that the sooner you get yourself clear of them, the better off you will be."

Tears trickled down her cheeks again.

"I don't want your pity," she said.

"You may not want what I have to offer, but you need it now."

Bea pulled the door open and hurried out.

Chapter Twenty

Bea hid in her bedchamber until her tears subsided and the puffiness receded from her face. With heavy limbs, she dragged herself to the great-aunts' chambers, avoiding the area of the castle in which her parents had taken substantial residence.

Lady Marstowe ushered her in. Her maid, Peg, sat in a chair by the bed. The curtains were still drawn.

"You have been crying, Beatrice," the dowager stated with her customary bluntness. "Have you allowed your mother's inanities to depress you?"

"I am well enough, Aunt Grace. How is Aunt Julia?"

"She has not yet awakened and I am terribly concerned. I don't know where Dibin could be with that physician."

"Milord has ridden off to hurry them along, ma'am," Peg said.

"Perhaps we will see someone before sundown, then." Lady Marstowe gestured to the maid. "You may go for a time, Peg."

Peg left the chamber. Lady Marstowe closed the door behind her, locked it, and fixed Bea with a hard stare.

"Is it Iversly, Beatrice?"

"Aunt Julia's illness?"

Lady Marstowe nodded her silvery head.

"Honestly, Aunt Grace, I don't know. He has not spoken to me today. Perhaps he is doing this. But I don't believe so."

"My thanks for your confidence, my dear." The deep voice echoed peculiarly hollow in the close space.

"Iversly, what are you doing to my sister?" the dowager demanded.

"Not a thing, madam. I am a mere spectator to this

unfortunate event."

"Are you telling the truth?"

"Almost always."

"Lord Iversly," Bea said, staring at her folded hands. Speaking with him without being able to see the dark loneliness in his eyes or the harsh slash of his mouth seemed wrong. "Is Aunt Julia's illness due to the curse?"

"I do not know. We must all await the conclusion of this trouble together. But . . ."

"But what, man?" Lady Marstowe's voice was clipped. "Tell us at once."

He remained silent.

"Please, my lord," Bea said. "I know you wish to help us, despite the façade you affect."

"I wished to help you alone, my dear. But as you seem fond of your kin, I will do what I can to assist you in this matter as well."

"What can we do?" Bea pressed.

"Nothing, I suspect. But I will seek answers where I may."

"In the library? I know you can manipulate objects, as you did with my garments. Can you read books in that manner?"

He scoffed. "What good would books do you? We are in need of counsel."

"Counsel? Whose?"

"The warlock who began this whole game, mayhap," he said, his tone like a threat of storm. "Mayhap another of similar powers. I know it not. I must be off, however, if I am to do any good in this matter."

"How are you able to speak to them now, after four hundred years?"

Silence met Bea's question.

"He has departed, it seems," Lady Marstowe said.

"It was much less disconcerting when I could see him come and go."

"But then you were in danger from him."

"I never really felt it. At least not very seriously. I do not think he intends to hurt people."

"He hurt that idiot woman Minturn. Though no doubt she deserved it, as he said."

"Well, I don't know if I agree with that," Bea mumbled. "No one deserves shabby treatment."

"Especially not my dear Beatrice." Aunt Julia's wispy voice came from within the draped bed.

Bea leaped toward the bed and drew back the curtain.

"Oh, Aunt Julia." She breathed a sigh of relief. "You slept for so long. Did you hear Iversly?"

"Was the dear fellow here?" Her eyes were dull, her cheeks two round spots of crimson.

"For a bit," the dowager said. "Do you feel feverish, Julia?"

"Yes, dear."

"Will you take some water?" Bea asked. They assisted her to drink and to change her damp nightgown, then Aunt Julia lapsed into sleep again.

"See to your mother now, gel," Lady Marstowe said. "And do not allow her to come near here. She is useless in the sickroom."

Bea went to her bedchamber to change her gown. As she pulled off the mussed one, her gaze strayed to the bed she had made up two mornings ago and had not slept in since. An eternity ago, it seemed.

She lay down upon the musty mattress and for the first time since her childhood, slept through the afternoon.

~o0o~

Bea dressed for dinner in her most becoming gown and arranged her hair in a fashion she had once seen Sylvia adopt. Her hair did not take to the style as did her eldest sister's golden curls, but it looked well enough. She pinched her cheeks and fastened a pearl-drop pendant on a filigree gold chain about her neck. When she looked in the mirror, a pretty girl with sad eyes stared back at her.

She stopped at the great-aunts' chambers before going downstairs. Aunt Julia's temperature was still high, and she was mostly sleeping, but the doctor had come and examined her, leaving fever powders and various instructions. The dowager looked exhausted, and Bea promised she would sit up with Julia tonight to allow Aunt Grace and Peg the opportunity to rest.

She went to the kitchen and ordered dinner for Lady Marstowe and her maid to be taken up, including a bowl of broth for Aunt Julia if she should wake.

Upon entering the parlor she saw Thomas first. He stood uncomfortably straight against the backdrop of the tapestry in front of which she had first noticed Iversly. He glanced across the chamber to her, then his brow crushed into lines and he looked to the floor.

"Beatrice, you are finally here." Her mother yawned. "You have made us all wait an additional quarter hour for dinner, and I was famished at least twenty minutes before that. Why didn't you assist me in unpacking this afternoon? Whatever were you doing?"

"Sleeping, Mama."

"Good heavens, you have developed shockingly slatternly habits in so few days away from me, haven't you?" Lady Harriet chided.

Bea's father stood at the opposite side of the chamber. Lady Bronwyn perched uncomfortably on a settle across from Lady Harriet, her entire lovely person silently screaming unease. The sparkle was gone from her eyes and her lips were unsmiling. Tip was not present.

Bea went to Bronwyn's side.

"I have just been in to see Miss Dews. She is sleeping, and Lady Marstowe will take dinner in their chambers."

"I hope we do not all catch Julia's horrid fever. How wretched it would be to come to Wales only to take sick and die," Lady Harriet exclaimed.

Bronwyn's eyes went wide. Bea grasped her fingers and drew her up.

"Let us go in to dinner then, shall we?" she said, tucking Bronwyn's arm into hers. The girl looked momentarily grateful.

"Do we not wait for Lord Cheriot?" she asked, a note of hope in her voice.

Bea glanced at Thomas, but he continued staring at his toes.

"Papa?" she asked.

"Cheriot brought the physician along hours ago, then rode out to Porthmadog to see to his business there. He expects to return late tomorrow."

So, it was to be abandonment after all. She supposed she should have expected it.

Bea drew her shawl more tightly about her shoulders and led Lady Bronwyn toward the door.

Dinner was a strained affair. Lady Bronwyn attempted conversation, but Bea was the only person to respond. Thomas provided no assistance whatsoever. When they rose from the table, Bea escaped tea in the parlor by claiming her duty in the sickroom. Lady Bronwyn said her good nights and hurried after her.

"Oh, Beatrice," she grasped Bea's arm, her eyes full of emotion. "I feel absolutely wretched for having left you alone here last night. However did you make it through to midnight? It must have been horrible waiting to discover if that horrid Lord Iversly would go through with his threat or not."

"I never thought he would." Bea started up the stairs. "How is Miss Minturn today?"

"Oh, Minnie is well enough," the girl said rather blithely. "I never imagined she had led such a dramatic life."

To Bea, the governess's life did not sound dramatic at all. Merely pathetic, like her own.

"Yes, well, she seems to have felt very deeply."

"Oh, and she still does. She speaks unceasingly of him, crying and bemoaning her unhappy fate." Lady Bronwyn's face grew pensive. "Do you think that true love never dies?"

Yes.

"Not really. My parents once believed they were in love,

and now they can barely speak to each other when they are in the same room. You may have noticed that."

"Oh. Yes. I see." Bronwyn was silent to the top of the stairs. "Beatrice." She laid a light hand on Bea's arm again. "I know you must think I am a flighty thing, and a person of loose morals."

Bea simply could not find words to reply.

"Oh, but you see," Bronwyn assured, "I was very frightened."

"Of course you were."

"I did not know Iversly was merely bluffing."

So, Thomas had not told her the truth. It was a surprising show of discretion on her brother's part.

"I would never have—" Lady Bronwyn continued. "Oh, you know. But I would not have done it if not for Iversly's threat."

"Of course not."

"Your brother has asked for my hand." Her brow puckered. "He told me he will await my response before announcing it to everyone."

"You are considering refusing him?"

Lady Bronwyn's lashes quivered and she seemed to study her interlaced fingers.

"I like him very much, but—but—" She stammered prettily.

"But what, Bronwyn?"

Her gentian eyes came up.

"I have not yet had my first season in London. I understand that there are a great many gentlemen there who pay calls on ladies, and bring them posies and poetry and ask them to dance ever so many times."

Bea held her mouth shut with effort. Her brother was as handsome as could stare—a striking male version of their stunning eldest sister—with easy charm, a more than comfortable allowance, and an excellent competence to anticipate when he inherited from their father someday. To Bea's knowledge, young ladies in town hung all over him when he deigned to pay attention to them, and he was beset by invitations the moment he entered the countryside. Bea had never yet heard of a girl turning up her nose at Thomas Sinclaire.

Perhaps Lady Bronwyn was even more naïve than she had thought.

"Also," Bronwyn said, more softly now, "I have been thinking. Or, rather, looking."

"Looking at what?"

"Rather, at *whom*."

Unease twined through Bea's belly.

"Whom?"

"Lord Cheriot."

Of course.

"Have you?"

"Oh, he is very handsome." Bronwyn dimpled, as though sharing a daring secret. "And a lord," she added a little breathlessly. "With no disapproving parents." An endearingly desperate cast to her fine features entreated one to sympathize.

Bea lifted a brow.

"True."

"Your brother told me the other day that Lord Cheriot is not promised to any lady."

Bea could say nothing in response. She could hardly inform this girl of her betrothal before she told her parents.

Lady Bronwyn's fingers tightened.

"I thought that since you and he seem to be such good friends, you might put a fly in his ear on my behalf."

"A fly?" Even this silly girl did not see the possibility of any connection beyond friendship between her and Tip. It didn't matter to Bea, really. She had his promise. She ought to be deliriously happy, as she had been that morning. And all night. Before he had deserted her at the precise moment when she most needed a friend.

"Oh," Bronwyn said, "you might mention my name a time or two in conversation, something about my pretty gown, my speaking eyes, and wouldn't it be lovely to invite me for a stroll in the garden. You know the sort of thing. Don't you?"

No, Bea had no idea. That was Sylvia's area of expertise, not hers. And she had never had any bosom bows of her own sex with whom to practice those sorts of games. She had always been too busy seeing to her mother's needs, comforting her woes, and quietly wresting Thomas out of scrapes.

"Yes, of course," she murmured.

"So you will speak to him about me?" Bronwyn's voice seemed lighter now.

"Bronwyn, I believe Lord Cheriot is under the impression that you intend to marry my brother."

"Oh, well," she said, a tiny furrow between her eyes. "That will be taken care of shortly."

Naive, indeed. But Bronwyn was probably so confident of her winning looks and sparkling charm she could not imagine what a pristine bride meant to a titled nobleman.

"My brother, I believe, is still in the parlor."

"Oh, I cannot go back there. Your mother—" She broke off, her cheeks coloring. At least the blush did not seem contrived.

"Of course. Perhaps later." Bea moved down the corridor. "I am needed in my aunts' room now. Good night, Bronwyn."

"Oh, good night, Beatrice. And thank you for your assistance!"

~o0o~

Bea spent the night watching her great-aunt Julia sleep, mopping her fiery brow with a damp cloth, and dosing her with fever powders. Peg relieved her at dawn. Too weary to eat and too agitated to sleep, Bea wandered into the fog-shrouded gardens, to the place where she had fainted days earlier. She stepped past the spot, then another ten paces. She breathed deeply of the misty, chill air of the early November morning, her blood sluggish from lack of sleep but her muscles and head in perfectly good order.

It could not have all been a dream. Tip had been there, and Julia confirmed it. Iversly had been telling the truth, and he probably still was.

The ghost had not visited the sick chamber all night. That was not a good sign.

Close to noon Julia's fever climbed, remaining high for several hours, then dipping again. Bea returned to the house and Lady Marstowe ordered her to rest. She went to her mother's chambers.

"Finally!" Lady Harriet sighed when she entered. "Begin with the gowns, then the undergarments. And when you are finished there, you will dress my hair for dinner. Do you think Lord Cheriot will return from Porthmadog in time?"

"I'm sure I do not know, Mama." She didn't know anything about Tip, his whereabouts, why he had left without a word to her, or why he had been so horrified when she cried. But men were like that, she supposed. Her own father complained of his wife's moods incessantly.

Tip had always seemed different, though.

Her mother's brow wrinkled.

"Why didn't Lady Bronwyn set her cap for him rather than your brother? She seems a conniving little thing, the sort who would look to a lord rather than a plain Mister."

"I couldn't say, Mama." Bea unfolded a glorious frock of sapphire muslin and lace.

"Put that back in the trunk, Beatrice," her mother scolded. "I cannot possibly wear muslin when I am so overset. Give me the silk instead." She held up a stocking to the light to examine it for tears. "I do not think she could nab him," she returned to her musings. "She is far too giddy. After his parents' disreputable behavior, I suspect he wants nothing to do with drama and tears. What a horrid scene they would make. But Clarissa Cheriot did have the most enviable taste in gowns. Why I have one here that I had made up by the modiste she employed."

Bea's mother continued her monologue, but Bea heard nothing of it. And her throat was so tight she was not even able to reply "Yes, Mama" when required.

~o0o~

Tip returned after dinner as the party was dispersing from the parlor for bed. He met Bea's gaze for a moment, then Lady Bronwyn claimed his attention, her slender hand making itself familiar upon his coat sleeve.

Bea turned away, irrational jealousy heating her cheeks.

He left the parlor before she did. When she climbed the stairs later, she conferred with Aunt Grace. Julia's fever was holding steady but not alarmingly high.

Bea returned to her bedchamber and fell into exhausted sleep. She dreamed of Tip holding her in his arms, making love to her, and refusing to let her go when her parents insisted that she must remain as a companion to her mother rather than marry a man she did not deserve.

He was not present at breakfast. Bea hadn't any stomach for food. She returned to the sickroom for the morning, quitting it only once to look in on her mother.

"Thomas refuses to leave without you," Lady Harriet exclaimed.

"I think he is concerned about Aunt Julia and does not wish to depart until we are certain of her recovery."

"He is a horrid boy, lacking all filial devotion. You must take him in hand, Beatrice, and make him see the right of it. I cannot go on another day in this wretched castle in the middle of nowhere."

"I will do my best, Mama."

After preparing her mother's midday repast, instructing the two maids Lady Harriet had brought from Hart House as to where in the castle they could find the necessary items for steaming and ironing their mistress's gowns, and relating everything she knew about Bronwyn's sickly grandmother to her mother, Bea escaped.

She ran her brother aground in an antechamber near the

kitchen, slouching on a barrel in an attitude of thorough defeat.

He started when she touched him on the shoulder, pivoting around to face her.

She peered at him.

"Thomas, are you hiding out here?"

"What gives you that idea? You're as nosey as our father sometimes."

She bit her tongue.

Contrition overtook his features.

"I beg your pardon, Bea. It's only that I'd rather not come across . . . someone in particular at this time."

"Lady Bronwyn? And Mama and Papa?"

His eyes opened wide.

"How do you know that?"

"Tom, we have been on this earth nearly the exact number of minutes, born from the very same womb."

"So what?"

"I guessed."

He cracked a grin. Bea wished she could return it.

"You're a great gun, Bea." He glanced around and lowered his voice. "Father is adamantly against the match, and Mama insults Lady Bronwyn every time they meet."

"Mother always insults women prettier than she. Avoiding them all will not help with any of that." Bea's mouth shut hard upon the final word. She could easily seek out Tip and speak with him. But she was afraid. Afraid to see the desire in his eyes now dimmed, and to read reticence on his handsome face.

"I know, I know." Thomas's shoulders hunched. He peeked up at her. "But, Bea, I might have made a mistake concerning Lady Bronwyn," he said in a rush.

"Oh?"

"Yes, oh. She is beautiful and spirited. But I don't know that she's a very nice girl after all."

"Thomas." Bea's blood spiked with prickly energy. "You are a thorough cad. At this moment, I am ashamed to call you my brother."

He staggered back.

"Wha—But it's better to know this now before I get caught in a parson's mousetrap with her. Or else I'll end up in a marriage like our parents' shamble of a thing."

Impatience got the best of Bea. She folded her arms tight across her chest.

"You should have taken that into consideration before you bedded her."

"Your sister is correct," Tip said at her shoulder. "As usual."

Bea's heart turned over. She pivoted and he glanced down at her, his expression unreadable.

"I should have, it's true," her brother said with a scowl. "But I didn't, and now I'm truly dished up."

"Tom," Bea said, more to allow time to wrest control of her racing pulse than because he deserved the reprieve. "Lady Bronwyn suggested to me that she might not be entirely amenable to a betrothal to you, either."

Thomas's pout of misery turned to affront with comical speed.

"Well, I daresay the tart could have told me that herself."

"Tart? *Thomas.*"

"Chit," he acquiesced.

Tip's presence behind her was a solid wall of silence.

"Did you tell her your feelings on the matter?" she asked.

Thomas stiffened.

"What are you thinking, Bea? A gentleman can't cry off from a betrothal, especially not under these particular circumstances. Would you do such a thing, Cheriot?"

"Of course not." His voice lacked color entirely.

Bea's insides twisted. She clutched her hands in her skirts.

"Nevertheless, Tom, I recommend that you find Lady Bronwyn and make a clean breast of it. If neither of you wish to marry the other, you certainly should not." She paused. "Unless it becomes necessary, of course."

"Well, there, you see, Bea, after only one time a girl doesn't always—" A flush stole over his cheeks. "That is to say—I took care—"

"I know how these things work, Tom."

Thomas's gaze shifted uncomfortably to Tip.

"Of course you do," he said hastily. Then his eyes lit with guarded hope. "But you've got something there, Bea. If I'm clever enough, she'll cry off before I have to, then I won't be in the wrong." He slanted a hopeful smile, pushed away from the barrel and headed off down the corridor.

Bea forced her body to turn around.

"I am on my way to inquire whether Lady Marstowe has need of anything for Miss Dews's comfort," he said. "Would you care to accompany me?"

Not if he continued speaking to her like a stranger.

"Yes, thank you." She fell in beside him. He did not offer his arm. "How did your business proceed in Porthmadog?"

"Well. Untroubled."

"Thank you for seeing to the doctor's quick arrival yesterday."

"It was nothing."

"Iversly came to speak with Aunt Grace and me. He is looking into Aunt Julia's illness."

"Is he?"

Bea's courage curdled. He was still displeased with her, as everyone always was. But never him before this past week.

She halted. He did as well. She looked up at his face and read absolutely nothing there. No anger, no pleasure, no teasing camaraderie. Nothing but handsome features set still as stone.

Words tumbled to her lips. "Would you like to cry off as well?"

His jaw hardened. "No."

"I only thought that perhaps you—"

"That I am as great a scoundrel as your brother?"

"No, I only—"

"I do not wish to speak of this." He started up the stairs. She went after him.

"We quarreled, and then you left without telling me."

"You were asleep when I departed."

"Lady Bronwyn has set her cap for you." Oh, Lord. She ought to cut out her tongue.

"Then she is doomed to disappointment."

Heat shimmered through Bea. *Ridiculous.* But she could not seem to halt herself.

"There must be dozens of young ladies in town, not to mention Derbyshire, who will be disappointed as well."

He rounded on her.

"What are you doing? Do you want to ruin yourself?"

"I already did that two nights ago."

"No. But you are doing so now. Do you wish to be released from your obligation to me, Bea? Is that what this is about?"

She couldn't breathe. She could save him now. He was offering her the opportunity. No one else would ever need to know about what had happened between them. Given his own situation, Thomas could be convinced this was for the best. Aunt Grace would be more difficult to persuade, but she would see the right of it once Bea explained. She must.

Tip's eyes seemed almost black in the dim corridor. He stood for another moment watching her as she searched frantically for words that would suffice. Nothing came.

"I will take your silence as assent," he said in a low voice. "Unless you find yourself with child, you are released."

Chapter Twenty-one

Bea's lungs felt as though they collapsed. She sucked in desperate breaths.

What had she done?

"I don't want criticism from you." She ached to reach out and put her hand on his rigid back.

"You have just assured that you will have nothing whatsoever from me now."

"Peter—"

"No, Bea. This is not how it works. I will not replay my parents' foolishness, arguing until someone weeps, then reconciling to the detriment of everyone around, most especially themselves." He swallowed hard. "Do you know how my mother died?"

Bea nodded.

"In a carriage accident?" he supplied. "As published in the papers?" His eyes shone with derision. "Elizabeth and I wrote that, inventing a faulty axle and a skittish lead horse so as not to be obliged to write the truth, that she went out alone at night on a horse that was barely broken. She sought the exact spot on the road where my father fell from his mount a year earlier while racing to apologize to her for yet another infidelity. She arrived there in one piece, amazingly enough. But she hadn't left matters up to fate. She brought a pistol in the event that the horse did not finish her off first."

Bea's hand slipped over her open mouth.

Tip nodded slowly. "So you see the way of it now, I trust." He took a hard breath, shuddering slightly on the exhale. "I will not have any part of that life." He turned to the door and knocked.

Bea hardly knew when Peg opened the door and Lady Marstowe came into the corridor. Her mind and heart were a sea of confusion.

"Iversly has been here," the dowager said, her sharp gaze shifting to Bea, then back to Tip. Her brow creased. "What is amiss? Beatrice, you look as though you are ill, too."

"I-I—"

"She has had an encounter with her brother that overset her," Tip said.

"The nincompoop." Lady Marstowe scowled. "I will see about him once we are finished with this."

Bea pushed away the tears surging behind her eyes.

"What did Lord Iversly say, Aunt Grace?"

"He believes he has found the source of Julia's malady, but he requires your assistance, Lord Cheriot. And yours, Beatrice."

"If it will help Miss Dews return to health, he has it," Tip said.

"Of course, Aunt Grace."

"You must go to the village," she said to Tip, "to that woman's cottage."

"Miss Minturn?" Bea asked. "Whatever for?"

"He wishes to speak with her."

"And if she will not return here with me?" Tip asked.

The dowager's assessing gaze shifted between them.

"He believes that he may be able to communicate through the pair of you."

"What do you mean, Aunt Grace? Does he wish for us to hold some sort of séance? I understand they are all the rage in London now. Mama attended one, though she would not take me."

"No," the dowager scowled. "Iversly does not need conjuring up. He is perfectly present here, of course."

"What does he wish us to do?" Tip's mouth was set in a line.

"He believes that if Beatrice remains here in contact with him, you will be able to speak on his behalf. He depends upon your bond with one another."

"That is ridiculous." His implacable tone hit Bea like a slap.

"It does seem improbable," she managed to say barely over a whisper. Her throat would not function properly.

"I told him the same thing," the dowager said, her lips pursed. "But looking at the two of you now, I am beginning to see his way of it."

Tip didn't move or speak. His jaw looked like stone, his shoulders stiff.

"If Aunt Julia's welfare depends upon it," Bea said, "I will do whatever he suggests."

"Why not prepare a speech that I may repeat to her?" Tip said.

"I asked him that," the dowager shook her head. "He says it will not suffice. She will only respond to him, apparently."

"Why, Aunt Grace? How can she help?"

"She will provide us with an antidote for Julia's illness. It seems that Miss Minturn is a witch. To take revenge on Iversly, she has poisoned my sister."

~o0o~

Bea stood across her bedchamber from Lord Iversly. He was by the window, as usual. He had informed her of his location, a strange consideration given how awful he could be at times. But he was not the man any of them had imagined. His actions now proved it. And his voice held a harsh note of anxiety, as though Aunt Julia's fate truly mattered to him.

"The woman has been teaching herself potions and the art of sorcery for a dozen years," he said.

"Since you broke her heart."

Iversly remained silent.

Bea crossed the chamber to her dressing table chair and sat on the edge of it. Aunt Julia's fever had risen again, and Lady Marstowe was seeing to her comfort while Peg ensured that Lady Harriet and the servants from Hart House were busily engaged elsewhere.

"How did you learn about the poison?" she asked. "You were gone for quite some time."

"I heard rumors of it, then needed only confirmation."

"Rumors? How?"

"The dead, my dear, practice methods of communication that would shock your innocent senses."

"After this week, I do not feel particularly innocent any longer. In many ways." She tilted her head. "I thought you could not communicate with other ghosts."

"Not all the dead are ghosts." His voice grated.

"I see."

"I hope you do not."

"Why must you speak with her yourself?"

"She fears no other. She will bend only to my will."

"Do you truly believe this will suffice, or is it merely another method to mend fences between me and Lord Cheriot?"

"I was not aware that those fences required mending at this time." His tone sounded lighter, as though the change of topic relieved him.

"I guess I have grown accustomed to you knowing the details of everyone's lives around here, I thought— But you were away all night and day, of course."

"Have you displeased him? I cannot imagine it of you. Nor of him."

Bea wished she had not broached the subject. She looked to the clock on the mantel. Nearly six. Tip would arrive at Miss Minturn's cottage in moments. He had left without a word, neither giving his consent to the experiment nor withholding it. Aunt Grace assumed his cooperation, of course. Bea suspected he would go through the motions of it, if only to please the dowager and Aunt Julia.

One more minute.

"We must begin soon," Iversly said quietly.

A shiver of apprehension went through Bea.

"What will you do?"

"I will enter you."

"What? You did not—"

"Not as you imagine. Though it is a pity, forsooth," he rumbled. "I may only take corporeal form once each century, as you know. Tonight, I will remain ethereal."

"Then how will you do what you must to communicate with her?"

"I will slip within your soul sufficient to use it and your young lord's as my conduits. Your intimate connection will allow it."

Bea's breaths shortened.

"Will it give him pain?"

"Ah, you think of his comfort before your own. True love." He chuckled, but it was a sound of derision. "No," he replied, his voice odd now. "No pain to speak of."

"Have you done this before?"

"I have walked this earth for so many decades, my dear, there are few things I have not done."

"That is not an answer."

Iversly remained silent. Then: "It must begin now."

Bea's gaze darted to the clock. The hands pointed opposite each other. Her fingers in her lap shook.

"All right," she said. "What do you wish me to do?"

"Stand, but remain relaxed."

"This will not work," she said, coming to her feet and resting her arms by her sides. She clamped her eyes shut. "He is very angry. He wants nothing to do with me now."

"So you say," the ghost murmured.

Abruptly, chill air swished around Bea's arms, blowing across her exposed throat and face. Like liquid, it crept beneath the fabric of her gown. Goose bumps lifted across her skin, her hair prickling with cold energy on her head and each down-like follicle along her limbs. She shivered, the sensations so intimate, as though she wore nothing.

Across her lips and cheeks an icy breeze seemed to pass, brushing almost tangibly, settling on her face and neck and above her bodice where her skin showed. Then on her breasts, down her belly, between her thighs and along her legs, circling back up to her buttocks. It caressed her back and shoulders with frozen fingers, and curled around her neck.

Then it delved within.

Her heart leaped, and then raced.

"Lord Iversly?" she gasped.

Frost grabbed at her lungs, crept around her stomach, bowels and heart, climbing up her spine, along her throat. Her body seemed suspended, floating, light like air, yet so heavy she could not lift a hand. She tried to move and her arm snapped back to her side. Ropes of tension bound her, icy straps clasping about her wrists, ankles, waist, and neck, bending her head back, splaying her palms upward, trapping her immobile. Her mouth fell open, her eyelids thick caps of frigid lead.

All thought fled, subsumed within emotion.

Apprehension, sharp and hard.

Fear.

Then, gradually, growing until it swelled in her head, her chest, and belly—

Terror.

Bea's throat worked and she tried to scream but no sound came forth. Only her breathing remained, hard and fast, panic-driven, the fox before the hunt.

Her blood slowed, thick and cold in each vein, every artery, the scent of ash all around. Her lungs drained. From inside she was beginning to freeze, becoming solid, no longer living flesh, but dead, chill matter.

She sobbed deep within where light no longer penetrated, no pulse of existence, only inky darkness, beyond all feeling but despair and grief. And consuming loneliness.

Endless . . . eternal . . . empty.

She slipped, slid, her body growing slack, releasing the remnants of her will.

Releasing life.

"*Peter,*" she breathed, a last hopeless whisper.

Warmth poured into her.

She gasped, heat surging up from her core into her belly, into her chest and neck, spreading along her arms and legs and around her head, filling her, replacing the cold like a maelstrom.

Hands touched her, strong and deliberate, spreading on her waist and curving around to her back, over her shoulders, drawing her close to encompassing warmth. They moved, stroking along her shoulders and arms, lacing with her fingers and then caressing her hips, dipping between her thighs. Intimate, tender. Seeking.

Giddy, luscious flame licked at her, gripping, stretching her arms wide and working her throat. A sound came forth from her mouth, a moan of ecstasy as a wave of heat spilled through her, seizing her around the hips, prickling her nipples to peaks. She moved against the sensations, shifting her body to feel the lap of hot friction. Damp scored her thighs, the taut peaks of her breasts so hard they ached. She felt no need, only the rapturous concourse of answered hunger.

She fell into pleasure, gasping, gulping in air, her flesh consumed with the sweetest delirium, convulsions of perfect delight. Joy shuddered through her, washing along her thighs, breasts, and hands, curling delectably in her womb.

Her palms sought her belly and mouth, pressing inward to hold herself together, clamping her lips to allow nothing to escape. Within, beneath her skin, deep and brilliant and miraculous, she trembled through a shower of illuminated rapture.

It came apart slowly, releasing her into awareness of her bedchamber, the scent of evening, the touch of fire-warmed air on her skin.

Her body sagged, legs shaking and then collapsing.

Strong arms surrounded her. Familiar and safe. Beloved.

She fell to the floor.

Chapter Twenty-two

Tip returned to the castle in a daze. Leaving his horse with Dibin in the drive, he went directly to Miss Dews's chamber and deposited the antidote cordial with Lady Marstowe. She woke her sister to administer it, and Tip retreated to the corridor. He must clear his head.

At the cottage, he had stated the case to Miss Minturn, and she had given him the antidote instantly.

Or so it seemed.

But something was wrong. He had entered her cottage the moment the castle bell struck the hour. Now, according to the clock across from him in the corridor, it was nearly seven o'clock. It did not require that long to ride back from the village, a mere ten minutes at best.

And the dream . . .

Had he dreamed it on the ride to the governess's house, or on the path back? Or not at all?

He could still feel Bea's body in his hands, her quivering pleasure. He could still taste her ecstasy. He had never before dreamed so vividly, and certainly not while awake. It left him stunned and shaking.

The door behind him opened.

"The fever has left her. She is sitting up and asking for dinner." Lady Marstowe's face showed calm relief. "Thank you for your part in it, my lord."

Tip glanced down the corridor.

"Is—has Miss Sinclaire—"

"When she did not come to us after some time, my maid went to her bedchamber. She has not yet returned."

"Pardon me, if you will, my lady." He strode to Bea's door.

Wanting to burst in, he knocked. The dowager's maid pulled
the panel open a crack, breathed a wide-eyed sigh of relief, and
beckoned him in.

"I found her like this, milord." She gestured toward the
hearth. Before it, Bea lay on the floor, a pillow stuffed beneath
her head.

He jolted forward and gathered her into his arms.

She was warm.

"I couldn't move her myself." The maid wrung her hands.
"But I didn't dare leave her so I could run and tell milady. And
what would she have been able to do? Someone needed to stay
with Miss Julia."

He lifted her and laid her on the bed.

"When did you come in here?" he said.

"Three quarters past the hour. Is she ill?"

"It's all right. You did well." He sat on the edge of the bed
by Bea's hip and rested his hand on her brow. She had no fever,
and her breaths seemed to be the regular breathing of sleep.
Her cheeks were dusted with the hue of a ripe peach. "She is
sleeping. Go tell Lady Marstowe. Miss Dews is already
recovered. Then wait nearby in the event that Lady Harriet or
Mr. Sinclaire should seek their daughter, and inform me
immediately."

"Yes, milord." She ducked an anxious curtsy and hurried
from the chamber.

He smoothed back Bea's hair from her brow. Even in
sleep she was beautiful, and she held his heart as securely as
though it were bound by chain and lock. He had gone to
Porthmadog to escape the tumult that touching her and
arguing with her created in him. But he had thought of nothing
but her, even while transacting his business. Now, still furious
with her for forcing him to cry off, he could not look his fill.

He hadn't meant it. Any of it. In the kitchen he had
bluffed merely to test her, and she had called him on it. If she
continued to refuse him he would somehow convince her to
wed him. He had taken her maidenhead. And he could no
longer live without her.

Her eyes fluttered open, and his breaths stilled. Her wide, dark gaze scanned his face, focusing, then returning to his eyes.

He whispered her name, his voice rough.

She drew in a slow breath and her body shifted. She returned the pressure of his hand. Tip swallowed through the desert of his throat.

"I must have swooned," she said unsteadily. "Again."

He nodded, not trusting his voice.

"Is Iversly here?"

He shook his head. His gaze traveled over her features, memorizing anew.

"Did he hurt you?"

"No." A flurry of emotion passed across her eyes— pleasure, doubt, then reticence.

Tip's heart lurched. What had Iversly done to her to leave her sprawled on the floor unconscious? Memory of his dream rapped at his senses, of Bea's body in his hands, her pleasure.

"What happened?" she asked. "Did it work? How is Aunt Julia?"

"Miss Minturn gave me the antidote. Your great-aunt has taken it and is already recovering."

Bea pushed herself to a sitting position.

"Oh, thank heavens. But how long have I been asleep?"

"Nearly three quarters of an hour."

Her eyes widened. "When did you return from the village?"

"Several minutes ago. She gave over remarkably quickly."

Bea stared at him.

"What did you—? What I mean to say is—"

"What did I do to effect her rapid acquiescence? I don't quite know." Her slender hand within his felt like an anchor to sanity. "She allowed me into her cottage with a great show of reluctance. I confronted her with the knowledge that she had poisoned Miss Dews, and . . ."

"And then what?"

"Then, I don't remember." He shook his head. "Moments, later it seemed, she gave me the bottle of antidote and professed her profoundest apologies for having done such a wicked deed. But as to what occurred until then, I don't know the words I spoke or the actions I took."

"You don't?" Her eyes were bright.

"Do you?"

Slowly, she nodded. Her cheeks flushed a delicate rose.

"Bea."

"Yes?"

"Did you . . . ?"

"Did I what?"

He scanned her face.

"Your cheeks are glowing. You look like—"

"Like what?"

He took a hard breath.

"Like you did in my bed two nights ago."

A small smile curved her lips.

"I do?"

Tip's hackles rose, his fist tightening around her hand.

"What did he do to you?"

"I don't believe he did anything. I know he did not, after a time."

"How do you know that?"

Her gaze remained direct.

"Don't you?"

As though scalded, he released her hand. It couldn't be. Only lunatics believed in such nonsense. But a sennight ago, Tip had not believed in ghosts. And he recalled her fast breaths, his hand caressing her tight womanhood as though he had been inside her minutes ago. He was hard now, wanting her.

"After I spoke with Miss Minturn"—he maintained an even voice with great effort—"upon my return here, I had the oddest memory."

"A memory?"

"Of a dream, in point of fact."

"A dream?"

He pulled air into his tight lungs. There was no way to

speak it aloud.

She glanced at their hands, separated now on the counterpane. Her brow seemed so determined.

"You are still angry with me," she said.

"I am not."

"You are. If not, you would speak your thoughts."

"Perhaps I am." The tight ball of unease in his chest could be nothing else. But it did not control him. Despite the tearful arguments and heated reconciliations, the passionate dreams and prickly disagreements, he wanted her with a certain, constant need that had nothing of drama or excess in it, only profound, utterly staggering honesty.

"Peter?"

"I dreamed of you, Bea."

Her lips parted on another smile. "I know."

A frantic knock sounded on the bedchamber door and it swung open.

"Milord." Peg curtsied swiftly. "Miss Beatrice," she whispered. "Your mother is coming."

Tip gritted his teeth. Bearing down upon his arousal, he stood and went to the window, turning his back. Behind him, Bea climbed from the bed, straightening her gown and smoothing her hair as Lady Marstowe's maid hurried to a chair and pulled needlework from a bag.

"Beatrice, are you in here?" Lady Harriet's limp voice carried though the door in advance of her person. Draped in flowing garments, she swept into the room in a flurry of perfumed elegance.

"We will not hold dinner again for you tonight, Beatrice. My lord, how do you do this evening? We haven't seen you all day. Have you been out riding again? I noticed your horse in the stable when we first arrived. He has such a beautiful bay coat, like pure satin, I told Alfred. A woman would pay money for hair like that, I daresay."

Tip's gaze slewed to Bea. Hers was downcast.

"Thank you, my lady," he replied.

"What on earth are you doing in my daughter's

bedchamber?" she asked without any evidence of interest. "Of course, you must be seeking out Lady Marstowe's maid for her," she gestured negligently toward the servant. "I hope Beatrice has not caused you nuisance?"

He could barely release his jaw sufficient to reply.

"Certainly not."

"Mama," Bea's head came up, beauty and quiet triumph radiating from her face. "Aunt Julia is well."

"She is? Well, that is to be celebrated, I suppose. Let us hope no one else takes the fever too. In fact, you are looking rather peaked tonight, Beatrice."

Bea turned to the mirror on the dressing table and a secret smile creased her lips.

"I think I look rather well, actually," she said softly as though to herself, then darted a heated glance at Tip that went straight to his cock.

"Put on some rouge before coming down," her mother said, "or your pasty cheeks will sour my stomach and ruin the meal for me."

"Yes, Mama." Her voice wavered. "I will change now and be down in a trice."

"No, no," Lady Harriet complained. "You will be too long and we will all end up eating cold food again. Come wearing what you have on now. No one will look at you anyway." She traipsed toward the door and held out her hand for Tip, smiling. "My lord, would you escort me to dinner?"

Tip looked to Bea.

"Miss Sinclaire?"

She shook her head.

He extended his arm to her mother. Lady Harriet started in on a steady stream of commentary about the damp castle, the cook's inadequate food, her useless servants, and the dismally misty climate. Bea followed in silence.

~o0o~

"Lady Bronwyn has gone to the village to comfort her old governess," Thomas announced when they entered the parlor after dinner. "It seems that Miss Minturn suffered a relapse of her recent illness this afternoon, just as Aunt Julia was coming out of her fever, in fact."

"Will Lady Bronwyn return tonight, Thomas?" Lady Harriet asked on a sigh.

"Not likely until tomorrow morning, Mama."

Bea's heady exuberance had ebbed to an agitated simmer but the relief in her brother's eyes acted like flint on her nerves.

"Is that so, Tom?" she asked. "Have you spoken with her?"

His gaze shot to her, confounded at first, then glowering.

Tip stood at the other end of the chamber, his expression still as severe as it had been all evening, a glass of spirits in his beautifully strong hand. Bea wished she could drink it. Spirits might serve to calm her fidgets.

What she really needed, though, was Peter Cheriot in the broom closet. For much longer than on the previous occasion. And with no arguing.

Although arguing with him was such a lovely pleasure. She had never quarreled with anyone else and now she recognized the gift of it. With him she was free to speak her mind. With him she felt fearless.

"Beatrice, have you had something to do with Lady Bronwyn's sudden disappearance?" Lady Harriet cast an irritated glance at her.

"Yes, Mama. I went to the village this afternoon and gave Miss Minturn an illness so that Lady Bronwyn would be obliged to care for her tonight rather than enjoy dinner with us."

Fearless.

Her heart raced. She darted a glance across the chamber. Tip's mouth curved up at the corner.

Bea's exhausted nerves tingled. He had dreamed of her. He would not marry her now. But he had dreamed of her while she felt him. It was . . . *extraordinary.*

"Beatrice," her father chastised, "You will not speak to your mother in that manner. What are you thinking, daughter?"

"Oh," she said, her voice quavering a bit. "Nothing, I daresay."

"I daresay." Lady Harriet fluttered a fan over her face. "You are ungrateful. All those years I kept you in town, searching futilely for a husband, and this is the thanks I get for it?"

Bea's giddiness abruptly clumped together. She bit the inside of her lip.

"I am sorry, Mama."

"Well you should be," Lady Harriet sighed.

"Beatrice, I have given the matter some thought of late," her father said, moving toward her. "I posted a letter concerning it this afternoon."

"What matter, Papa?"

"Lady Bronwyn has not yet had her come-out season in London."

"She is young yet. Eighteen, I believe," Bea said uncertainly.

"She ought to have a season to give her some exposure to the world she will live in as a member of our family."

Bea glanced at her brother. His eyes were wide as horseshoes. He shook his head back and forth quickly.

"That seems like a fine idea, Papa," Bea murmured.

"Her father, Lord Prescot, is an aging recluse without a female relation in London. So I have taken the liberty of writing Prescot to tell him that before the wedding we will bring out Lady Bronwyn. He must fund her wardrobe and pin money, of course, and a ball that we shall host. But we will take care of the rest."

"How delightful, Alfred." Lady Harriet sat up straighter than Bea had seen her sit in years. "When shall we go? Now? Or will we await the spring, when everyone is in town? How diverting it will be to have new gowns suitable for London entertainments again. You cannot know how trying it is to be confined to poor country amusements. Why, the other day,

Mrs. Smythe was wearing a chartreuse pelisse. Can you imagine that? Chartreuse? This year!"

"You, ma'am," Bea's father said, "will not be attending us in town. Beatrice will serve as chaperone to the girl. Since Thomas and Lady Bronwyn are formally betrothed, this will not seem unusual."

The blood drained from Bea's cheeks.

"But, Papa—"

"Now, I don't wish to hear a word of it, daughter. You must help your brother in this matter. You will have all the new gowns and other gewgaws you require to suit your station," he said with a wave of his hand. "I will hire a house and be in residence with you both there throughout the season."

"Papa, I am hardly fit—"

"Alfred, this is absolutely horrid of you." Lady Harriet leaped up. Tears trembled in her pale lashes. "I cannot fathom why you are sending Beatrice rather than your own wife. Who does she know to introduce our future daughter-in-law to?"

"She can begin with your sister. Audrey would be glad to introduce Lady Bronwyn to her friends, as she did when Georgie lived with her."

"I cannot abide Audrey." Bea's mother sniffed. "She is bookish."

"That is another reason I have chosen Beatrice for this task. She will not get in anyone's way and Lady Bronwyn will have her season as a pretty girl like her should."

"Papa." A lump of shame burned in Bea's breast. "I do not think that—"

"Beatrice, I have decided."

"He has decided," Lady Harriet pronounced in airy accents. "We must all bow to his high-handed ways. Oh, how could I be so unlucky to have a daughter who would betray me in this manner?"

"I am not betraying you, Mama," Bea said tightly. "Papa—"

"I will hear no more of it, Beatrice."

"But, Papa, I am only twenty-three," she forced through

cold lips, her hands trembling.

"Ladies four and five years your junior act as chaperones to younger girls. It is the least you can do."

"But, Papa, *I* am not married."

Chapter Twenty-three

"What does that signify?" her father said. "Plenty of ladies' companions are unmarried."

"Companions?" she uttered, but all the air had gone from her lungs.

"You will do as you are told, daughter."

"Alfred," Lady Marstowe's voice cut across the parlor from the doorway. "You are a fool. Beatrice, come with me." She snapped her fingers.

Bea went to her great-aunt. She could not bear to look at Tip.

"Julia wishes to speak with you before she retires," the dowager said.

"Of course." She sank her clenched hands in her skirts and followed her from the room.

"I was under the impression, Beatrice, that you are soon to be wed. Was I mistaken?"

"Aunt Grace, I cannot discuss this now. May I please go to Aunt Julia?"

The dowager fixed her with a firm stare then allowed Bea to precede her up the stairs. In the bedchamber lit with many candles, Aunt Julia was propped up in bed looking as healthy as ever.

"Beatrice, come closer." Julia's hazel eyes sparkled as Bea sat at her side. "How lovely you are this evening. Isn't she lovely?"

"Always," Tip said at the open doorway.

"Peter dear, do come in. I wish to speak with you both." She grasped Bea's hand and winked. "I don't mind a gentleman in my quarters every now and again, do you?"

Bea met Tip's gaze. He seemed pensive.

"I wish to thank you both for what you did for me this evening," Aunt Julia said with a cheerful smile. "I spoke with Rhys, and I know it must have been very trying, especially for you, dear Beatrice."

"Lord Iversly came to see you?"

"Yes, dear. In private. He does not feel up to much company at this time, I am afraid."

"Is he very unhappy?"

"He is searching for a companion, I daresay. A mate for his soul."

"A man should be allowed that, at the very least." Tip said in a peculiar, deep voice.

His words hung in the silence. Bea's insides felt hollow. He looked so severe again, his eyes indifferent.

"And yet," Julia said, her curious gaze still resting on Bea, "I am under the impression that he does not believe he deserves happiness."

Bea took a steadying breath.

"If Lord Iversly cannot accomplish this for himself, perhaps we should."

"That is a capital idea." Aunt Julia clapped her hands.

"What on earth are you suggesting, Beatrice?" the dowager asked.

"Gracie, I am trapped in the castle until this silly curse is lifted, of course. Why don't we remain here and help Iversly find his soul mate? It would be great good fun, and the poor dear ghost deserves it after all these centuries."

Lady Marstowe pinned Julia with an astonished stare.

"Julia, have you lost your mind?"

"No, that is our sister, Petunia, of course," Julia said with a cock-eyed twinkle of pure lucidity.

"You would remain here willingly?" Bea said. "Indefinitely?"

"Would you like to stay, too, dear? There is plenty of space, I daresay, and I don't believe Bronwyn's grandmother would object to a bit more company. She is such a retiring lady, of course."

"Well, I—"

"Lord Cheriot," Lady Marstowe said, "is my great-niece betrothed to you, or not?"

Bea's breaths froze.

Not a flicker of emotion showed on his handsome face.

"She is not."

The dowager's nostrils flared.

"I am fully willing to inform Beatrice's father as to the necessity of it."

Bea leaped to her feet, her heart pounding.

"Don't, Aunt Grace. Please." She wanted him, but her head was a muddle, and she could not have him like this. Aunt Grace's ice-blue eyes might as well be the barrel of a pistol. But if anyone were going to force him into marrying her, it would be herself.

"My lord?" Lady Marstowe asked.

Tip stood like stone.

"As she wishes." He could not sound more unmoved. Bea's courage wavered.

"Beatrice, you are being pigheaded and unwise. Both of you are," the dowager stated. "I do not intend to allow you choice in this matter."

"It has been an exhausting day." Bea hurried to the door. "I am tired. I am going to bed and will speak with you all in the morning." With trembling hands she turned the handle and slipped out.

Tip came after her.

"Bea—"

"First Thomas, then Papa and Mama, and now . . ." She bit her lip. "This is all unspeakably horrid."

"Which part? The part in which you willingly accept your fate as others have laid it out for you? Or the part in which you act contrary to what you know to be right?"

Her throat thickened. She ached to touch him and renew the mystery of bewildering intimacy they had shared hours earlier, to carry it straight into his heart.

Throwing prudence to the wind, she laid her palm upon his chest. His heart beat steady and swift. She spread her fingers and shifted her hand beneath his coat to feel more. He was warm and hard and *perfect*.

Tip grabbed her wrist.

"What are you doing?" His voice sounded rough.

"Do you know, earlier tonight," she whispered, "what happened to me, it was like nothing I have ever experienced before." She lifted her gaze. "Except with you."

His eyes shone. He wrapped his hand around the back of her head and dragged her to him. His mouth came down upon hers firm and open, his hands circling her face, sinking into her hair as he pressed her against the wall. He kissed her deep, hard, and wonderfully.

She clutched his shoulders and drank him in, trapped between solid man and her own liquid heart. Her palms slid down his chest, adoring him. She would never weary of touching him, not even when they were old and gray and barely able to totter around. The sensation of his heartbeats beneath her fingertips would always move her.

She should tell him now that she was sorry she had prodded him to cry off. She should end this foolishness and have the man of her dreams who desired her and cared for her. But she couldn't. Now more than ever, she knew she did not deserve that happiness.

Not yet.

"No." She shoved him away, pressing the back of her shaking hand to her mouth. "I will not marry you under these circumstances."

"These circumstances?" His breathing was uneven. "What circumstances are those, Miss Sinclaire? That I have not, in fact, asked you to marry me lately? Or that you cannot keep your hands off me? Or—"

"Go away, Peter." She slid from between him and the wall, sidestepping out of his reach. "Go to the village or some other place, and don't come back until tomorrow. I am excessively fatigued and cannot quarrel with you at present. But, frankly, if you remain here I don't believe I can withstand you, either."

He stared. "You are excessively fatigued?"

She nodded.

"And cannot quarrel with me?"

She bit both her lips.

"Beatrice Sinclaire, you are a strange and impossible woman."

"I *know*. The trouble is that no one has ever recognized that but you!" She whirled around and ran for her room.

She locked the door. This dramatic gesture did not, however, guarantee a restful night. She lay awake staring at the canopy atop her bed, her heart beating wildly at the memory of Tip's kiss and his outraged eyes, his wonderful words and everything between them, everything she had done wrong, and right, and had yet to do.

When she finally arose near dawn, her eyes were heavy with dark circles beneath them and her cheeks as pasty as her mother said. She dressed and descended to the breakfast parlor, but not even the servants stirred yet. Leaving the fortress, she went silently across the mist-shrouded courtyard, making her way toward the rear garden path.

She walked and thought and imagined until the cold Welsh morning eventually drove her inside again. Smoothing the mist off her cloak, she made her way into the breakfast chamber.

Everyone was present except Tip. Bronwyn was absent as well, no doubt still at the village with her governess. Aunt Julia enjoyed a bowl of porridge and jam, her elbow entrenched in a puddle of butter.

"Oh, are you awake this early, Beatrice?" Bea's mother asked with a lift of her pencil-thin brow. "How unusual for you of late. Lady Bronwyn keeps her servants to shockingly early hours. But this is the wretched countryside, after all."

Bea went to the sideboard to collect a muffin and tea.

"Beatrice," her father said, "have you given any further consideration to your poor attitude last evening?"

Bea took a slow breath.

"No, Papa, I have not." She set down her plate, a tinny sensation running through her blood, thinner and colder than her heady excitement the night before, but clear and thoroughly focused. "I believe I was entirely in the right of it."

"In the right of it?" His brow darkened.

She folded her hands.

"Thomas and Lady Bronwyn do not wish to marry."

Thunderous silence met her statement. She forged on, energy replacing the chill with each word. "Thomas's infatuation with her has cooled, and Lady Bronwyn, it seems, would prefer a titled gentleman."

"Thomas, my wayward son!" Lady Harriet exclaimed. "Your father has already sent his letter to Lord Prescot. Tell me your sister is spewing untruths."

"Why, Mama?" Bea asked. *Fearless, fearless.* "Only yesterday you complained that Bronwyn was not a suitable match for my brother. Have you altered your opinion on the matter so swiftly?"

"Insolent girl," her mother grumbled. "You are jealous of your brother's success and have intentionally botched this betrothal, haven't you?"

Bea's mouth fell open.

"Jealous? Of Thomas's happiness? I wish him nothing but."

"You are guaranteeing that right and tight then, aren't you?" Thomas shot her a glare, crossing his arms.

Heat ran up Bea's spine.

"What on earth are you talking about, Tom? You would rather marry the wrong woman than risk Mama and Papa's displeasure?"

"I would have done it my way," Thomas grumbled.

"How is that? After you are already married to her? Let me tell you something, that lovely girl you set your sights on just over a fortnight ago will not wait patiently to see the day." She balled her quivering fists. "Thomas, this is the last scrape I am wresting you from, and you should thank me for it. From now on, you are on your own."

"Beatrice, you have certainly done this, and your brother will suffer for it."

"I beg your pardon, Mama, but I simply cannot see how I am to blame for Thomas and Lady Bronwyn determining they will not suit," she said, her teeth clenched so hard they squeaked. "And that is another thing. Just because I did not hang out for every gentleman who crossed our drawing room threshold does not mean I had an aversion to finding a suitable husband."

Lady Harriet sniffed.

"You never showed interest in any of them," she said.

"I did. Some of them were quite nice. But I had little opportunity to discover whether they would suit. You chased them all away with your whining and complaining so effectively, I never knew. Then you took me out of society at precisely the moment I was beginning to feel comfortable in it, cutting me off from my friends in order to spend time with yours and making so many demands on me that it was nearly impossible to go out simply for diversion."

Her mother waved that away with a languid hand.

"You would never have accepted any of them if they had continued calling."

"That is true. I might not have." Most assuredly not, with her heart lodged securely in Peter Cheriot. "But that hardly signifies. At least I might have enjoyed better company than your gossiping friends. I should have adored living with Aunt Audrey, even visiting her on occasion." She turned to her father. "Why didn't you consider that for me, Papa? Why only when it came to bringing out Lady Bronwyn did it cross your mind? Didn't you think me fit to enjoy my seasons as well? You gave Georgie that consideration when she went down to town. Why not me?"

"Your aunt does not approve of your brother. You know that, Beatrice. You would not have been able to keep an eye on him from Audrey's house."

"How is it that I became my brother's keeper? Perhaps when we were children and we shared the schoolroom it might have made sense. But Thomas is a grown man now, Papa. To expect him to take instruction from a sister who has seen considerably less of the world than he has is ludicrous." She let that sink in. "And it is unfair to me, as well."

"Beatrice, what has gotten into you?" Her father stood.

"Myself, I think."

"You are a selfish girl." Lady Harriet sighed. "Alfred, tell your impertinent daughter that she is wretchedly selfish."

"Selfish to meekly rusticate to the country because you drove Papa to distraction in town?" Bea said, calm conviction filling her. "Furthermore," she looked to her father, "Mama does not need me at home. She needs you, her husband. You want me to be there so that you are not obliged to feel guilty about not being there. But acting as your substitute is not my life's ambition. I never wanted the position, and I only did it from duty to both of you. For too many years. As of now, I will no longer be filling that role."

Bea's father stared, eyes wide.

"What else would you do?" her mother said petulantly. "Go to live with your sister in Ireland? I daresay she would be happy to have you there to care for the children, at the very least."

"I have no doubt Georgie and Kievan would welcome me into their home, as a friend rather than an unpaid servant, of course. But I do not intend to go there." She gulped in air. Sometime during her tirade Tip had appeared at the doorway. She felt his presence like a wind strengthening her flame. Certainty filled her lungs and sang in her blood. "Lord Cheriot has asked for my hand, and I have accepted."

~o0o~

December 29, 1814

Today I made the acquaintance of Mr. Peter Cheriot. He is kind, clever, and well-natured, and when we speak he looks at me as though he is actually listening to my words.

He is also very handsome. Mama says handsome men are a woman's curse. But Mr. Cheriot seems handsome on the inside as well. Cousin Mirabella was excessively peevish due to the weather, and he spent an hour with her counting snowflakes on the window to distract her. She is not yet eleven, although he must be nineteen at least.

Mama also says I haven't the knack of flirting with gentlemen and will be a dismal failure during my first season in society. But Mr. Cheriot seemed perfectly happy to talk with me. He is very amiable.

Diary, when he looks at me, my insides grow warm in the oddest manner. I cannot explain it. I would say it was love at first sight, but I do not believe in such a thing.

Rather, I did not. Until perhaps today.

~o0o~

Chapter Twenty-four

Her parents gaped.

"Beatrice, how *could* you?" her mother exclaimed.

"I don't have any idea what you mean, Mama. And I could very well, thank you."

Her father cleared his throat.

"You might have asked me first, Cheriot."

"And you, Beatrice," Lady Harriet whined, "are an ungrateful girl not to have asked me first."

"As I understand it," Tip said, his voice perfectly even, "your other daughters' suitors did not ask your permission to pay their addresses. Nor did the ladies themselves require your leave to marry. Why should your youngest daughter be held to a different standard?"

Bea's breath left her. Could it be? Had he not asked them because he respected her—worlds more than her parents ever had—and he wished her to know it, even years ago? Bea's heart filled with gratitude. Sizzling anticipation curled around it. He was not denying their betrothal.

"Be that as it may," her father said gruffly, "someone must look after Thomas and Lady Harriet."

"As head of your family, sir, I should think that would be your duty."

"You listen here, young man. You may hold a title, but I will not stand for Richard Cheriot's son, of all people, telling me what my duty to my family ought to be."

"Papa, cease," Bea said. "He does not deserve your censure, and it is me that you truly wish to chastise. So go ahead. Do so and be done with it, because this is your last opportunity. After this, you will have my deaf ear, I assure you."

"You thankless girl," her mother muttered.

Bea turned a level gaze upon her.

"You, too, Mama. Have your say now. I will not be available for more forthwith."

The lady's mouth opened and closed like a fish.

"Harriet," Lady Marstowe intoned. "Julia and I will not be returning to Hart House at this time. Instead, she and I, *and you*, will remain here after the others have departed."

The crystal blue eyes went wide.

"Me? Whatever can you mean to say, Aunt Grace?"

"That you are a spoiled, overindulged child, and it is about time you looked after someone else for a change. Lady Bronwyn's grandmother requires more attention than the chit is willing to pay her, and as Julia and I are past our prime we cannot do it alone." She cast Bea a shrewd look. "Perhaps Beatrice might recommend some methods for caring for an invalid."

Bea smiled. She glanced at Tip. He seemed to be studying the shine on the toes of his top boots. Her heart tightened. Could he be unhappy about what she had done?

"Alfred, tell her I will not do it," her mother insisted.

"No, Harriet. It will do you good to spend a minute or two each day thinking of someone other than yourself." His gaze shifted back to Bea, troubled. He opened his mouth as though to speak.

"I think I shall have a stroll in the garden," Aunt Julia said brightly, standing. "Gracie, Beatrice, I would be so happy to have your company." She turned her twinkling eyes on Tip. "And dear Peter, too, of course."

"Ma'am." He smiled and bowed.

Spent exhilaration was washing through Bea. She felt drained and wonderful. Almost courageous enough to face him alone.

"May I come along?" Thomas asked hesitantly.

Their mother's mouth pouted.

"You are a faithless boy, Thomas. I always knew that."

"Oh hush, Mama." He came to Bea's side and offered his arm.

He had not done such a thing in years. Not even during those endless nights at balls and assemblies her first season in London, when she had known so few people and often stood alone awaiting a partner, had Thomas acted the gallant escort to her.

But Tip had. Whenever he had been present at a party or ball he had sought her out, teased and talked with her, made her feel comfortable. He had even introduced her to his friends, always gracious and solicitous. It had never bothered her that those eligible bachelors invariably disappeared into the ether as soon as they paid her a few calls. She only ever had eyes for one gentleman.

He still had not looked at her. She watched covertly as he took Aunt Julia's arm and led her from the breakfast parlor.

"Bea," her brother said as they moved through the courtyard toward the rear gate. The sun had climbed high enough to dissipate the mists, and the grass was nearly dry. Bea's slippers were already a soggy mess from earlier. But she didn't mind it. She walked five feet off the ground.

"I'm deuced sorry I've been so wretchedly addlepated," Thomas mumbled. "Will you forgive me?"

"Probably, but only after many years."

His gaze cut to hers, then relaxed with a great show of relief.

"You are gammoning me. My sister," he squeezed her hand in his elbow. "I don't know what I would ever do without you."

"Well you must become accustomed to it, Tom. I was perfectly serious when I said I am finished saving you from your mistakes."

"I know it, and I'm damned jelly-legged to do it alone, I'll admit, Bea. I depend upon you."

She blinked rapidly.

"You have never said such a thing to me before."

His brow beetled.

"I may not have said it, but it's the truth." He quirked a rueful smile. "I wouldn't be half the man I am if it weren't for you. The better half," he added on a chuckle.

"Thank you, Tom."

He did not leave her side for the remainder of the promenade, keeping her hand tucked on his arm and helping her over rough spots in the ground. Bea wished she had the heart to tell him to run off like he usually did. But as minutes passed into an hour, she began to despair of ever having the opportunity to be with Tip in private.

When they reached the house, her brother squeezed her fingers yet again.

"I'm off to the cottage to speak with Lady Bronwyn then."

"What will you say to her?"

His chest expanded on a deep breath.

"I'll leave it up to her to decide, I suppose. It's the gentlemanly thing to do." He shrugged. Bea patted his hand. He tipped his hat and headed toward the stable.

Heart climbing to her throat again, she turned toward her great-aunts and Tip approaching up the path.

"What a lovely outing. I feel entirely myself again," Aunt Julia said. "Where is Thomas going, Beatrice dear? To see that pretty girl, no doubt. Poor thing. He never knew what was coming from that direction, did he?"

Bea could not prevent herself from looking at Tip. He was smiling slightly at Aunt Julia. Would he avoid looking at her for the remainder of the day?

"Beatrice?" Her father stood in the doorway to the keep. "I would like to speak with you for a moment." His gaze shifted to a point over her shoulder. "I have at least a few more weeks to demand a father's prerogative," he added in a firmer voice.

Bea looked behind her. Tip stood close, his stance unmistakably protective. Her stomach somersaulted.

She ought to have expected it of him, of course, after the broom closet.

"All right, Papa." She followed him toward the parlor,

struggling not to glance back to see if Tip watched her go.

Her father closed the door and turned to her, his shoulders heavy.

"Daughter, I owe you an apology."

Bea's jaw loosened; she was not fool enough to let it drop. "Papa?"

"I have underestimated you." He seemed remarkably uncomfortable. "I never imagined you had it in you to defy your mother, and certainly not me."

"I am not defiant by nature, Papa. Only determined."

"I never knew that."

"I didn't either, until recently."

"And you are happy with this match with Cheriot?"

"Why shouldn't I be?"

"Your mother always told me how tame he ran around the place, like a brother. I noticed it myself when I could still bear to reside in—" He seemed to recall himself. "He is certainly well set up, but a man's situation in society does not always suffice for the ladies, I realize. I know what it is like to be in a marriage where the partners are not suited to each other. I don't want you marrying yourself off to someone you cannot care for simply to get clear of your mother."

"I am not, Papa." Bea's voice was not as stable as she liked.

"Because if you'd rather not, I will write to your aunt Audrey. I suspect she would be glad to have you live with them in town."

"Thank you, Papa. I am content with the situation as it is." Entirely. *Anxiously.*

"You are a good girl, Beatrice." He patted her on the cheek. "Perhaps too good for your own good."

He walked from the chamber stiffly. She had never seen him so discomposed, not even when he learned that Kievan had returned from Ireland to finally claim Georgie, and Georgie was his favorite.

Bea's gaze strayed to her embroidery bag, forgotten beside a chair days earlier. Her hands still shook a little, and she felt astoundingly light-headed. She could spend some time in quiet reflection with her needlework and rally her nerves before seeing others again. Or she could go find Peter Cheriot.

She marched toward the door.

He was leaning against the corridor wall, one foot propped against the stone, hands in his pockets. He drew them out and pushed away from the wall.

"I was just coming to find you," she said. Best to tackle the bull head-on. She hadn't an ounce of energy left after her morning's tacklings, but his enigmatic smile made nerves dance around in her belly.

"Lady Bronwyn's grandmother has come forth from her chambers and called luncheon in the dining room. Shall we?" He gestured her forward.

Bea went and he fell in beside her.

"That was an impressive show in there earlier," he said quietly.

"It was not a show. It was real."

"Good. Congratulations."

"Thank you."

"So you think to force my hand?"

Not trusting her exhausted tongue to behave, she nodded.

He glanced aside at her.

"I seem to recall at least twice vowing—out loud to you on both occasions—that I would not renew my suit."

"You needn't," she said. "I already have."

"Yes. Rather publicly."

Her stomach twisted.

"What will you do if I refuse to honor this one-sided agreement?" he said. "Return to your mother's home?"

"I would go to Georgie and Kievan in Ireland, or Aunt Audrey in London. Or"—she paused—"I could hire myself out as a governess. Then perhaps when I retire I might return here and learn witchcraft from Miss Minturn. I understand it is useful to know when one is crossed by a ghost, or some such thing."

Tip's eyes glimmered.

"Then when I am gone and done for," he said, "I will be certain to haunt this castle."

They halted before the dining chamber door. He reached for the handle. Steeling herself, she laid a hand upon his arm, staying him.

"I always thought you never asked my parents for permission to address me because you lacked sincerity."

His features sobered again. He shook his head.

"Thank you for your confidence in me, Peter. You are the best friend I have ever had."

He offered her a beautiful smile.

"I wondered if you would ever notice that." He pulled open the door and ushered her within.

Chapter Twenty-five

Lady Bronwyn returned to the castle after luncheon. She came to Bea tentatively, grasped her hand, and her pretty face was full of contrition.

"I am very happy for you, Beatrice," she said in subdued tones.

"Am I to wish you felicitations as well?"

"Your brother and I have decided on a long, private betrothal. We would like to become better acquainted first, to determine if we suit." Her grip tightened.

"How is Miss Minturn?"

"Oh, she is miserable." Bronwyn's gaze relaxed. "I had no idea she harbored such passions. Will Miss Dews seek out the magistrate?"

"I don't believe so. What magistrate would believe the story?"

"Thomas told me that your parents have no idea of Lord Iversly at all. My father did not believe it, either, although I wrote him countless letters."

"I understand he is something of a recluse."

"Oh, yes. And very old. My mama was his fourth wife."

For a recluse, Lord Prescot had been a busy man.

"Bronwyn, would you like a season in London?"

Bronwyn's eyes lit. "Oh, it is my fondest wish. But it is unlikely, I'm afraid."

Perhaps if she saw what a prize her betrothed was, she would not be so hesitant about him. Or, perhaps during their time in London together, Thomas and Bronwyn would realize they should in fact not wed.

"If Lord Cheriot does not object, I would be glad to bring

you out," and take Bronwyn to all the fashionable venues Bea's mother had neglected to take her to after those first few months, with Aunt Audrey to assist.

"Oh, Beatrice, you are exceedingly kind. Especially after—" Her cheeks colored up. "I am excessively mortified. I had no idea."

"No one did."

"That must have been very difficult for you."

Bea smiled and glanced across the chamber to Tip. His emerald gaze rested on her.

"No," she said, a flutter of nerves in her belly. "Not really."

~o0o~

Thomas suggested they all go for a ride. Aunt Julia remained happily in the castle. Casting her husband resentful peeks, Lady Harriet said she would stay in as well. But Aunt Grace agreed to the venture, and Bea's father enlisted his groom to fit up the old gig tucked away in the stable.

Because of the gig, the going proved slow along barely tracked roads and paths, but pleasant. The hills were bright green, straggling with mists, dotted with wooly white denizens, and tangled with copses of mottled trees. Tip made no effort to speak with Bea in particular, and said nothing to her that could not be heard by everyone.

By the end of the ride, Bea's head swam with bewildered exhaustion. After everything they had been through, he seemed perfectly at ease and just as always before—friendly, kind, laughing, and entirely unsatisfying to her hungry heart. She should feel like a fool for expecting something else from him, but her body still tingled each time he looked at her.

When they returned home, she went to her bedchamber and in weary relief fell soundly asleep.

She awoke to evening's gray peeking through the draperies and a knock on her door. She dragged herself from bed.

Her mother swished into the room, a vision in saffron taffeta trimmed with silk flowers.

"Beatrice, your father has commanded dinner at half past the hour. I have come to make you presentable."

This was a turnabout. Bea rubbed the sleep from her eyes. "Thank you, Mama."

"Do not thank me." Her mother dug into the traveling trunk. "It is the least I can do."

"Mama, you needn't—"

"No, I needn't." She drew forth a gown. "But you are to be a grand lady now, a baroness, and I will not have you believing your own mother an ungrateful puss." She swiveled around. "How will this one do? It suits your complexion nicely. I do not recall it. When did you purchase it?"

"I had the shop in York make it up last spring." She paused. "Mama, I don't hold a grudge."

"Then you are a better person than I, Beatrice, for I certainly would. But you deserve happiness now." A tear sparkled at the edge of her crystal eye. She held the dress forward, assessing it approvingly. "He will not be able to take his eyes off you in this."

~o0o~

Apparently he could not. It disconcerted Bea nearly more than anything had as yet. He said almost nothing to her throughout dinner and afterward in the parlor while everyone took tea, but he watched her as she never recalled him watching her before, his eyes unreadable. Bea found it extraordinarily difficult to eat. The longer it continued, the more her nerves jittered.

"Well I'm done up for the night," Thomas declared, setting down his empty port glass. "Mama, may I see you up?"

Lady Harriet glanced at her husband, a curious expression on her face.

"No, Thomas. I believe I would like your father to have

the honor." She stood and extended her hand. Bea's father rose and took it upon his arm, and they left the room.

Lady Bronwyn looked shyly at Thomas.

"Mr. Sinclaire, would you see me up? I would like to say good night to my grandmother before retiring."

Thomas bowed neatly, his gracious smile tickling Bea with pride. Perhaps the girl would make a man of him, after all. Or else they would come to despise each other.

She glanced at her great-aunts. Julia's head had fallen back upon the sofa. The dowager nudged her awake.

"Come, Julia. To bed. Lord Cheriot, Beatrice, see us to our chamber."

Tip went forward and took Julia's arm. She blinked, smiled cheerily, and patted his hand.

"Thank you, dear Peter. What a remarkable day it has been."

"A remarkable sennight, forsooth." Iversly's voice sounded through the chamber. Aunt Julia's attention went to the window.

"Good evening, Rhys. Are you turning in as well?"

"Perpetually, my lady."

Aunt Julia chuckled.

"Good night, Iversly." The dowager gestured her sister and the baron forward.

Bea paused. At the door, Tip cast her a glance, then went out.

"Lord Iversly," she said, "I wish to thank you for what you have done for me."

"You have what you desire now," he said without inflection.

"Well, partially, at least."

"Ah, but I believe you will find that you have more than you could have ever dreamed, my dear."

The knot of nerves in Bea's belly tightened.

"What of you, my lord? Will you ever find your dream?"

Silence met her, vacant and chill in the fire-warmed parlor. Bea waited, but nothing came, and she knew she was alone.

She climbed the stairs and walked the corridor to her bedchamber in a pensive humor. She grasped the handle but did not turn it.

Iversly was willing, even eager, to live eternally without hope of love. And Thomas seemed happy to wait indefinitely to learn if he and his betrothed would rub along well together. But Bea's blood still ran with impatient need.

She did not wish to wait months or years to know if Tip could love her. Her daring might never be higher than now, after finally telling off her family. She might as well learn the truth right away. At least then she would know what to expect from her marriage.

"Planning on spending the night here in the corridor?" Tip's voice came at her shoulder.

She spun around.

Being betrothed to him, this time publicly, permanently, did not make it any easier to stand close to him without losing her breath. A lock of dark hair fell over his brow, his jaw was ever so slightly shadowed with whiskers, and his eyes sparkled.

"I was th-thinking."

"And stammering again, apparently." He reached up and tucked a few errant strands of her hair behind her ear. His fingertips lingered on her neck. "What seems to be the trouble now? Has Iversly discomposed you?"

She shook her head, swallowing around the lump of wavering courage lodged in her throat.

"Not Iversly?" he asked, moving closer. A breath of air separated them. Bea had to bend her neck to hold his gaze.

"Not *him*." She curled her fingers around his lapel, turned the door handle, and pulled him into her bedchamber.

Tip caught her up in one arm, pushing the door shut.

"What's this? Have *I* caused sensible, practical Miss Beatrice Sinclaire to become overset?" He smiled, and heaven descended for Bea.

"Always," she breathed and drew his face down to kiss.

He dragged her tight against his body.

Given the half hour it had taken her mother to button her

into her garments, Bea's clothing came off with remarkable speed. But Tip seemed intent, his fingers on the hooks and laces certain. Her stays, shift, and stockings joined petticoat and gown on the floor.

He took in a heavy breath, tangled his hands in her hair, and covered her mouth with his. He kissed her with a hunger Bea had not dared to imagine. She tore at his coat and cravat, needing to feel his warm skin beneath her hands. He yanked his shirt over his head and pulled her into his arms again.

She fumbled with the buttons on his trousers, caressing his arousal beneath the fabric in tentative strokes. Tip sighed deeply, his hand covered hers, then he helped her divest him of the garment. Bea sought his hard satiny length, heat spreading inside her in anticipation.

He swept her up and deposited her on the bed.

For a moment he stood still, his gaze scanning her from toe to brow, and Bea thought she would die with delirious happiness. Heat prickled behind her eyes, so intense she sucked in breath to hold her emotions at bay. He joined her on the mattress, lowering himself between her thighs, and he brought his body intimately against hers.

He took her face between his hands.

"Beatrice Sinclaire," he whispered huskily, "you are beautiful."

She choked down a sob of overflowing joy, shifting beneath him to feel him more, reveling in his words and the caress of his body. He lowered his mouth to hers, and she kissed him. Whatever this was that he was giving her, whether love or merely friendship laced with beautiful passion, she could accept it. She would take anything he had to offer if it felt like this forever.

Her hands clutching his shoulders trembled and her breaths were labored as he kissed a line of perfect pleasure along her throat to her neck. Tears trembled at the corners of her eyes, then spilled out, marking twin tracks into her hair. She willed them away, praying he would not notice, but another sob shook her.

"What is it?" he murmured against her shoulder, a smile in his voice.

The intimate whisper only caused the tears to flow more heavily. She bit down on her lip in agony. He simply must not see her like this. But try as she might, the stream of tears only worsened.

Tip lifted his head. His eyes darkened with dismay.

"You are not laughing." He pushed back onto his elbows. "Oh, no. *No.* Don't, Bea, please. I knew it was too—I should have waited until after we wed. But then you seemed to want—Dear God, please don't cry." He pulled away and sat up on the side of the bed.

She pushed to a sitting position and reached for his arm. The sensation of his hot skin over firm muscle caught her breath.

"I did want to. I do. I'm so sorry." She hiccupped a staggered sniffle and sucked in a big breath. "I cannot seem to prevent it. I am just so filled with—with everything. I-I know I am stammering, but I feel as though I've sprouted wings, or perhaps only found those I always folded up tight before."

"Wings?" Through her tears, he looked confused.

"When I left Mama at Hart House to come here," she hurried to explain, "I was so excited for an adventure. But I discovered more than an adventure here. I discovered that I do not want to go back to being good, practical, sensible, obedient, wretched Beatrice. Ever! I want to be free. Not just here at the castle for a few days. Always."

"Free?" His jaw went taut, his shoulders rigid. "Don't even think of refusing to marry me again, Bea. It is far too late for that."

"No, of course not," she exclaimed, but the expression in his eyes was so strange. "It is only that I—" The tears began again, dribbling down her cheeks and dripping off her jaw.

"Dear God, this is a nightmare," he said in a thick voice, running a hand through his hair. "I want you so much it makes me crazy sometimes—nearly all the time. It used to be that making love to you was the only thing I could think about.

Now, more than anything, what I want most is to make you happy. I thought perhaps you felt the same. But if this is how it will be, I cannot do this to you. It's impossible."

"It doesn't have to be this way," she said through the tears, her heart singing from his beautiful words. Perfect words. Words she had never dreamed he would say. "I won't always cry, and you did—you do— What I mean to say is—"

"No. This was a mistake. I will go." He stood and moved across the chamber toward his clothing, hastily pulling on his trousers.

"Don't you dare leave, Peter Cheriot!" She leaped off the bed, grabbing up her wrapper and holding it tight against her— for protection or comfort she didn't know.

"Let me go, Bea," he said, his voice hoarse. "Then you will stop crying and tomorrow after we've both had some sleep we can sit down and calmly talk about how we are going to arrange this." He swallowed jerkily.

"I do not wish to sleep, and I do not wish to arrange it. No! Listen to me, for pity's sake."

"Your tears tell me everything I need to know."

"Curse my wretched tears. I'm crying because I am happy!"

Tip went absolutely still. But his eyes grew more fevered yet. Panicked. "Happy?"

"Yes, I am happy. And I cannot bring myself to believe you actually wish to marry me. Every time I think of it, I know I must be dreaming. Then, when you hold me, I feel as though—as though— I feel *heaven*." The floodgates of Bea's eyes opened wide now. Her heart poured through them.

"You are happy." It was a statement, uttered low and unsteadily.

She nodded.

He walked to her, grasped her arms tight, and swept her into a kiss that left her struggling for air and clinging to him. His mouth moved along her jaw, then lower, ravenous, and his arms encircled her, pulling her against him. She welcomed his caresses, sinking her fingers into his hair and sighing her pleasure through her soggy throat.

He pressed his lips beneath her ear, his hands gripping her close.

"I am lost, Bea." His voice was a ragged whisper. "Flooded with you."

"What?" The word stumbled between her lips.

"I need you like air." He pulled back, his eyes awash in bewilderment. "Even more so since you discovered your wings. I wanted you before, but since we came here, each time the spark of excitement lights your eyes, I want you more until I cannot see, can barely breathe unless I hear you, touch you. I tried to control it, to deny it. I even left here on the pretense that I could withstand it. But it was futile. You hold me in your hands. I am yours to do with as you will."

He wanted her, but he did not *want* to want her? His anguished eyes showed it so clearly. And it explained so much—his kisses, his anger, his proposals and retractions.

"I am sorry," she said upon a choke, swiping her knuckles across her damp cheek. "Perhaps it will pass. I mean to say, perhaps your strong feelings have arisen from this rather intense situation here, the castle, the danger, and the intimacies we have shared."

"I should say so. But only to strengthen what already existed."

"Already existed?" She clutched the dressing gown to her breasts. "I don't understand."

He stared at her for an endless moment, astonishment dawning upon his handsome face.

"Good Lord, Bea," he uttered in a low voice, "how can you not know it by now?"

"Not know what?"

His eyes glittered. "I am in love with you."

She couldn't breathe. "You are?"

"I have been in love with you for years."

"*Years?* You have?"

"Of course I have. Why do you think I've asked you to marry me a dozen times?"

"Because—" She could not think. He loved her. *He loved her.* "Because you did not actually wish to marry," she whispered, the words sounding ridiculous beneath the force of the glorious truth, all of her rationalizations tragically misguided now. "Because I was a safe gamble since you knew I would refuse you."

With a strong hand he tilted up her chin so he could look into her eyes directly.

"Bea, when a man does not wish to marry, he simply does not ask anyone." He smiled, and her knees turned to jelly.

"It does seem a rather far-fetched notion, now that you put it that way."

"It does indeed." His gaze scanned her face slowly, coming to rest on her mouth. He bent to touch his lips to hers, a deliciously tender caress. He drew back and took in a hard breath.

She flattened her palms on his chest, the dressing gown slithering to the floor between their feet.

"Would you—?" she whispered. "D-do you think you could—?" she tried again.

"More stammering? Am I always to have this effect on you now?"

His shining gaze was too much to bear. She laid her cheek against his chest, his skin so warm and taut and his heartbeat swift beneath her ear.

"Please tell me again."

"I love you, Bea. I have loved you for so long and with such hope that you have become part of my very soul."

Happiness swelled in her, grand and fresh and spectacular.

Tip's gaze sought hers. "I know you have given your heart elsewhere. But do you think that in time you could come to love me?"

Tears clogged her throat.

He stroked his thumb over her lips, determination in his eyes.

"I want your love, Bea, and I will win it however necessary. Whoever he is, he was a fool to have left you free.

But I have you now, and I will not give up, for I want all of you." With gentle fingers, he tried to wipe away the moisture collecting on her cheeks again. "Of course, if you ever let slip his name I may have to kill him."

She sobbed, turning her lips into his palm, then her cheek.

"Weep now if you must," he said roughly. "But I will make you forget him." He kissed her mouth and his hand trapped her hips against his.

"You cannot make me forget him." She sighed through her tears. "He is you."

He stilled. His lips parted for a long, silent interval.

"I beg your pardon?" he finally said.

Sweet laughter welled up in her.

"You are the man I gave my heart to, Peter Cheriot. I love you. I have loved you since the moment we met. No one else. Only you."

He shook his head once, his jaw slack.

"Forgive me if I appear astonished." His voice was wonderfully unsteady. "But I must venture to say, Bea, that of all the gentlemen of your acquaintance, I believe I can safely assume that for some time now I have been the *least* ineligible."

"You loved Georgie."

"I did what?"

"You loved my sister. I was certain of it." She rushed the words. "You were devoted to her, then when Kievan and she married, you showered upon me all the attention you could no longer give to her. She broke your heart and it comforted you to pay addresses to me so that you could continue hearing of her, perhaps even see her when she visited Hart House."

"Astounding," he murmured. Then firmly, "I showered you with attention because I was falling in love with you."

"I did not know that. You never told me."

"Because I—" He halted. "I asked you to marry me! Quite a few times."

"You never said you loved me!"

"And I assure you I will never regret anything so thoroughly for the remainder of my life."

"Why didn't you?"

His mouth opened, but he did not speak immediately. Finally he said, "I could not. Each time when we were together and the words came to my tongue—and it was often—I heard my father's voice pleading for forgiveness for his infidelity, my mother giving it to him, both of them suffering as they professed their undying devotion in the certain knowledge that they would do it all again."

"You thought it would be that way with me? With us?"

"I was certain of it. My feelings for you overwhelmed me. They still do."

"But you will not be unfaithful to me, will you?"

"Never," he said harshly.

Her heart ached with happiness. "Yet despite your hesitations, you persisted."

"I could not do otherwise."

"You were so careless in your addresses."

"It was either that or make violent love to you each time I saw you. I took the safer course, I thought, for both of us."

"I thought you didn't care. I thought you pitied me, trapped in Yorkshire with Mama. I could not bear you offering for me out of pity or perhaps even habit." Her hand slid over his chest.

"I see," he murmured. "You refused me because you wished to spare me from making a sacrifice of myself?" A wondering smile shaped his mouth. "You, my love, have much to learn about men."

"I refused you because the prospect of being married to you yet not having your love seemed infinitely worse to me than the rest of my life spent serving a hundred Mamas. Obviously, I did not follow through on that resolution."

"That's all right. You had a pressing reason to alter your plans. But what a ghastly image you've just conjured, Bea. One hundred Lady Harriets living under the same roof." He shuddered, his eyes alight. "Horrifying. You have a vivid imagination."

"I am more than happy to put it to rest." Her fingers

traced a circle on his skin. "I think I would like one of those lessons on men now. One man, in particular." She kissed his collarbone, loving the scent of him, his texture.

"Your sister never broke my heart."

"Oh, don't—"

"I was mildly infatuated with her for a time when I first went to London."

"You played the cicisbeo very convincingly at my great-uncle's house party."

"Unless a nineteen-year-old on the town is drinking, gambling, and—forgive me, Bea—whoring his way into rustication, like your brother, by the way, he must play the cicisbeo to someone. I wished to avoid entanglements like my father's, so I chose a lady to admire. Georgianna was my sister's bosom bow and close at hand. And she was by far the kindest lady with whom I was acquainted then."

Bea smiled. "She is wonderful."

"She never had my heart." His eyes looked very sober. "I was waiting to lose it to her younger sister."

She sighed. He pressed his lips to her brow and she wound her arms about his waist and breathed him in.

"Bea, I have a confession to make."

"Haven't you already made one?" She sighed again then grinned. Since when had she become so flighty?

"Another confession. This one shameful, I'll admit." He smiled. "Your mother did not frighten off your suitors in London. I did."

"You? How on earth?"

"I knew them well enough. I had introduced you to most of them, fool that I was. But I was proud of you. Proud of this lovely girl I had found."

"How did you accomplish it, scaring them away?"

He gave her a devilish smile.

"I told each one of them—confidentially, of course—that you intended to bring your mother to live with you once you were wed."

Bubbling laughter spilled from her.

"Thank you, my lord."

"For ruining your prospects?"

"For saving me for you." She lifted her lips to be kissed. Tip cupped her face in his hands and bent his head.

"I love you, Bea. Thoroughly." He brushed her lips. "Madly." This time he stayed for longer, tasting and giving pleasure. "Body and soul."

"Show me," she whispered.

He scooped her into his arms and carried her to the bed.

"I must look a fright," she said when she eventually had independent use of her tongue again. She said it very unevenly.

"You look beautiful. And you feel like heaven." Tip's eyes were dark with heat. He stroked into her in slow, tantalizing thrusts, teasing her need. "Now, where were we when those pesky tears interrupted us? Here, perhaps?" He took her earlobe between his teeth and pressed her into the mattress with a hard thrust. She gasped and lifted her hips to meet him, to feel him so deeply.

"Ah, yes. And here?" His hand curved around her breast. His fingers found the peak and caressed until the delectable pleasure undid her. In need and ecstasy, her body tightened—her breasts and thighs and belly, the tips of her toes. Her hands clenched on his shoulders.

"Yes, yes. Everywhere. Peter, I cannot breathe."

"No, my love," he said with a slow, deep smile. "You are only now beginning to breathe."

Then he showed her what he meant.

~o0o~

December 4, 1822

Diary, I married him.

~o0o~

Epilogue

"Another letter from Lady Marstowe, my love?"

Bea swiveled around on the escritoire chair and smiled at her husband coming toward her across the parlor. Early spring sunlight beamed through French windows, sparkling like Bea's heart did each time she saw him. Four months of marriage had served only to immerse her more deeply in love.

She grasped his hand, bringing his palm to cradle her cheek.

"I like it when you call me that."

"I like to say it." He dropped a kiss on the top of her head. "What is the news from Gwynedd?"

She offered the letter to him.

"Aunt Julia is happy as can be at the castle, engaging Bronwyn's grandmother in all sorts of useful projects. Aunt Grace has sent Mama home."

"Your mother is too taxing even for the old termagant to bear after so many months?" He scanned the letter. "Bea, you were a saint."

"Were?"

"Are, of course. No doubt I am as demanding as Lady Harriet."

"Only in ways that I am more than happy to accommodate," she replied, standing and placing her palms on his chest.

He dropped the letter onto the desk and his arms encircled her.

"Is that an invitation?" he said.

She slid her hands around his shoulders.

"Haven't you an appointment you were about to go to?"

"It can wait."

"I promised Bronwyn I would take her to the shops this afternoon."

"She can wait."

"She is already waiting, in the drawing room."

"That is what drawing rooms are for." He pulled her tight against him.

Bea laughed, the same tumble of complete joy she felt every day.

"Wasn't this morning sufficient to satisfy you until tonight?" she asked, loving the sensation of his wandering hands.

"I am making up for lost time. Four years is a long while for a man to go without." He bent, clearly intending to kiss her, but she pressed him away, her eyes widening.

"*Four years?* You did not."

"I did."

"But were you—? What I mean to say is, don't gentlemen—?"

"Most certainly." He offered her a delectable smile.

She narrowed her eyes. "What about that house party at Nancy and Averill's, that time? Everyone assumed you and that pretty widow—"

"Everyone?"

"Thomas can be very indiscreet. But don't distract me. I find it difficult to believe that you—What I mean to say is, you are not particularly reluctant . . ."

"I did not claim it was easy." He was still smiling.

"But why on earth didn't you?" The words barely crossed her tongue before she understood. Four years ago he had proposed to her for the first time.

As though seeing that realization in her eyes, Tip set his lips upon her brow, breathing in deeply.

"I was in love with you," he murmured. "I did not want any other woman."

"But I refused you," she said unsteadily. After months of marriage, she still trembled when he told her.

"Nevertheless, I considered myself bound."

She met his expressive gaze and turned her mouth up to his.

"I think Iversly considers himself bound in some manner," she said a few minutes later, rather more breathless than she had been since dawn when she was wrapped in his arms with the bed linens tangled about them.

"Perhaps." Her hair muffled Tip's voice. His fingers worked at the hooks along her spine. She ran her palms over his shoulders.

"Aunt Grace writes that they have not heard or seen him in all these months."

Tip's hands slowed and he drew away slightly. His eyes glimmered and she could see that he wished to tease, but then he sobered.

"I feel for the fellow. I was never all that cheerful after you rejected me, either."

"I don't think it was about me in particular."

"There I believe you are wrong, my love."

"Well, perhaps somewhat," she conceded. "But I think it was much more, really. I think he believed that through me he could avoid what he truly longs for."

"You may never know. Will it bother you?"

She settled snugly into his embrace again.

"I am truly sorry for him," she said. "But I have a living man whose future happiness I hope to assist in securing."

"Now, there is a venture I can applaud." Tip set to work again at the fastenings of her gown, his mouth moving to her neck.

"I meant Thomas, of course."

"He can wait too." He started in on her petticoat lacings.

She wrapped her arms around his neck. "Bronwyn wishes to purchase a new pair of opera glasses for him, in thanks for escorting her to the performance last night."

"How nice for him," he murmured against her mouth, his

palm stealing down to cup her behind and pull her flush against him. He was hard already—hard, wonderful, and hers.

Her breath caught on a sigh of anticipation.

"He likes her quite a lot," she said as her hand slid down his waist.

"Thank God."

"I thought you didn't care for her."

"I don't much," he replied huskily, his open mouth on her throat working sensual magic through Bea's whole body. "But if your brother had not become infatuated with her in Wales, your hand might not be where it is at this moment."

"You don't think so?" She wiggled to help him divest her of her gown, then set to work on his breeches. "Perhaps you would have devised some very clever proposal I could not possibly have refused."

"Assuredly." He pulled her close and started kissing her again, impatiently gathering her petticoat and shift to her waist.

"Or perhaps we would have simply gone on for years and years in the same vein," she said as he lifted her onto the table and parted her thighs. "Then would you still have considered yourself bound to me?"

"Forever." He pulled her forward and, carefully, fit himself to her. She sank onto him, loving how he filled her body now as he always filled her heart.

"And beyond." His voice was so deep, like his need buried inside her.

Bea tilted her hips, deepening her possession of him, and nestled closer.

"I love you, Peter."

"And I love you, my girl." He cupped her face in his hands. "My lady." He kissed her so that he was everywhere within and around her, entirely hers. "My Bea."

To My Wonderful Readers

Thank you, from the bottom of my heart, for your open, warm, and infinitely loving hearts. Your letters, e-mails, posts, tweets, and reviews make me happier than you can imagine. I am so grateful for each and every one of you.

To be sure you don't miss any of my book news and to receive a free short story, subscribe to my e-mail announcements www.KatharineAshe.com. And to receive beautiful bookmarks and postcards for each of my new books, send your street or post office address to me at Katharine Ashe, PO Box 51702, Durham, NC 27717 or via my website contact form.

I'm happy to announce that Rhys Iversly's story is on its way soon! In the meantime, I have another series I think you'll enjoy. In my Twist Series, the Goddess of Love is trapped in a statue in Regency-era England with nothing to do but stir up trouble of the most breathtaking sort. And one altar-shy family is about to discover how dedicated Aphrodite is to her work.

Turn the page for an excerpt from *Again, My Lord*, the first book of my Twist Series…

Excerpt from *Again, My Lord*

In the middle of the inn yard, shrouded in sheets of rain, her son stood as though paralyzed, eyes and mouth agape at the huge horse galloping straight for him.

"Harry!" Calista leaped forward. But she was too far away, the horse too close, Harry immobile, the rain driving down.

The horse shied, and reared, its hooves pawing the slanting rain above Harry's head.

Then its master was flying into the air, boots slamming to the ground, greatcoat swirling as he swept forward, fell to his knees and wrapped his arms around Harry, surrounding her son in safety. A shrill whistle pierced the downpour and the horse wheeled away.

Abruptly there was no movement in the yard except the rain pounding on the muddy ground.

Calista ran forward. Harry broke from the man's arms and flew straight into hers.

"Mama, did you see? Did you? It was amazing!" Words streamed from his mouth as he wrapped his skinny arms around her neck and she gripped his body to hers. "That man saved me from his horse! And then he made it turn away, with only a whistle."

"Yes." She pressed the word into his soaking hair, the raw terror of the moment subsiding and making her arms shake. "Yes, darling. What an adventure."

But he was pulling away already, turning to the rider. Calista rose to her feet, took hold of her son's hand, and lifted her eyes to the man.

In her life she had hated only one man as much as she had once hated her father and now her husband. Rather, almost as much: Tacitus Everard, the Marquess of Dare.

Now he stood before her, soaked by the sheets of rain that perfectly matched his beautifully intense gray eyes. Still as stone and severe of jaw and stance, he stared at her without speaking as water streamed off the brim of his hat and the cape of his coat. Even with rain washing across his features, he was as handsome as ever: tall and dark and broad-shouldered, with the sort of jaw a woman longed to stroke and lips that stole her reason. And as stiff as a steel rod.

"I beg your pardon," he said across the rain. "Is he all right?"

"Yes, sir!" Harry volunteered. "Grand horse you've got there, sir!"

"Yes, well, he's a goer." He looked at her. "Forgive me, madam. I was … That is …" He scowled.

A second horseman splashed into the yard and slowed, drawing his mount to a halt and sliding out of the saddle. He tossed the reins to a stable boy holding the marquess's horse.

"Damn and blast, Dare," he exclaimed upon laughter. "I would've had you if it hadn't been for that coach blocking that last bend." He took them all in. "Good Lord, have you run someone over?"

Calista grasped her son's slippery hand. "Come now, Harry. We must dry you off before you depart." She drew him back into the inn as he craned his neck.

Evelina stood in the doorway. "It's him."

"Who?" Harry said.

Calista glared at her sister. "No one." Going to her sodden knees in the foyer she dusted raindrops from her son's coat, and removed his hat and shook it out.

"But, Mama—"

"Harry," she said firmly.

Her son's lips shut tight. "Yes, Mama."

Her heart twisted anew. Despite the Chance spirit he'd been born with, he had learned to be docile from necessity.

Ignoring every lesson about stalwart strength in the face of adversity that she had taught her son over the past five years, she wrapped her arms around him again and pressed her face into the crook of his shoulder.

"I will miss you, my darling," she whispered fiercely.

"I'll miss you too, Mama."

She drew away. "Now, listen to your aunt and Grandmama this month."

"And to Cook," he said.

"Yes, and to Cook, so she will bake your favorite biscuits and allow you to taste the bread as soon as it is out of the oven," she repeated the comforting words she had been telling him the entire journey to this tiny inn in this little village where Richard had instructed her to leave him in her sister's care. She looked into his sober face that had never resembled her husband's, rather featured the Chance black hair, blue eyes, and defiant chin. Harry would be better off at Dashbourne than at home, free to be a boy. It was she who would hate every day of this month apart. She stroked his cheek, then stood.

Lord Dare filled the inn doorway, his coat dripping, knees and boots muddy, and face inscrutable. A scar now cut across his jaw, lending an air of danger to his male beauty.

"My lord," she bit through tight lips.

His attention shifted to Harry at her hip.

"Do you know him, Mama?" her son whispered in the comically voluble whisper of the young.

She reached down and clasped his little fingers. "He is Lord Dare. Bow to him now, darling."

Harry cut a neat little bow, his eyes remaining wide.

"Why doesn't he come in out of the rain?" His whisper filled the foyer.

"Because he is a peculiar man," she said. "Peculiar men who are very wealthy do anything they want."

"Even stand in the rain?" Harry asked skeptically.

"You should see me when it snows," Lord Dare said, and stepped into the foyer. His voice was as deep and velvety as it had been years ago. Adorned with a caped greatcoat and tall crowned hat, his presence dominated the small space. Were he atop a mountain, Calista thought, he would still seem to command the peaks with his quiet authority and stormy eyes…

Again, My Lord is available in ebook or paperback at booksellers everywhere.

In Gratitude

Many thanks to the generous souls who helped me prepare the 2017 edition of *Captive Bride* for publication, Carrie Divine of Seductive Designs, Lori Devoti, and Georgann T. Brophy, with special thanks and hugs to Mary Brophy Marcus and The Lady Authors—Caroline Linden, Miranda Neville, and Maya Rodale—whose help and support I depend on with every book I write.

Thanks as well to the people whose work made the original version of this novel possible: Georgann T. Brophy, Monica Burns, Kim Castillo, Judi Fennell, Sonja Foust, Melinda Leigh, Diane Leipzig, Karrie Matthews, Joan Swan, Martha Trachtenberg, and Marquita Valentine.

I am especially indebted to author's assistant extraordinaire, Cari Gunsallus, and to my fabulous agent, Kimberly Whalen of The Whalen Agency. As always I offer profound thanks to my husband, my son, and my Idaho.

Finally, thank you to my sister Georgie C. Brophy, without whom Gwynedd Castle and its ghostly overlord would not be. Our sojourn in Wales remains to me a dream out of time—a bit like Rhys Iversly, I daresay.

Bonus Material: The Soundtrack to *Captive Bride*

For each book I write, I create a playlist of songs inspired by characters or scenes. I don't usually write to music, but I do listen to these playlists during the months I'm writing a story while I'm driving, walking the dog, doing laundry, running, shopping, and then again each time I work on it after that.

I have pretty eclectic taste in music, and each book I write inspires a unique sort of playlist to reflect the tone of that couple's romance. For instance, the playlists for my Devil's Duke series are full of gorgeous Scottish folk tunes and epic movie scores. My Prince Catchers and Rogues of the Sea playlists include lots of gritty rock n' roll and heartachy female vocalists, while my Twist series books feature wry, angsty alternative rock and deeply romantic ballads. And many of my playlists are threaded through with chamber music and waltzes, music that my characters themselves would have listened and danced to.

Bea and Tip's love story is one of the first full-length novels I ever wrote, many years before I first published it. Perhaps because of that, their romance has an especially sweet tone to it—even a bit innocent. So their playlist turned out to include lots of pop. I suspect you'll be able to recognize which songs particularly influenced which parts of the story. Enjoy!

The Soundtrack

"Hearts on Fire" by Bryan Adams
"Anywhere But Here" by Hilary Duff
"Beautiful Soul" by Jesse McCartney
"Kiss the Girl" (Pop Version) by Ashley Tisdale
"Crash Into Me" by Dave Matthews Band
"This Is Me" by Demi Lovato and Joe Jonas
"Walls Fall Down" by Bedouin Soundclash
"Just Like Heaven" by The Cure
"Fall For You" by Secondhand Serenade
"Songbird" by Fleetwood Mac
"I Don't Want To Miss a Thing" by Aerosmith
"Fearless" by Taylor Swift
"I'll Be" by Edwin McCain
"I'm a Believer" by Smash Mouth

Made in the USA
Middletown, DE
27 May 2017